Sugar Island

Sanjida O'Connell

JOHN MURRAY

First published in Great Britain in 2011 by John Murray (Publishers)
An Hachette UK Company

First published in paperback in 2012

1

© Sanjida O'Connell 2011

FT
Pbk

The right of Sanjida O'Connell to be identified as the Author of the Work has been
asserted by her in accordance with the Copyright, Designs and Patents Act 1988.

Map drawn by Rosie Collins

All characters in this publication are fictitious and any resemblance to real persons,
living or dead, is purely coincidental.

A CIP catalogue record for this title is available from the British Library

ISBN 978-1-84854-040-8
Ebook ISBN 978-1-84854-509-0

Typeset in Monotype Baskerville by Servis Filmsetting Ltd, Stockport, Cheshire

Printed and bound by Clays Ltd, St Ives plc

John Murray policy is to use papers that are natural, renewable and recyclable
products and made from wood grown in sustainable forests. The logging and
manufacturing processes are expected to conform to the environmental regulations of
the country of origin.

John Murray (Publishers)
338 Euston Road
London NW1 3BH

www.johnmurray.co.uk

To Jaimie

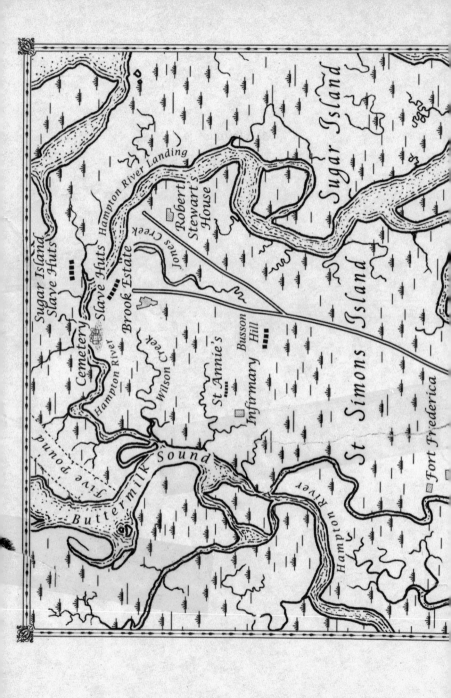

Atlantic
Ocean

Christ Church

Taylor Estate

The Halls

The
Dummonds

St Simons Island
and
Sugar Island

Kilometres

0   1   2   3

Chapter 1

April 1859

Emily could see only the front row distinctly and it was filled with the Harvard boys who'd been coming for days, slipping past their parents or dodging their landladies. Their upturned faces, gleaming like oiled bone in the wan yellow of the oil lamps, were creased with knowing pity, as she discovered what they knew already: that she, Juliet, a Capulet, had fallen in love with a Montagu. The smell of oranges, the peel lying thickly between the seats, melting candy and hot wood rose towards her as the theatre warmed beneath a fierce sun.

She bent over Romeo and kissed him softly on the cheek, at the crease of his lips. She tasted greasepaint.

'Thy lips are warm!' she whispered.

She searched through his clothes and pulled out a knife, turning the blade between her palms so it glittered in the light of the single candle. 'O happy dagger! This is thy sheath; there rest and let me die.'

There was a sharp intake of breath, a collective sigh from

the audience and a woman cried out as Emily stabbed the blade into her chest and collapsed over Romeo, her heart beating hard.

She felt Romeo's chest rise and fall beneath her and her back grew hot where she rested upon him, trying to still her own breathing. She'd lain awkwardly again and the corner of the tomb bit into the fleshy crease behind her knee. Someone was sobbing in the cheaper seats.

'For never was a story of more woe, Than this of Juliet and her Romeo,' the Prince concluded.

Emily counted for three slow beats and then rose as the audience, gently at first then growing in strength, started to clap and whoop and stamp their feet until they too staggered upright in one ragged mass. She held out her hand to Nate Doyle, who played Romeo, and they walked to the centre of the stage, where she curtsied and he bowed and she smiled at the Harvard boys, whose eyes glistened and mouths hung wetly open. She scanned the front rows for one familiar face: that of a young gentleman with curly, fair hair. He always sat on the third row to one side. Today, though, he was absent. She turned and, with a look, summoned the other members of the cast to join her. Mr Doyle's hand was clammy and she let his fingers slide from hers. She stepped forward to receive the warm tides of adulation, smiling, smiling into the dark.

In the dressing room there was, as usual, a neat bouquet of flowers: yesterday there had been salmon-pink dahlias and strawberry peonies cushioned on a bed of moss with a card that read, as it always did, 'To Miss Emily Harris,

From a Friend,' the last word underscored so hard a tiny splatter of ink had been left in its wake. This time the flowers were cream roses with a hint of green running through their veins.

Today, because it was a matinée, she opened the shutters in the dressing room to let the light flood in and a crowd of street urchins pressed themselves against the window. They stared and pointed at her dress, simple as she had had to insist, in white with a gold trim, and her gilt slippers and watched as she removed the faux pearl pins from her hair and the choker from around her throat. She closed the shutters again and began to wipe away the heavy stage make-up with cold cream.

There was a knock.

'Emily, it's me.' Her father was playing Capulet.

'Come in,' she called.

John Harris put his head around the door. He had already changed and his overcoat was hanging over his arm, his hat in his hand. 'The carriage is waiting.'

'I shan't be a moment,' she said, half muffled through the cream.

Without his help she would not possibly reach the carriage through the dense crowd of onlookers who wished to catch hold of her clothes, call her name, claim her attention so they could say they had seen Emily Harris, that they'd touched her skirt and that she had smiled at them.

It was early evening by the time they reached the house at Cape Cod and the white wooden walls glowed in the soft, dusky-pink light. Orange trees in terracotta pots were placed on either side of the door, the colour of the ripening fruit beginning to suffuse through the waxy green rind. As her father helped her out of the carriage, Sarah Crawford came to the door, stepping past the butler and the maid and holding out her arms.

'My dear,' she said, 'you must be positively shaken to bits.'

'It was somewhat uneven,' said Emily, laughing, 'but I'm becoming accustomed to your deplorable roads and dreadful conveyances.'

'Forgive her, Miss Crawford,' said John as he kissed Sarah's hand, 'she is terribly bad-mannered. She had a singular upbringing.'

Sarah smiled and tucked a wispy strand of hair back into her bun. 'Ely is looking forward to seeing you, but I knew you should like to freshen up first.'

'Thank you, Sarah,' Emily said. 'I'm always grateful for hot water – it seems to be rationed in this country.'

The Crawfords' house was as spare and elegant as they were: the walls were whitewashed, the wooden floorboards burnished. As soon as the maid had shown her to her room, Emily ran to the window and threw it open. The wind, sweet with salt, blew back the muslin curtains and the canopy around the bed until the room seemed full of fine, white fabric billowing like an unsheathed sail. Below her the beach stretched for miles, the sand a dull rose-gold. She would have liked nothing better than to run down its firm, hard length but the Crawfords were holding a dinner in her honour.

The maid returned with hot water perfumed with orange blossom and soft, white towels. Emily wet one and held it to her face, moulding it against her features, breathing in the heat and scent until it grew cool. The maid helped her change into a shell-coloured raw silk dress scattered with seed pearls and trimmed with white velvet, and then styled her hair. The curls were so dark and neat it looked as if she squeezed them she might wring out drops of precious essential oil. Emily looked at herself in the mirror. She was small with smooth curves. Her large eyes were almost black and her face was heart-shaped. Her skin appeared opalescent against her dress. She did not realize that she was beautiful for the simple fact that her mother had often told her she was not.

'Ah, my dear, you look magnificent,' said Sarah, taking her hand and leading her into the drawing room.

Sarah Crawford always dressed in black during the day and in the evenings changed into grey silk with a lace collar. She wore her brown hair scraped back from her face and pinned firmly into a bun but fine, frizzy strands constantly escaped. Her eyes were sharp and blue and her mouth was set in a straight, determined line. In her mid thirties, she had never married, choosing to live at home with her father, Theodore, and her younger brother Ely, and work as a novelist. The Crawfords lived almost spartanly but they entertained with great warmth and generosity. The room was filled with candles and gleamed with silver and crystal; a plate piled with delicate pastries was positioned in the middle of the table, around which stood a group of people, who turned towards Emily as she entered.

Emily nodded and bowed. Sarah began to make introductions. 'May I introduce a friend of the Bells, Mr Charles Earl Brook?' she said, handing Emily a glass of champagne.

'We have already had that pleasure,' said Charles Earl Brook, holding out his hand and bowing slightly.

'Mr Brook,' she said.

Charles slowly bent over and kissed her hand.

She sipped her champagne and remembered the first time she'd met Charles. It had been January and she and her father had just finished the Christmas season in New York. It was bitterly cold and they were both exhausted. She'd been in America since the previous October and she was homesick and missed her mother and her brother, William. She had been tramping around the streets through liquid snow until her boots were quite soaked and had arrived back at the hotel, chilled to the bone, her cheeks flushed, her throat aching, in a thoroughly bad temper.

Her father had caught sight of her and called her. He was sitting drinking and smoking in the public room with a young man whom he introduced to her as Charles Earl Brook. As the man smiled and said how delighted he was to meet her, had, in fact, longed for the pleasure of her acquaintance, she recognized him. He had attended many of her performances and once he had stood outside the theatre waiting for her. He had taken off his hat and stepped forward as if he might like to speak to her but her father had escorted her to their carriage and the moment had been lost. She had noticed his fair curls before; now at close proximity she observed that his eyes were an unusually pale grey, with the luminosity of fine crystal or labradorite.

He said that he was a lawyer with a practice in New York but he had travelled to other cities on the east coast particularly to see her act. He declared himself enchanted. In spite of his northern address, he spoke with a faint southern drawl. Delightful as he was, she wanted nothing more than to change out of her wet clothes and lie down in her room. Until, that is, she mentioned that she loved to ride and missed her horse at home and had, as yet, found no one willing to accompany her.

Charles's eyes had glowed and he had leaned forward slightly in his chair.

'Why, that is a singular passion of mine too,' he'd said in his soft voice. 'With your permission, sir, I could secure horses for us all,' he'd added, turning to Mr Harris. 'We could ride around Central Park. It is quite beautiful in the snow.'

Her father, though he loathed horses, acquiesced for her sake.

Charles Brook had been correct: Central Park was indeed spectacular beneath its frozen winter mantle.

'Allow me to introduce you to everyone present,' Charles Earl Brook now said, taking Emily's elbow and adroitly steering her away from Sarah.

It was, Sarah had told her, to be an intimate dinner and weekend with a select number of friends. Naturally

Theodore, Sarah and Ely's father, was there, as well as their aunt, Mathilda Fraser. Charles introduced her to a society couple, the Bells, and their daughters, Penelope and Catherine, with whom he had been staying for the past few days. In his typically flamboyant style, he presented her as the most celebrated actress of the day.

'My word, that is quite an accolade,' murmured Penelope Bell, bending very slightly at the waist towards her. She had thick, straight blonde hair and a heavy milky complexion. She looked sleek and well fed.

Ely was standing next to Miss Bell and Emily caught a fleeting expression on his face, the merest shade of anger. He looked down at her and smiled. He was in his early thirties, tall and thin with the same sharp blue eyes as his sister but his features were much finer than hers.

'Not everyone thinks actresses deserve to be celebrated,' Emily remarked to Ely after she'd excused herself from the younger Bells. 'It is only you Crawfords who have been so immeasurably kind to us, to Father and me.'

'The elder Miss Bell is used to being the most fêted female in the room,' Ely said quietly. He paused and then said, 'But far more important than the younger Bells – we have taken the liberty of inviting your publisher. Please, allow me,' and he took her arm and led her to the far corner of the sitting room where his father was leaning against the cherry-wood mantelpiece talking to Edward King. It did not come naturally to the elder Mr Crawford to host such a gathering, but Emily saw that he had quite taken the thing in his stride.

'How delightful to see you again, Miss Harris,' said Edward King. 'My favourite authoress.'

Mr King's skin had the nap of a white peach and his dark, almost navy eyes were deep-set and half hidden beneath wiry eyebrows. He had a penchant for waistcoats and today, with his grey evening suit, he was wearing mustard-coloured silk embroidered with fleurs-de-lis, and an ivory cravat.

'Are you familiar with Miss Harris's book on American life?' he asked, turning to Mr Bell.

'I should say we could hardly have missed hearing of it,' said Mr Bell. 'Most amusing but a little, if I may say so, Miss Harris, dismissive of the American way of life and somewhat restricted in its reach.'

'Restricted in reach, Mr Bell?' asked Emily.

'Miss Harris, you are such a young lady and have spent so little time in our great nation that I cannot quite believe you could have seen sufficient to warrant the title, *American Life*.'

'You are quite correct, Mr Bell. I have travelled considerably – or so it felt to me – but I see now that I have hardly made a dent in the vastness of the continent. I have not ventured particularly far south nor west and, indeed, have spent but little time in the middle. The book, such as it is, is meant only to be a slim volume of observations from one who expected, because of our natural kinship with America, to find that your customs would be as ours but, in fact, discovered them to be disconcertingly different.'

'Come, come,' said Mr King, 'you are doing yourself a disservice, Miss Harris. It is full of bons mots and spry observations.'

'Ah well, for those I thank my father,' said Emily, 'who retained a singular good humour throughout our travels whereas I, I am afraid to admit, was rather less pleasant company.'

'That I could not imagine,' said Charles Brook, who had drawn near, leaving the women, the two Bell sisters, their mother and Sarah Crawford together. Mrs Fraser and Emily's father were deep in conversation on the far side of the room. 'I thought the book delightful, Miss Harris, and we are lesser men than I had presumed if we cannot take a little gentle teasing from the fairer sex.'

'A fair observation, young man,' said Mr Bell, inclining his head. He raised his glass in a toast. 'To Miss Harris.'

As the others followed suit, Charles Brook said quietly to her, 'I have taken the liberty of bringing my horse with me.'

He was half watching Penelope who had swayed across the room to speak to Edward King.

'Mr Crawford has been so kind as to offer you one of his geldings. That is, if you wish to ride tomorrow.' He smiled at her.

How self-assured of him, Emily thought, to arrange a horse for her at her own friends' house.

'Mr Crawford, would you excuse us for a few minutes? I need to borrow Miss Harris for a moment,' Charles Brook said, half bowing to Theodore. Turning to Emily he said,

'Dinner is almost ready and I wish to speak to you privately beforehand. I may not have another opportunity.'

He led her on to the veranda at the front of the house.

'I had thought we surely should be able to see the stars,' he said, strolling ahead of her, his hands in his pockets, looking up at the sky.

A fierce wind had sprung up since the afternoon and dense clouds obliterated the stars and the moon. The sea felt very near, the waves crashing on the shore, coating her skin with a fine spray of salt. There was something exhilarating in its strength.

'Miss Harris,' he said, turning to her.

Emily gripped the rail of the veranda, feeling the day's residual warmth in the wood. She shivered. She had an oily feeling in the pit of her stomach. She glanced up at him and he walked back towards her, half smiling. He stopped when he was very close and leaned against the rail, one hand almost touching hers. She looked down at this hand, so white and clean, the gold ring on his little finger glinting dully in the dark. Her throat felt as if it might close.

'What was it that you wanted to say, Mr Brook?' she said finally, forcing herself to look at him.

The iris of his pale grey eyes appeared almost the same shade as the cratered moon she had once seen through a telescope. He leaned closer to her and she could feel the heat rising from him, smell the cigar smoke trapped in his suit and his cologne, like Christmas in a grand house.

It started to rain, heavy drops at first, driving in at an angle and then suddenly a deluge, sheets of water, almost milky white. They stepped back against the side of the house where they were more sheltered.

'Mr Brook . . .'

'Not quite what I had anticipated,' he said and she felt the entire right side of her body burning where he pressed against her beneath the eaves.

He cupped her chin in one hand and very gently traced the outline of her cheek and her jawbone with one finger. It felt as if he were drawing a bead of liquid mercury across her skin. His face was in darkness now and he bent towards her. Emily felt the rush of hot air from his breath, the biscuit scent of champagne, and then his lips met hers, so much hotter and softer than she had imagined. He stretched his hands flat against her shoulder blades and pulled her towards him. She turned her head away and drew back from him and after a moment he released his hold.

He dropped on one knee. Elongated puddles of water glistened around him, crackling with the force of the rain.

'Mr Brook . . .'

'Miss Harris, Emily, if I may, you are quite the most beautiful and the most talented woman I've met.'

'Mr Brook, please . . .' she said awkwardly.

'Will you marry me?'

'Mr Brook, do please get up. I am terribly sorry but I hardly feel that I'm the marrying kind. I'm an actress and actresses are not known for making excellent wives.' She began to shiver. 'And I think you ought to have spoken to my father first, Mr Brook,' she said quietly.

He rose to his feet. 'Emily, my dear, we both know that you do not like acting. If you married me, why, you'd never need to perform in public again.'

The rain was coursing down his face now, running into his collar, crushing his curls.

'And I do believe you like me, just a little. Please, do reconsider,' he said, reaching out to touch her wrist.

She took a step back and felt the wooden deck slick beneath her feet. 'Had you asked my father, Mr Brook,' she persisted, 'he would have given the same answer as I have.'

As she turned to go back inside, lightning cracked across the sky and there was a heavy roll of thunder. She hastened upstairs to dry herself as best she could. She could see what Charles Brook had wished for – a proposal beneath the stars on a warm June night, the sea murmuring below – and then, tinkling his spoon against his glass, he would have announced to the assembled diners, her closest friends and some of Boston's most influential people, their engagement. Emily felt sorry that she had hurt him and angry that she had been forced to do so. She patted her ringlets, now ruined, shook out her damp skirts and wrapped a cashmere shawl around her bare shoulders before descending. She paused just before she entered the dining room, still conscious of the imprint of his lips against hers.

When she went in, the party were already seated. They stopped speaking as she appeared. One of the servants pulled back the empty chair between Sarah and Edward King and it scraped across the wooden floor. Ely, seated opposite, looked at her with concern. Penelope Bell glanced ostentatiously from Charles Brook to Emily and back, and frowned.

'You are quite soaked through, my child,' said Aunt Mathilda.

'I'm afraid I ventured outside just as it began to rain,' said Emily, shivering slightly as she tried to smile.

'I will blame you, Mr Harris, if that child catches a chill. She should not be allowed to run about so unsupervised.'

'My daughter has a tendency to do as she pleases, Mrs Fraser,' said her father.

In the silence they could hear the rain lashing against the window panes, which rattled in their frames, and there was a clap of thunder.

'It sounds like a terrible storm,' said Sarah, motioning to one of the servants to light the fire.

The maid began to ladle out the soup.

'I know it is rather dull of me to comment on it each time we meet, but your accent is quite delightful,' said Edward King, turning to Emily.

'On the rare occasions that I hear it, the English accent makes me simply homesick,' she replied. 'But I feel quite at ease here. The Crawfords have taken me under their wing,' she said. 'I had not realized in what little regard actors are held over here. People are prepared to pay us very handsomely yet not allow us to dine with them. It is most curious.'

Mr King took a delicate sip of his soup and laid down the spoon. He dabbed at his full lips with a napkin. 'It grieves me to see you received with anything less than the utmost hospitality. We are such a new country and yet we cling to outmoded values and conservative customs.'

'Isn't that exactly the prerequisite of the new – to extract comfort from the old?' said Emily. She glanced up to see Charles looking at her. She smiled back gently.

Over dessert the conversation turned to politics.

'The poor man! What an utterly tragic waste,' said Sarah.

'Well, perhaps his death was not entirely in vain. It has, at least, roused the Democrats,' replied Theodore.

'To whom are you referring?' asked Emily.

'Dred Scott,' said Sarah. 'You may well not have heard of him. The trial took place before you arrived in America.'

One of the maids brought in a tray laden with thimble-sized glasses full of clear liqueur and placed one in front of every guest.

'He was a slave,' explained Ely. 'Dred Scott was owned by a general in the army, John Emerson, who was transferred to states where slavery is illegal. Technically he should have emancipated the man, but instead he hired him out as a labourer and kept his wages and when Emerson died his wife carried on the practice. She refused to let him or his wife and child leave and so Scott actually sued the American government for his freedom. This was back in 1840 and he was, after several court cases, granted his freedom.'

Emily took a sip of the viscous liquid. It burned her throat and tasted of oranges.

'But then,' interrupted Sarah, 'the Supreme Court over-turned the decision last year. It was eventually ruled that Scott was not and could not be an American citizen.'

'Typical example of a jumped-up darkie with ideas too big for his britches,' said Mr Bell in a low grumble.

'The wider political ramifications, of course, are that Taney's ruling suggests that slavery can occur in any state,' said Theodore. 'And, as you know, northern states are anti-slavery and wish, if not to abolish the practice in southern states, at least prevent other states from taking it up.'

'I have never seen a slave,' said Catherine Bell. She had thin hair and sharp features and lacked the creamy glow of her elder sister. 'I am quite curious to see what one looks like.'

'They say that in general they are kept very well, cos-seted even,' said Mr Bell, 'the way one might treat a racehorse.'

Ely Crawford glared at Mr Bell but said nothing.

'Well, surely, Mr Bell, it does not matter how well a man is treated – how much fresh hay and exercise he's given – if he is to be deprived of his liberty,' said Emily.

'I am merely pointing out that the southern states believe they can justify their customs. Furthermore, a man's pos-session does not cease to be a man's possession simply because it happens to reside elsewhere in our great country. By your own admission, Miss Harris, you are somewhat inexperienced regarding our American ways.'

'Well, I am prejudiced against slavery, though, as an Englishwoman, the absence of such a prejudice would be utterly disgraceful.' Emily took a mouthful of her tart. The berries burst in her mouth with a sweet astringency.

'The story has an even more unhappy outcome,' said Ely. 'Scott's former owner, who had originally sold him to Emerson, bought him and freed him but barely six months later he died of tuberculosis. I'm writing a pamphlet about his life,' he added.

'How dreadful,' said Emily. 'I do find it hard to comprehend,' she added thoughtfully. 'Slavery was abolished in England before I was born. I simply cannot understand how one man can justify owning another – as if he were a horse.'

'As you have admitted, Miss Harris, it is a prejudice. Perhaps if you were to journey to the south you might see the truth for yourself,' said Charles smoothly. 'The situation is potentially more complex than you have allowed.'

'Shall we adjourn to the parlour for coffee?' suggested Theodore Crawford.

The following morning was beautifully still: the sea like glass, the sky a clear, fresh blue, but the shoreline was littered with great swathes of seaweed and chunks of driftwood. There were also grey piles of something that appeared to be moving. As she opened the door Emily saw that the wind had devastated the two little orange trees: the unripe fruit were strewn across the front porch like lime-green marbles. When she reached the beach she laughed out loud at the incongruity of it: the sand was heaped with lobsters. They waved their pincers and moved their legs like mechanical objects. She looked up to see Ely walking towards her carrying a basket.

'Good morning, Miss Harris. The debris will make riding this morning somewhat hazardous, but I thought you might want to help me fetch our lunch,' he said as he drew near.

'I've never even seen a live lobster before!'

'Take care of the pincers,' he said, as she bent to pick one up.

She grasped the lobster's hard carapace behind the claws, as he instructed, and picked it up, shaking it slightly to disentangle its legs from its fellows. It was a large, old beast, draped with skeins of weed, and with barnacles growing on its back leg. She dropped it in the basket and Ely replaced the lid firmly.

'It's going to be the very devil to put them in when there's already a few in there trying to get out,' he said.

They could hear the lobster inside, clicking its claws.

'How do you cook them?' she asked.

'They're dropped into boiling water.'

'Alive?'

'I'm afraid so. It's a quick way of dispatching them though.'

'Oh, how horrid. The ones we choose are going to suffer a vile death.'

He looked out to sea and then back at her. 'Perhaps in the future people will view killing animals the way we view slavery. Some of us view slavery,' he said, correcting himself.

A lobster walked past her and Emily swiftly grabbed hold of it, a little too far back, and it seized her wrist, pinching the skin. She cried out in shock and dropped it. Ely picked it up expertly instead.

'Are you hurt? Their claws are rather powerful for such small creatures.'

'No,' she said, rubbing her wrist, 'only taken by surprise. But all beasts wish to live so I should not have been.'

She plucked another lobster from the heap and Ely helped her pull its legs free. The crustacean was a dark vitreous green with smooth, black, blank eyes on tiny stalks. A group of seagulls were squabbling over a dead lobster a few yards away, shrieking at one another, pulling the animal apart, stabbing at its flesh. In the bright, flat sunlight she could see all the faint lines on Ely's face, the threads of silver in his hair.

'How curious that their shells turn red,' she said, carefully putting the lobster in the basket, pushing its curled tail in before closing the lid.

'It sounds as if they are screaming when they're dropped in the water, but I'm told it's the air escaping, hissing through their joints. I think we've sentenced enough to death though, don't you?'

'Yes, let's return to the house. I'm feeling famished. I ran out here without any breakfast.'

He smiled. 'I noticed. Would you care to stay here longer, Miss Harris? I can see the sea air agrees with you.'

'I should dearly wish to.' She sighed. 'But we have to

return tonight. We have rehearsals tomorrow and then the performances continue. Those endless performances!'

'Everyone is talking of you. What a wonderful actress you are. So natural. And so beautiful. But you don't like it.' He smiled gently.

Emily thought of the theatre in Boston: the dark mass of the audience, the young men with their pinched faces who hung outside, the ticket touts in their greasy shirts loitering by the theatre entrance; of the gossip columnists.

'I don't like being discussed,' she said. 'And I detest acting.' She hesitated. Ely Crawford waited quietly for her to continue. 'You know, Mr Crawford, my father and I have been here seven months in total and we will stay for two years altogether and then return, having made our fortunes. I must say that, apart from the sadness of losing you and Sarah, I am counting the days until I can return.'

When Emily entered the dining room, Charles Brook was seated at the table. He looked up at her and smiled as she walked in, greeting her in his usual charming way, as if her rejection of him the previous night had not been a disappointment. He was drinking a glass of sweet wine and eating a thick slice of brioche slathered in marmalade. He slid two teaspoons of sugar into his coffee cup and stirred, his spoon clinking against the china sides. Penelope Bell was sitting next to him. She looked as if she too had eaten something very sweet for breakfast but it did not stop the shiver of distaste that passed over her face, like a ripple across a pail of milk, as she took in Emily's dishevelled hair, disordered dress and sandy shoes. The two of them cordially took their leave of her, then followed the maid to the parlour, leaving her alone with Catherine Bell. The young woman rose to her feet and looked down at Emily.

'I hope that it's at an end, Miss Harris.'

'That what is at an end, Miss Bell?' Emily asked, surprised.

Catherine made a small gesture with her white hand. 'Whatever it was. Between you and Mr Brook.'

Emily swallowed and took a sip of her coffee.

'You do realize that they're engaged, don't you?'

She shook her head. 'No, I did not. Mr Brook has never mentioned it. Nor had I heard it announced.'

'Well,' said Catherine sharply, 'it has never been *formally* announced, but it is understood by all.' She glared at Emily.

'I see.'

'They're perfect for one another.'

'Quite.' Emily took another sip of her coffee. 'I wish them the utmost happiness. Mr Brook, my father and I occasionally ride together and I hope that will continue for the time being. It can hardly affect Miss Bell; at least, until her wedding.'

'It's improper,' said Catherine, two red spots appearing on her cheeks, 'but I hardly expect someone like you to understand that.' She swept out of the room.

The day that had started so freshly and so beautifully seemed ruined.

'Whatever is the matter?' Sarah Crawford walked in just in time to see Catherine leaving.

'I had not realized that Mr Brook is betrothed to Miss Bell,' said Emily.

'Ah,' said Sarah, sitting down next to Emily. 'The Bells and the Brooks are two old, respectable families with money. It's always been understood that they should be united. When the Brooks' oldest son, Emmanuel, refrained from taking the opportunity, it was assumed that Charles would fulfil his obligations. But as far as I am aware, there has been no formal announcement. Mr Bell awaits one daily,' added Sarah dryly. 'I was wondering whether you perhaps have any feelings for Mr Brook?'

'He asked me to marry him. I refused.'

'Ah,' said Sarah again, tucking a stray wisp of hair back into her bun.

'You can't simply say "Ah" when I've divulged such monumental news,' said Emily, playfully pulling the strand of hair out again.

'Well, my dear, I have two pieces of advice I can give you. One general and one particular.'

'So early in the morning?' said Emily, taking a bite of her toast.

'The first one involves marriage. You should not marry.'

'And how, may I ask, have you ascertained that?'

'Currently you enjoy a privileged position in society because of your celebrated status and, as a result of your work, you also have money. If you marry, you may well lose both. You certainly won't be able to continue to work and your fortune will be at your husband's discretion.'

'What if he's rich?'

'There's plenty to be said for a rich husband. But you are not ideally suited to be someone's wife. You are used to being of some note and having your own way. You will have to pray for a very rich and very lenient man.'

'And the particular advice?' Emily pushed away her toast.

'Charles Earl Brook, dear child, is not of your calibre. He is like this' – Sarah raised the silver sugar bowl – 'in comparison to you,' and here she chinked the capacious fruit bowl that stood in the middle of the dining table. The bowl made a clear, ringing sound. 'You are petite and beautiful and many gentlemen will find that combination charming. But it is a rare man who will remain in love with a woman who is both intelligent and independent.' She stroked Emily's shoulder. 'My dear, you are only twenty-two. Aunt Mathilda is right. Your father should have brought a chaperone for you.'

Emily found that in spite of her objections she was able to eat a great deal of the lobsters' sweet, fresh flesh drenched in butter at lunch. Afterwards she and her father set off in their carriage, Charles Brook following behind in his. Edward King had left earlier with the Bells.

As the carriage turned out of the Crawfords' drive, Emily felt the familiar dread steal over her. She hated the endless rounds of rehearsals with mediocre actors and the constant travelling from one lacklustre theatre to another bad hotel. And then, of course, there was Charles Earl Brook. She thought about Miss Bell and the life she would have as Mrs Brook and something in her envied its settled nature and the security it would offer. She wondered if Charles really would marry Miss Bell now that she had refused him. Apart from Miss Bell's looks and class, Emily failed to see why he was attracted to her.

Their journey from the Crawfords' had initially been along sandy roads with the scent of pine trees in the air but as it grew dark, the roads grew muddier and more pitted. Because of the storm the night before there was a great deal of water in trenches and ruts, and the carriage bumped and tossed even more than it had on the journey there. It had been lurching unevenly but steadily for some time when suddenly there was a loud creak and the oil lamp at the front swung wildly, sending light flickering through their windows.

'Dear God,' said her father and that was the last thing she remembered him saying before the carriage tipped over.

Emily was thrown violently against the window. She must have passed out momentarily. When she opened her eyes, it was dark and she was hunched in the corner in an odd position. Her head throbbed, and something trickled down one side of her face. Outside, she could hear the horses neighing and the coachman calling frantically. She shifted and the carriage rocked alarmingly. In the dim star-light she could make out her father lying silently against the broken window, blood streaming over his face.

'Father! Father!' she screamed.

When she touched his neck, she could feel his pulse. He was still alive. The carriage started to rock as the coachman wrenched open the door and reached in to help her out.

'We have to get my father out,' she said, as she perched on the side of the carriage and then slid to the ground. In spite of the coachman's steadying hand, Emily was much higher up than she'd anticipated and she fell awkwardly, landing in a puddle. She saw that one of the wheels had caught in a ditch and as the horses had struggled to pull it out, the axle had snapped.

While she stood there, unsure what to do next, she glimpsed a light in the trees behind them and heard the sound of horses – Charles's carriage. She ran towards him, shouting.

'What's happened? What's wrong?' he said, jumping out as the carriage came to a halt. He took her by the shoulder. 'You are covered in blood!'

'There's been an accident,' she said. 'I'm perfectly fine, but Father is not.'

Charles looked around wildly. 'Stay here,' he commanded.

'But we must get my father out. He's hurt,' Emily cried, but Charles had stridden away and was shouting at his driver. Emily ran back to her carriage and called to the driver, who was tugging ineffectually at the lodged carriage wheel, 'You've got to get my father out!'

'I can't do it on my own, m'am,' he said. 'I need a light and another man.'

'Mr Brook, please, come over here and help my father,' she called.

Charles joined her swiftly, looked inside the carriage, and when he turned to Emily his face was white.

'Well now,' said Charles, his voice trembling slightly, 'we need to think about this, how we get him out. He might have hurt his back. We don't want to do more damage.'

Emily dashed over to Charles's carriage, climbed up and unhooked the oil lamp and returned, holding it as steadily as she could in front of her. By the light of the lamp she saw a man riding towards them, slowing to a halt as he saw the horses at an angle across the middle of the road and then turning his head to take in the broken carriage.

'Sir, over here,' she shouted and waved, holding out the lamp.

The man trotted over to her. He was a Negro, wearing a grey suit that had been patched repeatedly, particularly around the knees, and a broad-brimmed hat. He dismounted as he reached her. Instantly Charles was by her side.

'Quick,' he commanded. 'There's a man trapped inside the carriage. Help the driver to carry him out.'

'Yes, sir,' the newcomer said quietly and handed Emily the reins of his horse. 'Pardon me, missis,' he said, taking the light from her.

'Climb inside. Pick him up. Pass him to the driver,' ordered Charles.

'Sir.'

As the driver held the carriage steady, the man climbed

over the smashed wheel and lowered himself inside. He hefted John into his arms, though he was not a small man, and passed him to Charles and the driver who pulled John out.

'Gently,' said Charles, cursing under his breath. 'Good God, man, he's not a bale of cotton.'

Once John was free of the wreck, the Negro and the driver carried him back to Charles's carriage and, with some difficulty, hauled him in and laid him on the back seat. Emily tied the horse to a tree and climbed in after them.

'You got a little liquor?' the man asked.

Charles pulled a hip flask out of his pocket and the man gave her father a shot. Abruptly, her father woke and groaned and coughed. The man soaked his handkerchief in water from his own flask and wiped John's face.

'A few cuts and bruises.' He wet his handkerchief again and offered it to Emily. 'Missis, right there on your face.'

'I'll do it,' said Charles, snatching the handkerchief.

He wiped her face gently and then finished by dabbing a drop of alcohol on the cut. She winced.

'Now, let's drive your father home and get him to a doctor. You stay with the other driver and attend to the horses and the broken carriage,' he said to the man. He took a swig from his flask, watching him closely.

'Yes, sir,' the man said and he looked away.

Emily turned to him. 'I can't thank you enough. Mr Brook, please give this gentleman some money for his trouble.'

'No, missis, I just help you folks out.'

'I insist. I don't know what would have happened without your help.'

Charles handed a few notes to the man, who nodded and jumped out of the carriage. Emily watched him as they drove away until the man had melded with the darkness.

Chapter 2

May 1859

They'd started rehearsals for a new play, *Undine*, beginning in the mornings when it was passably cool. It would be the last play before the summer. Emily's role was the fairy water nymph, Undine, who, with a kiss, kills her mortal husband. This play had been extremely popular when she and her father had toured with it before – even more so than *Romeo and Juliet*.

Emily felt wretched. The heat made her restless. Worse, her father was still ill. Since the accident two weeks ago he had barely been able to get out of bed. He'd been bled and she had placed poultices across his back where he complained of the pain but neither remedy seemed to be working.

She thought about the day her father had suggested they should travel to America. It was the morning after the final performance of *Undine* at the Theatre Royal in Bath. The entire run had sold out and they had celebrated late into the night. Emily had felt light-headed with relief – that the play had been received so well and had been so uncommonly well attended, and that now it was over she hoped she could perhaps retire from acting. It was late by the time she, her brother Will and her mother returned home; they left her father singing with his manager and some of the other actors.

The following morning felt quite different. Emily woke late to a silent house and with none of her former *joie de vivre*. She felt fragile and the beginning of a vicious headache pulsed behind her eyes. Her mouth was dry and her cracked lips were stained maroon from the red wine she had drunk. She washed and dressed and sat alone in the dining room, still laid for breakfast although it was almost noon. She was about to ring for the maid when Rachel knocked and entered.

'Miss, it's your father.'

Emily's heart lurched. Her father always seemed so hale but, nonetheless, she worried for his health. He ate too little and drank too much and he was showing the first signs of gout.

'He wants you to meet him at the teashop, miss. He said for you to go as soon as you was ready.'

She knew where he meant, of course. It was his favourite haunt during the day, by the river not far from the theatre. Rachel was already holding her cloak and she helped Emily put it on and then ran for her bonnet. Emily hurried as fast as she could. It was early summer and the lime blossom was out; the air was as thick as treacle and as sweet as honey and the pollen and tiny chartreuse-green florets dusted her shoulders.

Her father was waiting for her, sitting at a table outside, smoking. In front of him he had a black coffee and a measure of whisky, the liquor glowing in the light bouncing from the black, sun-stippled river. When he saw her he stood and embraced her. This morning he looked like another man. As a young man he had always played the lead. Age had given him gravitas, a statesman-like quality. He was tall with luxuriantly thick, dark hair, a large, slightly hooked nose, deep-set eyes and square jaw. Today the pouches beneath his eyes were puffy and tender-looking; in the harsh light his skin seemed almost translucent, with a faint greenish pallor, the lines from his nose to mouth deeper, and he had not shaved.

'Have you not been home, Father?' asked Emily.

He summoned the owner and ordered Emily a Sally Lunn bun with cinnamon butter and a weak tea, then he turned to her.

'You were wonderful. Astounding,' he said.

Emily made an impatient gesture. Her father had said all this the night before with great eloquence and this morning it rang hollow.

'What ails you, Father?'

'It's the theatre. We have still not saved it.'

She took a bite of her bun. 'So, we'll have to continue. Another play. Perhaps tour,' she said sadly.

'It needs more than that,' said John. 'My love, I think you and I will have to go to America. They pay uncommonly well over there, you see. More than we could ever hope of making here.'

She said nothing but stared out over the river, banded with emerald and mustard drifts of scum.

'For how long?'

'Only a few months.'

He took a pull on his cigar and the smoke hung in the air in front of him. She knew he was lying.

Emily picked up her bun and was about to put it down on the plate again without taking a bite when she realized with a start that a picture of herself was printed in indigo in the centre. It was now smeared with butter and sugar.

She turned the plate around so that he could see. 'Of course I'll go with you,' she said quietly.

'That's my girl,' he said, and enfolded her tightly in his arms.

She left him sitting there as she walked back beneath the avenue of lime trees. She managed to make it all the way home before she started to cry.

Charles had turned up on the second day of rehearsals for *Undine* with a flute and had joined the orchestra. She hadn't even known that he could play. He caught her eye and smiled. He'd been most attentive, bringing her father flowers, ripe peaches and chilled slices of watermelon, and he'd paid for a doctor who had come with extremely good recommendations.

Now, as the rehearsal entered its third hour, Charles left the orchestra pit and handed her a glass of cold water. She thanked him and held the glass, beaded with condensation, momentarily against her forehead. She watched as Charles left the stage and whispered something to the director.

The director clapped his hands. 'Ladies and gentlemen, that's quite sufficient for today. We shall begin at the same time tomorrow with a full read through.'

'Do you think you might have time for a ride with me before you have to start learning your lines?' Charles asked quietly.

'I know them already,' she said.

'Well, good. It'll be cooler in Mount Auburn too.'

She nodded. 'We can't be long though, I'll need to return to my father.'

He smiled and she realized that there was something different about him, some subtle change in his attitude towards her. She couldn't quite put her finger on it but, whatever it was, it made her feel triumphant. Miss Penelope Bell had not been mentioned once since their weekend at the Crawfords'.

'Shall we say in an hour?'

She nodded again.

Back at the hotel, she washed her face, put on her riding habit and pinned up her hair beneath her hat, then looked in on her father. He couldn't accompany her but she wanted, at least, to ask his permission. He was asleep, his face pale with pain; his breath rattled in his chest. Dark shadows exacerbated the hollows beneath his cheekbones. She crept out and stood in front of his door for a moment to collect herself.

Charles was waiting outside the hotel for her, mounted

on a fine bay and holding the reins of a rather beautiful roan. As soon as he saw her he dismounted and helped her on to her horse. As usual, he had picked a good one, wonderfully responsive to her touch. Even so, she felt thoroughly uncomfortable: the thick cotton of her habit irritated her skin and she hated how tight the bodice was around her chest.

She followed Charles through the town but it wasn't until they passed beneath the great granite gateway into Mount Auburn that a sense of calm descended upon her. Charles had been right, it was cooler. A slight breeze had risen and the shade from the trees provided welcome relief. The sky was brilliant blue and cloudless and a faint scent of pine came from the avenue of firs; the white marble of statues and gravestones glimmered through the green light from the trees as if they were at the bottom of some great torpid river. Mount Auburn was a beautifully landscaped cemetery; its park-like lines of trees, the small lake, rolling lawns and hidden glades reminded Emily of England.

As usual, they galloped through the pines and then came to a halt near the ornamental lake, its surface scaled with the glossy plates of water lilies. Charles pulled out a heavy green bottle of chilled white wine from his saddlebag, along with a couple of glasses and a handful of peaches. He shook out a blanket and laid it on the grass.

'How perfect!' exclaimed Emily, holding one of the peaches to her cheek to feel its soft skin and inhale its ripe scent. She would take one back to the hotel for her father.

'I've been racking my brains why your play should be so

popular – sold out before it's even opened. Everyone wants to see you, of course, but it's something else too and I think I've got it. We are so darned scared of you.'

'Scared of me?'

'Of womankind. You have a power over us men; you bind us with spells and wicked kisses like Undine.'

'What nonsense, Mr Brook,' she said.

'It doesn't matter what you say, it's true. Women charm us and they torment us. We love them and we're frightened of them, of their hold over us.'

'And meanwhile you run the country while we remain at home. As if we have any hold over you – we women have no power.'

'What is politics but posturing? It's merely men showing off to each other. We don't want you to see that, we don't want you to be involved in what is degrading and ultimately meaningless. You have no need to envy us this power – men are nothing and have nothing compared to you.'

'I have a feeling that Miss Sarah Crawford would not agree with you there,' Emily said, shifting her position so she could feel the sun on her face.

'Ah, but that is because Miss Crawford is not as pretty as you.'

'But what in the world do a woman's looks have to do with inequality?'

'Looks have everything to do with it. You, my dear, have quite a stranglehold over me. And if you were less delightful and even a shade less beautiful, I might be able to free myself,' he whispered.

He bent down and kissed her softly on the lips, his pale grey eyes suffused with light. She wished she could lie there in the heat, absorbing the smell of crushed moss and Charles's musky odour, his weight pressing against her. Then she thought of her father and felt a cold, slippery sensation around her heart. She twisted to one side, away from Charles, and sat up.

'I must go. I've left my father alone for too long.'

She stood up abruptly and staggered; the wine and the sun had gone to her head. He caught her elbow, his hand hot beneath her arm, and helped her on to her horse.

As she rushed through the lobby of the hotel, Emily caught sight of herself in one of the mirrors: her face flushed, her hair escaping from under her hat, her cream riding habit blotched with green grass stains. She looked, she thought, as a woman in love must look.

She knocked on the door to her father's room and waited, adjusting her skirts and brushing back her hair. There was no reply so she pushed the door open. Inside it was dark. A few rays of light slid through the shutters and spilled over the bed. There was a sour smell of stale sweat. A plate of biscuits in congealed gravy stood untouched on the side table. Her father looked asleep, his head thrown back, his mouth open. She walked towards him slowly, waiting for him to snore. His eyes were open slightly and the whites looked cloudy. A thin trickle of saliva had dribbled from his mouth and hung stickily against his chin. A couple of flies were buzzing noisily around the room. She put her hand over her mouth to stop herself from making a sound. She should touch him, she knew she should, and she stretched out her hand, but at the last minute could not bring herself to do so.

She broke into heavy, silent, juddering sobs. She rang the bell for the servant and stood waiting for what felt like a long time. Eventually the Negro maid pushed open the door without knocking and said, 'What?'

Emily couldn't answer. She stood to one side and the maid said, 'Lord,' under her breath and then, 'Missis, you just go on next door to your own room and I gone fetch the doctor.'

Emily didn't move. The maid turned to her and Emily felt her put one heavy hand on her shoulder and steer her out of her father's room. Things seemed to happen in a disjointed and unconnected time frame after that. The doctor arrived and gave her some drops. Charles appeared and hugged her to his chest. She started to cry again and he wiped away her tears. She heard him shouting in the corridor and the maid appeared with a basin of hot water and helped her undress. A short while later a tray of cold chicken and a hot rum punch was brought up. As she sat at her table, unable to bring herself to eat a single mouthful, she was, she suddenly realized, completely alone.

The following day she stayed in her room and Charles came and went. He sent a telegram to the Crawfords; he spoke to the theatre manager who released her temporarily from her contract. A seamstress arrived, the one who had made her costume for *Undine*, with yards of black crêpe and a new black bonnet edged with black satin ribbon. She measured and pinned and cut, laying the fabric out on the floor, and said she'd have the dress ready for the day after next.

'The day after tomorrow?' Emily asked stupidly.

'Why, m'am, that's when the funeral will be. But there's no need for you to worry yourself. Your fiancé has arranged it all. Now, I'll stitch a veil to the ribbon here, and you can unpick it later and use the bonnet again. For a happier occasion. I'll retrim it for you if you like.'

My fiancé, she thought slowly.

And finally Charles reappeared and knelt almost jubilantly at her feet.

'I've managed to secure a place for your father at Mount Auburn.'

'But he should be buried at home. In England,' she said, snatching her hands out of his.

'Emily,' he said firmly, 'that simply ain't possible. It takes at least three weeks to reach England. You know that. He needs to be buried now,' he added gently. 'And this way, he'll be in a place that means something to you. To us. And we can, at our leisure, choose his gravestone and have it carved. He'll be buried near the Avenue of Firs.'

She said nothing.

'It was uncommonly difficult, you know,' he said softly, 'obtaining permission to bury him there.'

'Thank you,' she said at length, 'thank you for everything you have done. I am not myself. But please, Charles, before you go, would you do one more thing for me?'

'Anything, my dear,' he said, kissing her hand.

'Would you ask Sarah to come to me?'

'She will be with you by midday tomorrow. Mr Crawford and his father will arrive later, for the funeral itself. I have taken the liberty of inviting a few more people, those who had the highest regard for your father.'

There were always young men hanging around in the public bar in the hotel hoping for a glimpse of Emily and, as news of the tragedy spread, their numbers had increased.

'My dear,' said Sarah, hugging her gently and looking around with distaste, 'let's get away from this horrid place.'

They walked along the quay where it was a little cooler and Sarah held her parasol over Emily who dragged along beside her listlessly. They leaned over the railings and watched the steamers and barges, crates of deep green watermelons and barrels of oranges being unloaded on to the wharf, seagulls screaming above ships netting shrimp.

'You're most welcome to stay with us, you know,' said Sarah quietly.

'Thank you. I think I shall remain in town though, dismal as it is. After all, I am required to finish the play.'

She began to cry again, raw sobs that burned her throat. Sarah offered her handkerchief and waited until she'd stopped.

'I'll return home after the play. I've saved enough to pay for Will's university fees and there must be some sort of work I can undertake to help keep Mother and me. I'm hungry,' said Emily abruptly. 'I can hardly remember when I last ate.'

Sarah took her to a restaurant near the waterfront and ordered sherry, a selection of cakes and a pot of tea. Emily ate ravenously while Sarah watched her. She herself took half a slice of Madeira cake, but barely ate any of it, instead playing with the crumbs on her plate as she listened to Emily.

'Mr Brook is being marvellous,' Emily said, through a mouthful of cake. 'He's arranged it all. I am not even sure who will be attending the funeral. But if he, you and your brother and father are there I shall be content.'

She felt the sweet cake and sherry curdling in her stomach and pushed away her plate.

'We'll be there,' said Sarah, taking her hand. 'But just be careful, Emily. This is a difficult time and I'm afraid to say you shall most likely feel worse before you begin to feel better. Nothing can prepare you for the loss of your parents.' She hesitated. 'It can become easy to rely on people upon whom one would not under other circumstances.'

Charles had managed it beautifully. A hearse pulled by a team of clinker-black horses followed by a carriage dark as oil containing the Crawfords arrived promptly at the hotel. Emily had been waiting anxiously in her room. The tightly laced corset beneath her new black dress contributed to her feeling of suffocation and nausea. Ely jumped out to clear her path but, for once, the small crowd gathered in the bar stood back and allowed her through without jostling her. Ely helped her into the carriage.

Sarah gripped her hand; Emily could see the ink stains on her fingers through the dark lace. She said, 'I've brought you a buttonhole.'

As the carriage jolted along the street, Sarah pinned a single white rose to Emily's lapel and then adjusted her bonnet and veil a fraction. It was what her mother might have done had she been there. Emily felt her throat constrict as the carriage stopped in front of the church. She took Sarah's arm and they walked slowly through the great doors and into the cavernous chill. Her father's coffin was placed at the front with a wreath of white roses in the centre. She looked around at the almost empty church, echoing with their footfalls: there were Charles and the Bells, without their daughters, the theatre manager and a few of the actors. How much more crowded the church would have been had he died back in England, she thought. How sad that those who loved him best would not be able to mourn him and honour his memory befittingly. Her letter to her mother and brother would not even have reached them; her father was being buried and they were not aware that he had died. She wept silent tears.

Towards the end of the service Theodore Crawford stood and spoke a few words about John, his voice echoing in the semi-empty church: he said he had been a man of integrity and wisdom, of wit and charm.

'It was not that he was an ambitious man, but he drove himself and others to perform as well as possible on every conceivable occasion. He did not aspire to lead roles but he pushed himself to become the best because he wanted to see his profession flourish and his theatre in his home town of Bath blossom. Anyone who saw him perform could not help but be swept along by his skill and craft, his ability to inhabit so perfectly another human being, if only for a couple of hours. For, as Hamlet said, "Speak the speech, I pray you, as I pronounced it to you, trippingly on the tongue: but if you mouth it, as many of your players do, I had as lief the town-crier spoke my lines. Use all gently; for in the very torrent, tempest, and, as I may say, whirlwind of passion, you must acquire and beget a temperance that may give it smoothness." We can all imagine that if John Harris had played Hamlet, he would indeed have given the part characteristic smoothness,' concluded Theodore.

He had played Hamlet, Emily thought, and with magnificent smoothness – the last time when she was sixteen years old. His performance had been, perhaps, a little too silky, with insufficient depth to hint at the prince's hidden torments, but it was only now, with the benefit of age, that she had grown aware of the surface sheen of his acting. Mr Crawford had given a fine speech for a man who had known her father for such a short amount of time but he had omitted what was for her one of John's greatest gifts: his capacity to enjoy life.

They followed the hearse to Mount Auburn. It was a beautiful day, the clouds like perfectly formed balls of cotton. As they drove beneath Mount Auburn's great granite archway she considered all the many happier occasions she had spent within the confines of this exquisitely landscaped park. And then she thought of the last time she had been here, of sitting by the lake with Charles Brook, and all the while her father had been dying, alone in his room. It was when the coffin was lowered into the raw earth and the first clods shattered the roses and scattered their pale petals across the sleek wood that she started to sob. It did not seem right, that her life-loving father should be laid to rest when he was still a comparatively young and healthy man, in an alien land beneath foreign soil. And it came to her afresh and with devastating force the full weight of her loneliness; her loss and her isolation from all that was familiar and dear.

The wake was in an inn and consisted of mediocre sherry and first-class seafood. She could imagine her father laughing and shucking oysters, regaling all and sundry with his tale of the first time he ate turtle soup from its shell in Baltimore. She tried to imagine the wake he would have had at home. How his friends would have drunk his health while imitating his sonorous voice and the slow majesty of his acting; how they would have drunk another toast and quoted his anecdotes and his jokes, the ones he liked to repeat over and over after a pint of stout in the tavern. How soulless this perfectly orchestrated funeral would have seemed to a man like him.

She excused herself and took the Crawfords' carriage back to the hotel. She had decided that the best thing was to grit her teeth and return to the play and to ask Charles to book her a passage back to England as soon as *Undine* had ended. She would hold that date in her mind as a talisman to see her through the weeks ahead. She must speak to the manager about returning to the theatre and to Sarah about hiring a maid who would be willing also to accompany her back to England. She would keep going until then by working as hard as possible.

The play was to open in three days. In the meantime Emily was trapped. She hardly felt able to venture out, given the young men lingering by the hotel entrance, the braver ones drinking in the bar. Without her father she was acutely aware of how unprotected she was. She could not even stroll along the promenade without men calling her name or trying to hand her roses. In her room it grew stiflingly hot. She lay on the bed, staring up at the stained ceiling, feeling the lumps in the mattress pressing into her back and listening to the constant clamour: doors slamming, the cook shouting, the clatter of crockery, the hum of voices from the public room, the clink of glasses. At regular intervals carriages pulled up outside the hotel with new guests, or carts stopped with barrels of beer or sides of meat to be unloaded and she could hear the shouts of the stable-hands and the porters. She felt wrung out with grief and loneliness. It would be at least another three weeks until she received a letter from her mother. She imagined them in Bath, still behaving as if the world were unchanged, not yet knowing that John was no longer in it. She started crying again, without bothering to rise or dry her eyes, letting the tears flow down her temples and run coldly into her ears.

She thought of the very first time she had read for her mother and father. They'd been sitting taking tea in the parlour when she entered and the way they both turned and looked at her made her feel awkward.

'Sit down, love,' said her father.

Her mother silently poured her a cup of tea, stirred in milk and sugar and passed it to her.

'We would very much like you to read to us,' said her father.

'Read to you?' she said stupidly.

'This passage here, from *Romeo and Juliet*,' he said, handing her the script, and pointing it out with one thick finger.

'But why? I've never—'

'Just try, Emily, for us,' said her mother in the particularly gentle and light tone of voice she used that meant she'd lose patience if thwarted.

Emily took the script and her tea and sat on the ottoman by the fireplace. She read through the passage several times and looked over at her parents. They were waiting expectantly. Emily took a breath and read aloud.

Her mother and father regarded her solemnly when she'd finished. She could hear the slow, metronomic tick of the clock on the mantelpiece. Then her father suddenly started clapping and laughing. He leapt up and hugged her, crumpling the script.

'That was wonderful, Emily, wonderful.'

Her mother smiled thinly and put her head on one side and did a little clap next to her cheek. 'A little more expression, but we can work on that,' she said. 'My fear is that her voice will not carry.'

'Well, we shall see. The theatre is empty this afternoon. Emily, my love, try to commit that passage to heart and then we'll put you on the stage.'

'But why?' she asked again in bewilderment.

She had never in her life wanted to act and her parents had always heeded her wishes.

'Just do as your father asked you, Emily,' said her mother.

Emily trailed listlessly up to her room with the script.

That afternoon at the theatre her father lit the oil lamps at the front of the stage and then retreated to one of the seats at the back. She stood in the centre, squinting at the lights, watching him until he was engulfed by the darkness. She swallowed, her throat dry. Motes of dust spun in the columns of light above the lamps; the thick velvet drapes smelled like ancient books newly opened. Her hands, clasped together, were slick with perspiration. She started to speak.

> . . . *bid me lurk*
> *Where serpents are; chain me with roaring bears;*
> *Or hide me nightly in a charnel-house,*
> *O'er-covered quite with dead men's rattling bones,*
> *With reeky shanks and yellow chapless skulls;*
> *Things that, to hear them told, have made me tremble;*
> *And I will do it without fear or doubt.*

When she'd finished she shivered, her breast heaving. There was the sound of clapping, but not from the back of the stalls where she thought her father was but from high up to her left. She looked up, shading her eyes. A man stood and applauded in one of the boxes. She could barely see his features but she had the impression of white hair and long whiskers before he stepped away from the balcony. She hurried backstage where her father met her. He was tense with excitement.

'That was Mr Thomas Williams,' he whispered.

She had heard of him from her father and read his reviews in the paper. He was an exacting critic.

'He liked you,' said her father, kissing her on both cheeks. 'Now run home, my love, while I speak further with him.'

This meant, she thought, as she tied her bonnet, that the two of them would retire to the tavern and that her father would not return for some while. She felt irritable and deflated as she walked back home.

'What did he say?' asked her mother, as soon as she entered the house.

'So you knew?'

Her mother looked pleased, almost smug. 'We wanted a professional opinion,' she said. 'Mr Williams did you a great honour, appearing merely to see an ingénue. So what did he say?'

'He said he liked me,' said Emily sullenly.

In fact Mr Thomas Williams had been more precise than that. He had said to her father: 'Put her on stage straight away.'

Emily had not understood the extent to which the theatre was haemorrhaging money nor quite how drastic a

47

change of direction was required to appease the creditors. She soon realized: her father wanted to open a new production with her as the star within three weeks. She had to learn the role of Juliet, rehearse with the rest of the cast and have a new wardrobe fitted. Her mother coached her and was by turns exasperated and delighted and Emily's mood followed suit, sinking from euphoria to despair. Her brother, whom she saw infrequently at this time, was the only person in the increasingly fraught household who remained untouched by the strain and was constantly ebullient. For, though it was never directly stated, Emily had grasped that the theatre was in serious financial difficulties and that she was, perhaps, their last chance. She also realized that it was not simply their future income that rested upon her but the livelihoods of all the actors who depended upon the Royal.

The morning of the day of her first performance she woke feeling sick.

'I can't do it, I simply can't,' she told her mother, starting to cry and clutching her stomach.

'But you must, my love,' said Lily gently, moving one damp curl from her forehead.

Emily gagged and Rachel ran forward with the washbasin. Emily retched again, a thin yellow bile.

Her mother tried another tack. 'Emily, you're marvellous. You shall be superb. Come now, rouse yourself.' She stood up and opened the curtains a fraction to let a sliver of daylight into her daughter's bedroom. She turned and frowned. 'Perhaps if you ate a little toast and took a small cup of tea you might feel better. All actors suffer in this way. No matter how experienced, we all feel stage fright, you know.'

'But I'm not an actress,' wailed Emily, hiccupping through her tears. 'I never wanted to be on stage.'

'Nonsense, Emily, you will be wonderful. Now, please, wash and dress yourself and come and have some breakfast.' Her mother, her patience at an end, left the room.

She must think I'm self-indulgent, thought Emily, for she had so loved to act and resented the lack of roles for a woman of her age. Somehow, she got through the day and the performance although she was so ill with nerves she could remember only stepping on to the stage into that pool of brilliant light and the end, when the audience stood and clapped and clapped until her ears rang. That had been three years ago. It was the beginning of what others saw as a luminous career and what she herself thought of as a sentence, one that would be served as long as her father was alive and he willed it so. Now it was almost over. But the cold and cruel thought that remained was that without her father how would she and her mother live if she did not continue to act?

For two days after the funeral she saw and heard nothing of Charles. On the third day, he arrived at the hotel in the morning.

'Tell Mr Brook that I'm not well,' Emily said to the maid.

It was all she could do to rouse herself for the

performance that evening. Her clothes were creased and stained, her scalp itchy. She had a headache, a dull and muffled throbbing.

The maid knocked again. It was the same woman who had attended her on the day her father had died and she looked at Emily with some sympathy.

'Missis, Mr Brook say the fresh air gone do you good. He say he have a horse for you.'

She sighed. She did not want to go riding but she felt a certain obligation towards Charles.

'Please tell him that I will be down shortly.'

She rose and changed her dress and tucked her unkempt hair into her bonnet. As she walked along the threadbare carpets in the corridor, she caught sight of herself in a mirror hanging at the end of the long, dark hallway. Her cheeks were drawn, she had lost the glow of summer sun and there were purple bruises beneath her eyes. She tried to ignore the people who turned to stare at her as she passed through the lobby.

Outside the hotel, Charles was waiting with two white horses, polished to a sheen, their hooves varnished and bridles gleaming. She noted his almost imperceptible hesitation as she came over to him.

'I thought a ride along the beach would refresh your spirits,' he said.

He held the horse steady at the mounting block and one stirrup out for her. Emily felt as if she no longer knew how to smile and perhaps never would again. It was already hot and the heat radiating from the street seemed like solid matter that they must forge through. The smell of rotting vegetables and spoiled fish hung in the air. It made her queasy and she clung to the horse's white mane. Gradually, as they approached the sea, the heat dissipated and the stench faded. She remembered how they had raced each other along the strand, Charles laughing as she nudged her horse ahead of his, their hooves churning up sand and spray. She could taste salt on her lips and smell the tang of seaweed freshly washed up on the shore.

'It's a relief to be out of the hotel,' she said suddenly. Even speaking seemed like a trial and she had exhausted her slim reserves of energy.

He smiled at her. 'I knew a short ride along the beach would be just the tonic for you.' His face clouded. 'But you mustn't tire yourself. Shall we stop for a moment?'

She nodded. She followed him back down the beach a little way and then he turned and cut through the dunes along a narrow path. He dismounted and led the horses into a sandy hollow, fringed by marram grass and with wide, flat logs of driftwood.

Emily slid off her horse and, handing him the reins, sat down on a log. Charles tied up the horses, looping their reins under one of the larger pieces of wood.

'You are bearing up magnificently,' he said, coming to sit alongside her.

She smiled to herself. His charm was such that she almost believed him.

'I still can't accept it. I keep thinking of things I should like to tell him.'

'I know how you must feel,' he said. 'My mother and father are both dead.'

'I'm sorry.'

'They died together. In a railroad accident. My brother and I were quite young.' He glanced at her and then knelt in the sand by her feet.

'I know this is not the best of times for you, dear Emily, but if you would consent to be my wife, I would cherish you always and would, I hope, try to make up for the loss of your father through my love for you.'

She looked at him and felt numb, consumed with grief. He was still kneeling in front of her, still talking, but his words were being whipped away on that pale wind and she could barely hear what he had to say.

'I know you said you were not the marrying kind,' he continued, 'but please, do reconsider. You have no one here to protect you and safeguard your good name and if you were to marry me, why, I would look after you. You could stop acting. I don't have a ring,' he said quickly, 'you have such singular taste I thought if you would accept me you could choose it. But I do have this.'

He felt in his jacket pocket and pulled out a white whorled shell. He held it out to her.

Emily looked down at the shell, ground soft and matte by the sea. She didn't know whether she would laugh or cry. There was a gaping hollow at the centre of her. In the end, she merely smiled thinly and enfolded the shell within her hand. But that seemed to be enough.

*

She stood at the window in her hotel. She'd requested one of the back bedrooms as it would have more privacy and when she looked out it was upon a jumble of brickwork, so soot-begrimed it hung in ledges from the pointing, windows glazed black and shrouded with tattered curtains, rows of crooked chimneys wheezing smoke. If she craned her neck she could see a slash of blue sky and seagulls fighting on the rooftops.

Charles had engineered her withdrawal from the play. The wedding seemed to have developed a life of its own. Charles had set it in motion and came to report on its progress as it grew in strength and wilfulness like a strange and capricious creature. She listened silently. She did not have an opinion, for it seemed to have little to do with her.

Instead she thought about her mother and her brother. They would now know that John had died. Her mother would have written to her. She imagined the letter crossing the Atlantic, drawing slowly towards her through the vast desert of the ocean, lying jumbled in a sack of other mail, an inky tangle of loss and love and longing. She thought of her mother sitting in the parlour in her favourite window seat, her lace handkerchief in a wet ball in her palm, weeping until her eyes were bloodshot. She thought of Will, in her father's place in the tavern, the chair polished smooth as bone, drinking glass after glass of bitter ale with no one to witness his sorrow. Will, who was always so lively. She thought about the last time she had seen him when he was home for the holidays.

'All the chaps in Cambridge want to meet you,' he'd said, bounding into the parlour and throwing himself on the settee next to her, upsetting her basket of thread. 'And now I can give them this instead.' He tossed a scarf in her lap and laughed uproariously. It was white and printed with tiny lozenges but when she looked closer she saw they were pictures of her. 'First plates, now scarves. Perhaps we should print you on tobacco so we can put you in our pipes and smoke you.'

Their mother frowned. Emily wasn't sure whether it was because she disliked seeing her daughter made fun of or because she considered the attention might turn her head.

'It'll all be over soon enough,' said Emily, smiling at her brother and gathering up the reels.

Her mother frowned even more. 'I should hope it won't. We need to keep selling tickets.'

'I'll sell tickets to the fellows at Cambridge. How much could we charge them for tea with Emily?'

'Will,' said their mother sharply.

'And should I be expected to discourse on theological matters over tea too?' Emily asked.

Will was studying theology. He had a fine, sonorous voice and the Bible sounded magnificent when he read it aloud, but as he had no desire to become an actor, he was intensely grateful that Emily's success had allowed him to escape his fate and run away to college.

Now, feeling utterly alone, she took out her father's dark navy Bible, the leather worn as soft as butter beneath his thumbs, and read from it, hearing the fine timbre of Will's voice in her head.

On the day of the wedding the weather broke. It was dark and gusty with a shiver of rain in the air. It reminded Emily of England. She felt cold, her hands icy, and ill with apprehension. Sarah and Theodore Crawford accompanied her from the hotel to the church and it was like some terrible sense of déjà vu: the two of them in their best dark clothes, Theodore helping her into the carriage, Sarah plucking a white rose from her bouquet and pinning it to Theodore's lapel, wearing those same torn gloves, her hair spilling unruly from beneath her hat. There were a handful of people waiting – a few of Charles's friends she had never met, Ely, Aunt Mathilda and some actors from the theatre company. It was unsettling that she had seen them all in more sober circumstances barely a week ago, then as now surrounded by white roses.

She had dressed in the raw silk dress scattered with seed pearls that she had worn at the Crawfords'; it was the only one remotely suitable and there had been no time to have another made: the only addition was a veil Charles had arranged to be sewn with pearls and trimmed with white velvet to match. She walked down the aisle on Theodore's arm; the faint scent of roses from her bouquet intermingled with the smell of hot hymn books and varnish bubbling from the wooden pews, made her stomach churn. It was like a performance, she thought, yet another performance she did not want to give, and the stage fright was equally vicious. She had to fight back the tears that threatened to overflow.

As they neared the priest, Charles turned and smiled. In his elegantly cut black suit, he looked relaxed and handsome and his grey eyes were heavy with tenderness. She felt her heart swell and beat faster. The ceremony seemed to pass so quickly – she had almost no recollection of it – and then they spilled out on to the steps above the street and it was as if everyone's spirits were suddenly released after being pent up in the church. Charles's friends threw their hats in the air and an urchin caught one and ran off with it. Two of the men chased the little boy, who flung it back to them and it sailed over the sidewalk and landed at the foot of the steps where the wind took it and tossed it down the cobbled street. One of the actors popped a champagne cork and the foam flew as if it were sea spray, bubbles winking on their clothes like sequins. Emily looked at Sarah, half expecting to see disapproval in her face, but her eyes were full of tears. She came over and embraced Emily.

'I hope you will be very happy,' she said. 'And that you'll live terribly near.'

Emily smiled through her tears. 'You must come round for coffee and cake every day. If I'm not acting I won't know what to do with myself.'

Ely, who had followed his sister, said, 'You could write another play.'

Ely's expression was unreadable. Was he teasing her? Emily wondered. She had confessed to him that she'd had a play published when she was still a teenager and he had once challenged her to read a scene from it. She had refused; she could see now that it was overlong and excessively melodramatic.

'Ely will talk you into writing treatises against slavery if you're not careful,' said Sarah.

'Well, as a matter of fact I *do* have a meeting with Mr King tomorrow,' said Emily, looking at Ely. 'He has suggested I should write a diary of our travels across Europe. It would be a sort of sequel to *American Life* perhaps.' She paused. 'But without my father's observations, it will be less humorous.'

'Nonsense, my dear,' said Sarah, taking one of her hands in both of her own. 'You will make plenty of witty observations of your own. And you'll have your husband's to draw upon too.'

It started to rain, softly at first, but the wind tossed it in handfuls so that, coming from every direction, almost at once, it appeared to be worse than it was. Charles approached them with a servant bearing a tray of full champagne flutes.

'May I propose a toast?' he said, raising his glass and smiling at her, his face lit up. 'To my beautiful new wife.'

She looked around at her friends and colleagues with their charged glasses raised in that milky rain and wondered how quickly she would be able to return to Bath.

It was late morning but Emily was still in bed drinking coffee and reading a book. Ely had given her *Slavery* by the theologian William Ellery Channing along with one of his pamphlets when he left his family's wedding present. Charles had snorted when he'd seen it. As an actress Emily had always risen late but even now there didn't seem any point in getting up early. Charles walked in and she hastily brushed crumbs off the bed and straightened the cover. They'd been married for one week and were staying at the house Charles had leased until they set off for Europe.

'I've got the tickets,' he said, flapping the papers at her and the day's newspaper and coming to sit on the end of the bed.

'How wonderful, Charles. When do we leave?'

'In a week. I've hired a villa.'

'A villa? But we can stay with my mother. There's plenty of room.'

'Ah – but Emily, my dear, we're going to Italy. And the villa is in Tuscany. It sounds delightful, views across a valley filled with rustic olive groves and vineyards.'

'And how long have you booked it for?'

'Six months. It was cheaper than taking it for a few weeks.'

'But I thought we were travelling through Europe! Not staying in one place.'

'This way we can do both. We will be near Florence, Pisa and Sienna so we can go on day trips and you can have your fill of culture.' He stood up and looked down at her, as if willing her to agree to his sudden change of plan. When she did not reply, he turned and flung open the shutters abruptly, letting light and noise from the street below flood into the room. 'And then we will travel to England, and see your family,' he said.

He left the room. Why could they not see her family first? she wondered. It would be a small torture to have to wait a further six months. She felt both confused and angry; she would have to try to persuade him to leave Italy early, she thought. She shook out the paper and turned, as she often did, to the gossip column. The writer hadn't mentioned her since the death of her father, but there was a piece about her today, describing her marriage to wealthy society gentleman Charles Earl Brook, and the 'some might say, tragic end' of her career. And in his true poison-pen fashion, the columnist concluded: 'He who weds her for an angel will discover, ere a fortnight, that she is nothing more nor less than a woman, and perhaps one of the most troublesome kind into the bargain.' It made Emily laugh out loud. She was about to run to Charles and show him the article, when it suddenly occurred to her he might agree with it.

Chapter 3

December 1859

They were hot and bad-tempered. It felt as if they'd been travelling for months; the food had been bad and the roads worse, the carriages uncomfortable, the horsemen unreliable. It was now seven weeks since they'd left America. Emily's spirits started to lift as they climbed the steep hill towards the villa. They passed beneath olive trees, bowed under the weight of heavy clusters of plump, black fruit, the underside of the leaves silver, and skirted rows of terraced vineyards, the grapes ripening in the late afternoon sun.

As they reached the top of the hill, spread before them were field upon field of golden sunflowers, the heads blazing towards them. A line of cypresses, so dark green they were almost black, flanked the driveway leading to a crumbling honey-coloured house. Emily shouted for the driver to stop. She kissed Charles and jumped out and ran towards the house, pushing open the ornate, rusting iron gates. The garden was full of lavender and rosemary, the violet blossom dense with bees; roses wept saucer-shaped petals on to terracotta brick paths, and the bay trees were pin-pricked with fluffy yellow flowers. Starlings shouted from the eaves and swallows swooped perilously close. The housekeeper was standing at the steps wearing an apron and she wiped her hands and opened her arms to welcome Emily to the house. Inside it was cool and dark; the walls were covered in pale frescoes, the plaster chipped in parts, and the smell of hot bread, fried garlic and freshly torn basil emanated from the kitchens.

'It's delightful,' she said, as Charles walked in a few minutes later, and she flew to his side.

That night they sat outside and drank a velvety red Chianti.

'There's the Milky Way,' said Charles, pointing to the swathe of stars stretched across a sky already bright with stellar light.

Emily felt giddy looking up. They were wrapped together in a heavy damask quilt in case the night grew chill, cocooned within the throaty hum of cicadas.

'We're so snug, we're like two oysters,' she whispered and he stopped looking at the stars and bent to kiss her, his tongue tasting of wine. After a few minutes, he wrapped the damask around her shoulders like a cloak and led her inside, up the wide, white marble steps, veined as a fine cheese, and into the bedroom with its four-poster bed shrouded in silk where a breeze redolent of jasmine was blowing through the half-open window.

She liked to think that the baby had been conceived that

night but in truth it could have been any one of a number of those first early, heady days at the villa. When Charles found out he was delighted, and immediately insisted that she rest. Emily was lucky enough not to suffer much from morning sickness and at first she had indulged him, lying for long periods under the vines and in their bed, luxuriating in such unaccustomed indolence, or basking in the sun, letting Charles boss the housekeeper into bringing her thick slices of lemon polenta cake and slivers of *castagnaccio*.

'Imagine,' she'd said to him once, 'all of this – pasta and *parmigiano* – are miraculously being turned into a baby as we speak.'

In the early evenings he liked to rub oil scented with vetiver on to her swelling stomach and then make love to her slowly and gently. But before too long, the wonder of her pregnancy ceased to be such a novelty and she was walking and riding again. She was, however, taken aback by how breathless she had become and once she felt a liquid fluttering in her stomach and stood still as she realized it was the baby turning in her belly.

One day, though, they had argued vehemently. She'd been sitting in the garden writing her diary, revelling in the smell of warm rosemary and the heady perfume of roses. Swifts were darting around the pond, as quick and slight as bats, siphoning off the insects that adhered to the water's surface, and their high-pitched chatter filled the air. Beads of condensation clung to her glass of chilled wine and in that moment she felt indescribably content. Charles joined her.

'What are you writing?' he asked.

'My diary,' she said, smiling at him.

He'd smiled back and looked a little smug. 'I hope you're not disclosing all my secrets.'

'Of course not! This diary is quite discreet. I will be adapting it for publication on our return so it needs to be. Although I don't have quite the amount of material I thought I'd have as we've been so insufferably lazy.'

Charles's expression changed. 'What do you mean, for publication?'

'You remember my publisher, Mr Edward King, whom you met at the Crawfords'? It was his idea.'

'And his firm is paying you for this?' he said with incredulity.

'Of course,' she said, more coolly.

'Well, tell them you're not doing it,' he said vehemently.

'I shall do no such thing. I've worked all my life and I'm not going to stop now. Thanks to you I no longer have to be an actress – but I can still support myself.'

'You are utterly ridiculous, Emily. Don't you realize how wealthy I am? I can easily keep you in shoes and frocks and whatever other fripperies you desire.'

'Thank you, Charles, but that's really not the point.'

'Well, what is the point, if I may ask?'

'The point is my independence. Don't you see, Charles? People value my mind, my opinions, my thoughts. Being a writer is a worthy, valued profession.'

'I simply don't understand you,' said Charles, his voice heavy with frustration. 'We're married. And I don't choose to have you provide for us when I am perfectly capable of doing so.'

'I don't care what you choose or don't choose,' shouted Emily, finally losing her temper, 'I'm writing this book whether you like it or not.'

Charles rose to his feet, pale with anger, and said, 'I forbid it.'

For the rest of the day he avoided her and the next day he barely spoke to her. Emily had plenty of time to think and to register the beginnings of a heavy and bitter disappointment. She had hoped that marriage would be a meeting of minds, of an equality and intimacy she had hitherto never experienced but had yearned for. Still, she thrust these thoughts away and while she could not understand Charles's point of view, she had stood at the altar and agreed to 'honour and obey' her husband. More to thaw his icy demeanour towards her and to secure his companionship once more than due to any change of heart, she agreed to write the diary purely for her own pleasure and not to publish it.

The change was instant. Charles seemed to melt before her. He pulled her towards him and kissed her hard. Later he made love to her as gently as he ever had.

It was late in the season but the skies were gloriously blue and it was still just warm enough to sit outside for short periods. Emily and Charles were drinking coffee outside the villa beneath a tangled profusion of fuchsia-pink roses when the mail arrived.

The summer had been beautiful. Their cultural forays to Florence had been infrequent and short but Emily had also enjoyed the long rambles and horse riding around the hills of Montaione. It had turned out to be no hardship to rest in one place after all, particularly as her American stay had felt, at times, as if she were constantly living out of a trunk. There was only one month left of their trip and Emily hoped to prevail on Charles to visit Sienna or even Carrera before their departure, although she feared he would use her confinement as an excuse not to go.

Charles opened a telegram. As he read, the sun seemed to seep out of his expression. He looked across at her.

'We are going to have to cut our trip short,' he said. 'I have to return to America straight away.'

Emily sat up, alarmed. 'What's the matter?' she said. 'Is someone in your family ill?'

He shook his head, irritated. 'No, no – nothing like that.' He paused. 'But we will have to live in the southern states for a short while on our return. It ain't something I hoped we should have to do, particularly in your condition. But there it is. It can't be helped.'

'Charles, what has happened?'

'My brother and I inherited a plantation on the death of our parents. The manager has unexpectedly handed in his notice. My brother is travelling there now to look after the place but he lives in Baltimore and can't leave his family for long. As we have no home yet, my brother asks if I can relieve him as soon as we can until we are able to make other plans.'

'A plantation? What kind of plantation?'

'We grow cotton and sugar. It's in Georgia. My brother and I grew up there until we moved to the north to attend school.'

'You never told me this!' Emily was profoundly shocked.

'You never asked,' he retorted. 'Just where did you think the money came from?'

She swallowed. 'I – well – I assumed . . .' She tailed off. 'I assumed you had inherited it – or from your work as a lawyer?'

'As a lawyer?' He laughed bitterly. 'You assumed wrongly.' He got up. 'Now I need to book our passage back. Perhaps you would be so kind as to start to organize our luggage. We'll have to leave quickly.' He went inside.

There had, of course, been no time to visit Bath. Instead, they began the long journey towards the plantation, travelling through Italy, back to America and then heading south by train. It was not until the end of December that they neared their destination.

Emily looked listlessly out of the window. She was tired and bored and too hot; she was six months pregnant and the coal-burning stove in the middle of the railroad carriage pumped out heat incessantly: the resulting smell made her feel nauseous. Charles was in the men's carriage where he had spent the entire journey, which meant she hardly saw him except in the evenings when they stopped at a hotel for the night. He was being particularly solicitous at the moment but she thought she might try his patience if he had to sit with her all day.

The train was passing through a dank, dark and swampy wood, festooned with creepers. Rotting trees poked out of black pools barely illuminated by the ghostly beams of weak December sun. Hardly a living thing stirred in these woods; the only people she'd seen for two days were some Negroes sitting on the front steps of their broken huts, watching the train pass by. Her carriage was packed with noisy American women who insisted on engaging her in conversation and offering her pieces of pound cake, commenting on her condition and giving her advice. Quite simply, most of them said, she should not be travelling. Emily felt inclined to agree. Gradually it grew dark and the embers in the stove glowed; the carriage was quiet apart from the odd snore and Emily stared at her reflection in the window, moth-pale against the darkness outside. She pulled out the last letters she'd received from her mother and Will. The paper was worn smooth from reading and rereading them.

'You cannot imagine how lonely I am,' wrote her mother, 'with Will at university and without you and your father. I keep expecting your father to come bounding in, full of light and life. Even the actors rarely visit; the house used to be quite full of them . . .'

Emily thought of her mother, alone in that tall, thin house, watching and waiting at the window, only their maid Rachel breaking the silence with the rustle of her skirts, the laying out of fires. There was, in her mother's letters, a thinly disguised resentment at the way her life had turned out; perhaps also she felt that her daughter had stolen her husband away, depriving her of his company in what had turned out to be the last months of his life. Emily folded up the letter carefully, along lines that ran like milk-white veins through the pages. She opened Will's and almost immediately started smiling.

'When are you coming home? I need to meet this husband of yours. Is it too late to send him back if he does not meet our exacting requirements? Cambridge continues to be wonderful but I miss coming home and telling you of our theological discussions over tea and buttered toast. And naturally my friends are most disappointed to hear that you are married, for secretly they all hoped to win you as soon as they had completed their studies, travelled the world and made their fortunes.'

She glanced up and saw Charles's reflection in the glass.

'We're here,' he said gently, touching her on the shoulder. 'I'll fetch our luggage.'

The train juddered to a halt. Emily wrapped herself in her shawl and climbed gingerly out of the carriage. She hated feeling so heavy. Charles was already at the far end of the platform collecting their trunks. It was cold, but the air was warmer and damper than it had been in the north. They were in Savannah, the last main town. Charles had said they would have a couple of days to buy provisions before they caught the steamer to St Simons Island and the Brook plantation. Emily shivered and wrapped her shawl more tightly around herself as she watched Charles organize the Negroes who had been sent with the boarding house's carriage to pick them up. Now he tried to smile as he helped her into the carriage.

'Almost there, my sweet,' he said, climbing in after her and taking her cold hands in his and rubbing them to warm her fingers.

Emily could see little of the town but had the impression of broad tree-lined streets. It didn't take long to reach the dark wooden boarding house that Charles had booked. A woman stood on the front steps of the veranda that encircled the house, waiting for them. She was plump with tawny blonde hair set in waves and piled upon her head.

'You're most welcome, Mr Brook, Mrs Brook,' she said, helping Emily out of the carriage. 'I'm Mrs Caroline Wyatt Baker. Do come on inside and refresh yourselves.'

She showed them to their ground-floor room, flinging open the shutters so they could see their portion of the veranda with two rocking chairs. 'I'm guessing Mr Brook will need to run round town some and purchase all your provisions. Now, there's hot water here and clean towels. I expect you didn't have much of either on the railroad. I'll bring you some cold meat as it's so late and tomorrow morning we'll have a regular feast for breakfast and show Mrs Brook proper southern hospitality.'

The Negroes brought in the last of the trunks and Caroline Baker ushered them away and closed the door softly behind her. Emily felt as if she might never be able to get up again.

When she woke the following morning, Charles had already left. Emily pushed open the windows on to the veranda. The wide streets were lined with wooden houses and in the distance she could see the red brick warehouses of the port. Even at this time of day the streets were busy with carriages and horses and women taking the air.

There was a knock on the door and Mrs Baker came in carrying a pot of coffee. She put it on the side table and poured her a cup.

'I've checked the times of the steamer, Mrs Brook, and she sails tomorrow morning. You'll be at your new home by midday.'

'Do sit down and have a cup of coffee with me,' said Emily.

'Well, now, I will, I've been rushing about all morning. Wait one moment and I'll fetch a cup.'

Mrs Baker returned a few minutes later and poured herself a coffee, adding a generous amount of cream and sugar. She sank into one of the richly upholstered chairs. She said, 'I've known Mr Brook ever since he was a small boy. His family have always stayed here before they travel to St Simons Island. And I've read about you,' she said, looking at Emily from beneath her thick, sandy-coloured lashes. Noting Emily's surprise, she continued, 'Oh, yes, even this far south we've heard about the beautiful, brilliant and perfectly modern young actress who's come all the way over here from England. I had never imagined—'

'That Charles would marry me?' Emily interjected quietly.

'That I should have the pleasure of meeting you. We southerners are rather conservative, Mrs Brook, and we all fully expected Mr Brook to marry one of the Bell girls, or any one of a number of society ladies. But that Mr Brook would make such an interesting match, that I had not anticipated.'

'Well, thank you,' said Emily awkwardly.

'I expect you're wondering what it will be like.'

Emily sighed. 'I expect I shall find out soon enough.'

'I guess our ways may look a little strange to an Englishwoman.' Mrs Baker rose and picked up her coffee cup.

'Are your Negroes slaves?'

'No, my dear, they're free men. I pay them. But I keep that to myself. When you're ready, come and have breakfast.' She smiled at Emily and left.

The steamer had seemed unbearably slow: chugging through wide stretches of the Altamaha River, almost grinding to a halt between the mudflats and the marshes, stopping to pick up passengers and drop them and their copious amounts of luggage off at every little pier and dock. Emily had been nervous the whole way to St Simons Island, twisting her handkerchief in tight knots. She had no idea what to expect but she felt the journey like an ache, taking her further and further from England and her family. The coffee-coloured river was churned into thick cream foam where it met a blue-green arrow of ocean current. Trees trailed their leaves lazily in the water, the branches dark with damp and bound with fleshy creepers.

At last they rounded a corner of the river and the bank opened out to reveal a jetty poking out from a manicured lawn surrounded by live oaks trailing curtains of pale grey Spanish moss. The steamer belched clouds of fumes and juddered to a halt by the rickety pier.

'We're here,' said Charles, laying one hand on her shoulder.

He ran down the gangway, leaving her to follow him cautiously, helped by one of the stewards. He embraced the man waiting for him.

Emmanuel Brook was taller and thinner than Charles and had dark hair cut very short but the same pale, grey eyes, the same sculpted jaw, only his features were longer and leaner and he had a more pronounced dimple on his chin. In spite of his angularity, there was a slight roundness to his belly. He smiled and half bowed to her.

'Charles was right. You are uncommonly beautiful,' he said. 'Welcome to the family.' He turned slightly, making a curious gesture behind him, and suddenly six tall black men rose to their feet from where they had been crouching by the reeds and came jogging towards them.

Emily took a step backwards. The men crowded around, their slow smiles breaking the dark of their skin, touching Charles as if to ascertain whether he was real. She felt nauseous and clutched her stomach as the reality of her situation struck her. Her husband was a slave-owner. How else could he run a plantation in the deep south? As soon as he had told her of his family's estate she had known. She had simply not wanted to admit to herself that the man she loved – and now she too – owned other human beings.

'Master, we so please to see you,' said one of the slaves, and the others joined in.

And then they turned to her. She felt herself grow pale.

'Missis so lily-white. So pretty,' one of them said.

'Missis bring we a baby?' asked another hopefully.

'Yes, soon, soon,' said Charles, and at that they smiled and shuffled their feet.

Charles looked at them tolerantly for a moment and then said, 'Now go and fetch our trunks.'

Emily watched them run up the gangplank to where the luggage was piled. No one looked at the six men save for her. She realized how shocked she must appear and tried to compose her features. The men were wearing almost nothing – torn, dirty and ragged trousers, the frayed hems barely reaching their calves. One wore the remnants of a shirt, another had a battered hat.

As she turned back to the brothers, she saw Emmanuel watching her closely. He smiled.

'This way,' he said. 'We could have taken a carriage to the far end of the island but the road is simply dreadful and it would have been gruelling for you in your condition. So I've brought one of the barges – a smoother ride and more room for your trunks. Our people will row us back.'

It was one of the most surreal experiences of her life. The barge was clearly used for transporting cotton; she sat in the middle of it on a bale, surrounded by their luggage and boxes of goods, sharp shards from the cotton bolls prickling her skin through her clothes, skeins of it flying freely around her. The boat itself was flat and rectangular, the sides barely higher than the level of the water. As they veered away into a tributary, the marsh, which seemed to stretch for ever, appeared to close in, the reeds brushing past the edge of the boat. The overriding smells were rotting fresh seawater, seaweed, fish on the edge of decomposition. Three cattle egrets took off, disturbed by their passage. To her right lay an island of dense, deep green tangled jungle; the dark grey sky pressed in on them. She'd spent the whole journey trying to dissect her emotions and now she realized that at the heart of all her arguments and counter-arguments was one very simple thing: she felt as if she were slowly being pushed into a trap.

As the slaves rowed she saw how they strained, their muscles taut, coated in a thin film of sweat though there was a chill breeze. She noticed how their palms were peach, in sharp contrast to the rest of their skin, and that their pale soles were fissured with deep cracks and rimmed with dirt. Many of them had weals and raised scars, white and black and a curiously intimate pink, across their backs. Charles was more animated than she'd seen him for months, talking to Emmanuel, who listened silently and cast sidelong glances towards her.

Suddenly, one of the men sang a line from a song and the others joined in with the chorus, their voices merging with the dip and splash of the oars.

Mother, master gone to sell we tomorrow?
Yes, yes, yes,

Oh, watch and pray.
Gone to sell we in Georgia?
Yes, yes, yes,
Oh, watch and pray.
Farewell; Mother, I gone leave you,
Yes, yes, yes,
Oh, watch and pray.
Mother don't grieve after me,
No, no, no,
Oh, watch and pray.

'That's why they are so pleased that you are about to have a child,' said Emmanuel quietly, leaning towards her. He had left Charles at the front of the boat, staring straight ahead. 'It means our family – your child – will continue to own them in the future and their families won't be split up by being sold at auction.'

Emily could feel her face colouring. 'How many slaves do you have?' she asked.

'We call them involuntary servants,' said Emmanuel.

Emily winced.

'Around seven hundred,' he said proudly.

She blanched. She resolved to say nothing until she had seen the slaves for herself. Perhaps the Brook Estate was a model plantation. For all she knew the situation could be unlike anything she had read about or thought before: after all, Charles was not a cruel man. She looked away and cradled her belly with one hand: even so, it disgusted her that the child she was carrying would be a slave-owner too.

75

Mother, we gone see you in heaven,
Yes, my child,
Oh, watch and pray.

Their voices were deep and haunting and heavy with sadness but held nothing of the effort of their labour, as slowly the barge pushed its way through the clotted marsh.

As they rounded the tip of the island the land was all at once denuded of trees and instead filled with a wide, flat expanse of fields full of straggly, dead, brown stalks.

'Welcome to the Brook Estate,' said Charles.

The slaves turned the boat with difficulty and bumped it into the jetty. Charles and Emmanuel both climbed out and helped her step on to the edge of the boat and then on to the jetty. A crowd of small, dirty, naked children had gathered at the far end and quickly surrounded them, grasping their hands and tugging their clothes. Charles smiled at her and took her hand. He was genuinely happy to be home, she could tell, and proud that his people were pleased to see him. The three of them and their impromptu retinue walked along a rudimentary path, made of broken shells, which crunched underfoot. The path wound between two rows of waxen-leaved trees.

'Orange trees,' said Charles, though at the moment the trees neither possessed flowers nor fruit and many of the branches were dead.

At the end of the row of trees stood a boxy, white wooden house with a veranda and steps leading up to the front door. It had nothing that could be called a garden and the land around the house merged almost seamlessly into the fields. They crossed a number of muddy, fetid-smelling dykes and she had the impression that the land was at the same level as the water behind them. Outside the house a ragged assortment of slaves and one white man were waiting to meet them.

'This is Robert Stewart, our overseer,' said Emmanuel. 'He has been holding the fort until you arrived.'

Mr Stewart was short and a little stout, with pale skin, red hair and freckles. When he muttered a greeting, she noticed that he had a faint Scottish accent.

'And these are your house servants,' continued Emmanuel. 'Virginie, your maid . . .'

The woman curtsied but wouldn't look at Emily. She was beautiful, tall and slender with a regal, almost despotic look, full lips and arched brows.

'Your boy, Caesar . . .' He indicated another slave but this one was so pale as to be almost white, with African features, grey eyes and wild, corkscrewing blond hair. He looked about fourteen.

'June is the cook and Joe, her husband, the carpenter.'

June was small and wore her hair, a mass of tight ringlets, pinned back. She looked shy and frightened. Joe was tall with large, downward-sloping eyes. He put his massive hands behind his back as she turned to him.

'The driver, Edward. He's the head Negro here and helps Mr Stewart, and his wife Molly, who is Caesar's mother.'

Edward bowed to her. He had an aristocratic-looking

nose, deep frown lines between his brows and an air of sad-ness about him. His wife looked much older than he did, and had an extraordinary face, both still and sharp with cat-like, piercing eyes. Her hair was almost white at the sides of her head but black on top. This sober couple didn't seem to bear any resemblance to Caesar, who stood there grinning, exposing a large gap between his two front teeth.

'And Bella here will help keep the house clean.' He pushed forward a pretty young girl with shoulder-length straight hair and large lips and eyes. She glanced up at Emmanuel and Emily with a look that seemed both flirta-tious and dismissive. 'You ought to watch this one, she's got a tendency to talk back,' said Emmanuel.

Apart from Edward and Molly, Emily noticed the house servants were all light-skinned, the colour of newly planed wood. They were at least fully clothed, the women in plain shifts, the men in shirts and trousers, but their clothes were dark with dirt and encrusted with sweat stains and they all smelled.

'I'm very pleased to see you all,' she said quietly.

'Work hard for the mistress or Mr Stewart will see that you do,' said Emmanuel. 'Come, dinner should be ready. Virginie will show you to your room.'

Virginie silently followed Emily up the steps to the veranda and then upstairs to the first floor. She passed her on the landing so that she could hold the door open for her. There were three large square rooms. The one for herself and Charles was dark, the shutters still closed. Emily quickly flung them open and breathed in the fresh salty air. The large four-poster bed and the bureau were made of heavy rosewood and the wallpaper was a deep green velveteen with an endlessly repetitive pattern.

'Would you bring me some hot water and a clean towel, please?' asked Emily.

Virginie, still without uttering a word, left her.

Emily leaned out of the window. She could hear but not see Charles and Emmanuel below her, laughing. Her window looked out over the cotton fields and the lines of dykes running away from her, the water pewter grey, mirroring the sky; to her left was the vast reach of the river and the marshes and at the far end of the fields thick jungle, and beyond that the sea. To her right was the beginning of a road, running inland towards the centre of the island.

Virginie silently returned with a bowl of tepid water and a small, grey towel. She nimbly unhooked and unlaced Emily's dress and helped her into a new one – the first one she could find at the top of her trunk. Once dressed, Emily went downstairs to join her husband, her brother-in-law and Mr Stewart who were already sitting at the table drinking claret.

It was the strangest meal she had ever eaten, served on a rough-hewn pine table, marked and stained and without a tablecloth. The silverware was tarnished and the crystal cloudy. The meal was prepared somewhere outside the house and by the time Virginie and Bella carried it to the table and served it the food was lukewarm. The main course was a stew, the meat in great chunks riven with thick sections of bone. Mr Stewart picked up one hunk with his bare hands and sucked out the marrow. The stew was accompanied by biscuits, cornmeal, cold ham and some greens that had been boiled to oblivion, and followed by a rhubarb pie with a heavy, thick crust and a lumpy custard, flecked with charred spots. Coffee and port completed the lunch. Even though she was hungry, Emily could eat hardly any of it. She watched Virginie and Bella's hands with fascinated revulsion; their nails were black with dirt, and dirt seemed to be ingrained into the skin of their arms as if they had reptilian scales. She shuddered to think how the meal had been cooked. She could see the alcohol rising in the men's faces. Virginie brought her a small glass of sherry at her request and then left the room.

'I thought we were handsomely provided for,' she suddenly burst out.

'We are,' said Charles, tipping back his chair and blowing out smoke towards the ceiling.

'Are you objecting to the lack of table ornamentation?' asked Emmanuel, looking at her with some amusement.

'Of course I'm not just talking about the tablecloth, I mean everything. The food was cold and almost totally inedible and the slaves are filthy. How can you bear to eat like this?'

'They do smell disgusting, but what do you expect?' said Emmanuel, still not taking his eyes off her.

'Well, my dear,' said Charles, rocking his chair back to the upright position, 'this is exactly what you're here for.'

'What do you mean, what I'm here for?'

'Isn't that what wives do? Sort out the kitchen and make

sure there's table linen. Attend to the finer things in life. That's what we look to women for.'

Emily laughed mirthlessly. 'Charles, you cannot be serious. I've never presided over a kitchen in my life and I don't intend to start now.'

'That's right. You've had your meals served to you from countless hotels and bars; in restaurants and cafés and at high society soirées. Well, my sweet, do you see a hotel around here?' He unhooked a set of keys from Mr Stewart's belt and pushed them across the table to her. 'The keys to my kingdom,' he said softly.

Emily picked up the bunch of keys and tossed them back at him. He ducked and they hit the wall and he laughed. She got up and marched towards the stairs but not before she saw Emmanuel looking at her. There was not a trace of amusement in his expression.

Emily lay on her bed all afternoon, drifting in and out of sleep. Once, as if in a dream, Virginie came in and closed the window and the shutters. It grew dark and a tide of frog calls rose and fell like an alien dawn chorus. Charles came in quietly and took his clothes off and rolled into the bed.

'I'm sorry,' she said, without turning towards him.

'I'm sorry too,' he replied, as if responding to an invitation.

He angled her further away from himself and hooked his arm under her leg and pushed himself inside her and she could smell the alcohol on his quickening breath.

*

They followed the road through the fields, the earth damp and red, the remaining cotton bushes dead and brittle, and entered the wood at the far end. It was the next day and their neighbours, the Halls, were holding a party in their honour. Hardly any of the plantation owners lived on the island – only two families, the Halls and the Drummonds – but Charles had told her proudly that people had travelled from Darien, the nearest mainland town, to see them. They were in Emmanuel's carriage and he had been right about the state of the road. Emily cradled her stomach as the carriage swung from side to side and slammed into potholes. They left the woods behind and crossed over the eastern causeway; the bridge was alive with ghostly crabs that skittered sideways out of the way of their wheels. A dark purple heron rose from the marshes and flapped slowly across the reeds. Above their heads two turkey vultures circled on the thermals. It all felt so very primitive, Emily thought, as if they had been transported to an ancient time and place. It was growing dark and as the sky deepened to the colour of a plum, faint wisps of cloud glowed fuchsia-pink. As they neared the Hall residence, the soft smell of the sea and the marshes strengthened: sweet and sour, salt and iodide.

The Halls' estate was at the far end of the island on the opposite side to the Drummonds' and overlooked the island's only beach. The house itself was a white mansion with palisades and a balcony running all the way round the first storey above the veranda. It was surrounded by a ring of palm trees and the pristine lawn sloped down to a white sand beach. It looked fresh and clean and neat and the picture was completed when Louisa Hall came to the door in a pure white muslin dress and white slippers.

Mrs Hall did nothing to make Emily feel anything other than large and ungainly as she heaved herself out of the carriage. Her hostess was tiny, almost the size of a child, with a minute waist and long, blonde hair looped in fashionable curls framing her elfin face. Her husband, Joel Hall, appeared beside her. He was a thickset man, running to a paunch, slightly older than Charles with dark, shoulder-length hair. Emily felt herself being appraised by Mrs Hall's sharp eyes and smiled at her.

'It's most kind of you to have us, particularly in my condition,' she said, holding out her hand to Mrs Hall.

'Why,' said Mrs Hall, turning to Charles, 'your new wife is utterly charming. Mrs Brook, we simply had to see you,' she said to Emily, 'and round here no one will expect you to shun company when we all wish to welcome you as warmly as we can to St Simons.'

She and Mr Hall ushered her into the parlour where the assembled might of Darien immediately stopped talking and turned to stare. Emily was glad she was wearing her best dress, made especially for the confinement, of damson-coloured silk, but it had crumpled in the carriage. She blushed and smiled weakly; as if that were enough, the southerners beamed warmly at her. The room was so full of people that she could barely tell what it was like but she had the impression of modernity and elegance: candle-light sparked from a crystal chandelier, the walls were whitewashed save for one which was papered in gold fleurs-de-lis and the air was thick with the rich, spiced scent emanating from cut-glass vases crowded with white roses. A flute of champagne was pressed into her hand and Mrs Hall took her arm firmly.

'I should like you to meet someone. I believe he'll be a vital acquaintance. Dr Samuel Walker.'

She gestured towards a tall man with short white hair, thin sideburns and an elegant goatee, who bowed.

'Delighted to meet you, my dear,' he said. 'It will be my pleasure to attend you when the moment arises.'

'A most useful gentleman to know but quite the irritant: he knows everyone in Darien intimately and yet is dreadfully discreet,' said Mrs Hall, smiling at Dr Walker. 'Now, allow me to introduce you to the only other neighbours you will have on St Simons,' she continued, steering Emily away, 'Mr Hamish Drummond and Mrs Ann Drummond.'

The Drummonds were in their late fifties. Ann Drummond had steel-coloured hair bound into a tight bun, small dark eyes and a tiny button nose. Her high, round cheekbones were the colour of dried apricots. She looked tiny alongside her husband who was tall and bony with a large, beaked nose, thin lips and a lean face. His grey hair was long enough to reach his collar but thinning on top.

'This must all seem so terribly sudden,' said Mrs Drummond, smiling at her, 'being quite thrust into the limelight as soon as you have arrived. But, you see, everyone was so terribly excited to meet you. We have not had the pleasure of having anyone quite so brilliant living on our island before.'

Hamish Drummond bowed and took her hand. 'You must come and visit us, Mrs Brook, as soon as you are able to. We should be tremendously pleased if you would grace us with your presence.'

Mrs Hall smiled graciously at them all. 'You will excuse us, won't you, Mr Drummond, Mrs Drummond? As you can imagine, everyone here is looking forward to having the pleasure of meeting Mrs Brook.' She inclined her head towards Emily and led her further into the crowd. Emily felt as if she were a great, sleek animal being towed through the throng on a golden cord.

Eventually Emily managed to disengage herself from her overly hospitable host. She looked for Charles and found him standing in one corner of the room with Joel Hall and Emmanuel who was speaking heatedly.

'. . . convicted of insurrection, treason and murder. He was hanged when you were travelling,' Emmanuel was saying to Charles with some satisfaction when she approached them. 'Plus six of the bastards who helped him.'

'Who was hanged?' Emily asked, hooking her arm through her husband's.

'John Brown.'

Ely had written to her about John Brown when she was in Italy: Brown and a small band of twenty-one men had held up the armoury at a tiny town called Harpers Ferry in Virginia. Brown had declared he was going to give the guns to the Negroes to defend themselves and obtain their liberty. He was caught, tried and hanged.

Now Emily quoted: "'John Brown did not recognize unjust human laws. No man in America has ever stood up so persistently and effectively for the dignity of human nature, knowing himself for a man, and the equal of any and all governments. In that sense he was the most American of us all." Henry David Thoreau.'

'This is no way for a Brook to speak,' said Emmanuel to Charles in an undertone, a muscle tightening in his jaw. He was slightly flushed with drink.

Charles scowled and disengaged his arm from Emily's. He said patiently, as if speaking to an imbecile, 'No matter what you people think, here John Brown is viewed as a traitor to his country. What is worse, from a practical point of view, is the message it sends to our bond people. It might give them the wrong idea.'

'And what idea might that be?'

'Try not to be so patronizing, my dear,' he said quietly, but loud enough for Joel Hall to hear. 'That they have something to gain by rising up and revolting. There's already been unrest in the region. Now that John Brown has been executed, we all hope that will be an end to the matter.'

'If a white man can't steal the guns, what hope has a black man?' asked Emily.

'You have it, my dear,' said Charles dryly.

'I believe this is a truly inappropriate topic of discussion to have in front of a lady,' said Mr Hall, breaking in to their conversation as if she herself had not participated at all. He turned to her and said, 'I apologize on behalf of the Brook men. They have clearly grown unused to polite society. And I sincerely hope we haven't tired you in your present condition in our eagerness to meet you.'

'Thank you for your consideration, Mr Hall,' said Emily. 'It's been a wonderful evening and we're most grateful for your hospitality but it's hardly good for me to continue to spend so much time on my feet.'

'I'll call your carriage for you now,' said Mr Hall, bowing to her.

Charles and Emmanuel escorted her through the parlour to the door of the Hall residence without a word.

The following morning Emily rose late and bad-tempered. When Virginie had finished helping her dress, Emily told her to tell June to make a fresh pot of coffee, calling after her, 'Please ensure that the water is hot.'

'Have some breakfast, won't you? You ought to keep your strength up,' said Charles as she entered the dining room.

Virginie laid out a clean napkin and silverware for her and placed a white bread roll and a boiled egg on her plate.

'And on our discussion last night, about John Brown,' he said, lowering his voice, 'kindly don't raise these issues here in front of the servants.'

'Servants are paid,' said Emily sharply. She saw Virginie cut her eyes sideways at her. She turned to Emmanuel. 'I imagine you must miss your family, Mr Brook. You are, of course, most welcome here for as long as you are to stay, but I wondered if you had made any plans for your future travel arrangements?' she asked.

Virginie silently poured her a cup of coffee, added sugar and cream and stirred it until Emily took it from her.

Emmanuel frowned. 'I plan to leave tomorrow morning. Today, though, I will need your husband. We have much to discuss as regards the plantation. Charles, shall we?' he said.

Charles lifted his feet off the table and rose. He kissed Emily on the cheek and followed his brother out of the house. She watched them leave and then said, 'Virginie, I want you, June, Bella and Caesar – in fact, anyone who enters this house and handles my food – to wash thoroughly.'

'We don't have no soap,' said Virginie flatly.

'Charles bought some in Savannah. Take a couple of bars for now and tell June to make some.' She looked up at her surly maid. 'I will pay you a cent a day for every day that you are clean.'

'Yes, missis,' said Virginie. She picked up a platter of cold meat and bread and left the dining room.

Emily wrapped her shawl around her and put on her bonnet before stepping out of the house. Today was a lot brighter, the sky the colour of a hyacinth, but it was still relatively cold. As she wandered towards the double row of orange trees, she was suddenly aware of someone following her. She turned round to see Caesar tagging along behind her.

'What are you doing?'

'I see if missis want anything?' he said diffidently.

'No, I don't. Please go back.'

He hesitated, standing on one foot and looking away.

Emily carried on walking and shortly heard Caesar's footsteps again. 'I told you to go home,' she said impatiently.

'Master say I stay with you. When you leave the house.'

'Why?'

He shrugged. 'Keep you safe, missis, from snakes. Him bite you. And alligators in them swamps.'

Emily wondered how likely it was that a fourteen-year-old boy would protect her from savage wildlife. He took her silence for assent and scampered up to her.

'Well, since you're here, you might as well make yourself useful. Take me to the nearest village where the slaves live.'

'No villages here. Camps. The closest one that way.'

He pointed to a grove of magnificent trees a few hundred yards away from the Brook house. She followed him slowly, the path becoming little more than mud but with piles of oyster shells scattered along it every so often.

'What are all these shells doing here?' she asked.

'We eat the oysters, missis, then throw them shells down.'

The trees, she now saw, were the south's famous live oaks, their small leaves glossy green all year round. They were huge, much taller than the house, with great sturdy branches from which moss hung in ragged clots.

'This where we live, missis,' he said.

The huts were white and seemed to be made with crushed shells in the mortar and wooden roofs. Chickens and ducks wandered freely in and out and a gang of grubby, mostly naked children were playing outside. Behind the huts was a drainage ditch that stank and had a fetid grey scum on the surface. She peered inside one hut. There was nothing in the dark hovel apart from mattresses made of Spanish moss, some filthy blankets and a dark fireplace with a few burning embers. She put her hand over her mouth to stifle the smell.

'How many people live here?' she asked.

Caesar shrugged. 'Depend. One or two families. Maybe ten people. Expect more.'

'And this is where you wash?' she asked, pointing to the ditch.

He nodded. 'The women get water from the river in the evening.'

'And what about beds? Tables? Where do you cook?'

He pointed to the blackened coals in front of the house. 'There on the fire, if we have meat. Most days in the cook-house by the cotton gin. After we work in the fields, we have hominy. Like porridge, but from corn,' he explained.

'That's all?'

'Yes, missis. Only if we kill our chickens or catch something – maybe a fish – we have more. Some people, like my mother, Molly, she grow a few things.' He shrugged. 'Mostly we too tired for that. Missis,' he said, and his face lit up, 'you ask master to give we meat.'

At the word meat, all the children, who had been cowering in the corner of one hut when Emily had approached, came rushing over, shouting, 'Meat, missis, give we meat!'

They took hold of her dress and shook it, looking at her pleadingly. Emily shuddered.

'Go back to the house, Caesar, and see if there's any cold meat left from breakfast and bring it to them. And a bar of soap too. And as for you children, you are utterly filthy,' she said, trying to keep the shiver out of her voice. 'Now, I will give every child who washes himself one cent, and one cent for you older ones if you keep the little babies clean.'

At this the children shouted even louder and rushed back to the dyke, plunged in and started splashing. Emily thought she might cry. The water was disgusting and she realized that when the children climbed out, they would have no towels to dry themselves with and no dry clothes, no clothes at all, in fact. They might catch a chill. She was about to head back to the house when a very old woman hobbled out of one of the huts and held up a hand to stop her leaving. Emily watched her, horrified. She was bent double. Her hair was completely white and her skin was so black it held a blue sheen. As she neared Emily she stretched out one twisted hand and grasped Emily's hand, craning her neck upwards to see her. One of her eyes was filmed with white.

'My name, it Mary,' she said. 'I done work for Mr Brook, Charles Brook's grandfather, in the big house.'

'I'm Emily Brook, Charles's wife.'

'I know who you be. We so please to see you. When I done work there, it different, so grand. Full of servants. All in uniform. A beautiful garden and oranges every year. They sweet back then, but oh, so bitter now. We make them into orange wine – they no good for eating. I have eleven children, missis, and only one of them live,' she said with a sigh, still holding Emily's hand. 'I work every day through dew and damp, and sand and heat, and done good work; but oh, missis, I old and broke now.'

Emily looked down at the old woman's head, her fragile, bent neck, corded with veins, and started to cry. She said, attempting to wipe away her tears with one hand, 'I'll send you some meat and some warm flannel.'

She gently disentangled herself from the old woman's grasp and turned and walked back to the house as fast as she was able. She approached from the back, past the house servants' quarters and the building that housed the kitchen. Joe was standing with his back to her, sawing something on a wooden table. Clouds of flies hung around his head and settled on something dark and fleshy lying on the table in front of him. Emily stopped abruptly as her stomach cramped and she bent double. Joe came running over to her, still clutching the saw.

'Missis, no well?'

'I'm quite well, thank you. I simply need to catch my breath. What are you doing?'

'I chop up the sheep for dinner.'

Emily walked more slowly over to the table. A dead sheep was lying on it and Joe had been using his carpentry

skills to saw off pieces at random. It explained the unidenti-
fiable lumps of meat and bits of bone in the stew.

'Joe,' said Emily, feeling a wave of nausea rising at the
grisly sight, 'I don't believe that is how one butchers a
sheep.'

They both looked at the animal. It had been hung until
bloodless, skinned and gutted and its head lolled at an odd
angle, tufts of wool clinging to the wine-dark flesh. Its teeth
with their blackened roots were spayed out and the eyes in
their raw sockets were enormous, dark and clouded as
grape skin. Emily wiped her clammy forehead and thought
back to Rachel, carving lamb on the kitchen table, her
apron bloody, her forearms slick with sweat.

She picked up a knife and held the blade against her
thumb to test its edge. She grasped one of the legs and
inserted the point of her knife into the flesh, feeling for the
hip bone and wriggled the blade until the bone popped
from the socket and then she sliced through the rest of the
carcass.

'There. Now you do that for all the legs so that you have
shanks. This bit is the loin. You need to put your hand
inside and count five ribs up. And you'll need the saw to
sever the spine.'

She stood back to let Joe turn the carcass over. The
sound of metal against the bone set her teeth on edge.

'Then cut down here, either side of the spine.'

Joe butterflied the meat apart and pressed down on the
ribs.

'Now you have two racks of ribs and that section you can

slice into chops and then cut there, for the belly. This part is for sirloin. And make a cut here for the neck.'

She ran her knife through the thin fat of the beast, showing Joe where he needed to make incisions. The animal was unpleasantly moist in her hands, and smelled of stale blood. It was old, the meat tough and fibrous. The flies clustered thickly on the eyes, buzzed around the ribcage and alighted on her face. She took a pace away from the table again and watched Joe. He hacked off the head, which fell in the coarse grass. As if from nowhere Caesar came running over and snatched it up, making her jump. He grinned at her and ran off, the head tucked under his arm. Joe sucked his teeth. He placed his knife in the groove she had cut and sliced through the neck.

'You may keep that bit,' said Emily quietly, and she turned to go indoors, holding her hands away from her sides so she wouldn't soil her dress.

Chapter 4

January 1860

When Emily woke, it was to an increasingly familiar feeling of dislocation. Outside, she could hear the rustle of palm trees, the leaves rattling as harshly as scabbards, the Negroes' sweet, guttural songs as they hoed the fields, the cries of alien birds. As she gradually realized where she was, she could almost feel the dampness of the swamp rising through the bones of the house. She shivered. Charles had already left and the room was cold; the fire had gone out. She lay disconsolately in bed, the sheets rising in a mound over her protruding belly. She felt bereft, as if all those she loved most in life had died instead of being merely physically separated by the Atlantic.

Charles had tricked her. What was worse was that she felt complicit: in the shocked aftermath of her father's death she had failed to question him properly about his background. But although there was little she could do about that now, she felt she owed it to someone – perhaps herself – to find out what the situation was truly like. She struggled out of bed and rang the bell for Virginie.

Outdoors, the first narcissi were blooming around the house. As she descended the veranda steps, Caesar suddenly stood up, startling her. He'd been crouching in the mud underneath the wooden struts supporting the house.

'I'd like to see the rest of the plantation today.'

'It a big place, missis,' he said, scuffing the ground with his toe and regarding her steadily with his large, pale eyes.

'Nevertheless,' she said.

He reluctantly walked ahead of her, leading her along a path next to one of the innumerable dykes. In the fields on either side of them the slaves were hoeing the stubble left from last year's cotton crop. Where the stubble and the weeds were particularly dense, they had set fire to them and over the island rose columns of smoke that stained the sky pale grey. It reminded Emily a little of autumn at home.

At length they turned towards the tip of the island where they came to a cluster of buildings beneath a giant live oak.

'That the cotton gin,' said Caesar. 'My brother, him in charge.'

'I didn't know you had a brother.'

Caesar shrugged and ran off, shouting, 'Hi!' A few moments later a slender young man came out of one of the buildings.

'This Frank,' said Caesar.

Emily looked from one to the other and could see no likeness. Where Caesar looked plain odd with his wild hair and pale eyes, his almost white skin and Negro features,

Frank was dark. He had a lean face with slightly downward-slanted dark eyes and a serious expression; Emily could see the man he would become.

'You look very like your father, Edward,' she said.

'Yes, missis.' He nodded. 'The cotton, it almost ready,' he said. 'You want to see?'

Emily followed him inside into a dark, hot shed, which contained several large wooden contraptions with great toothed rollers and wooden chutes.

'Them take off the leaves from the cotton boll, then we bale it,' he said.

In the gloom, heavy swathes of dust rotated in shards of sunlight. Towards the back of the barn several men were piling the cotton into sackcloth bags. Scraps of the stuff floated everywhere, like dense dandelion seed. Perhaps because of the long walk or the heat and the dust, Emily suddenly felt faint. Frank noticed and grabbed her arm. He let go almost immediately, as if her skin had burned his fingers.

'Missis, over here.' He pointed to a rickety chair by the door. 'I fetch you some water.'

He reappeared with a battered tin cup. The water was cool but tasted brackish. He saw her expression and said, 'It all we have. Them no wells here, we have to drink from the river.'

'Thank you,' she said.

She dipped her handkerchief in the cup and wiped her forehead. She looked up to see Frank staring out towards the horizon where the dense marsh seemed to stretch for ever. His expression was the same one almost all the slaves she'd seen had: a blend of intense sadness and fear.

'Them men there,' said Caesar imperiously, pointing to the slaves laboriously filling the cotton sacks, 'they carry you home.'

'Thank you, Caesar, but I can walk.'

'The cart here, for the cotton. We take you home in that,' said Frank.

'I can walk,' Emily repeated, but Frank quietly and efficiently rounded up the men, the cart and the oxen and hauled a couple of sacks full of cotton on to the base for her to sit on.

It was a rough and bumpy ride and Emily wondered if she would not have been better on foot. Still, it was faster and she shouldn't be far from the house so close to the end of her confinement. How surreal, she thought, as they finally reached the grove of orange trees, to be transported towards the house down a driveway with delusions of grandeur in the back of an ox-drawn cart.

'You done ought to let them carry you,' said Caesar in a surly tone as he lolled beside her, chewing a blade of cord grass. The two men walked by the oxen, encouraging them with shouts and slaps. 'You got niggers enough.'

Charles was standing smoking on the veranda as they approached. When he caught sight of her, he threw away his cigarette and came running down the steps scowling.

'What on earth are you doing?'

'I didn't feel myself. This, apparently, was the quickest way back from the cotton gin.'

'If you'd wanted to visit the gin, you only needed to ask me,' he said crossly, helping her from the cart.

Caesar skirted the side of the house, heading towards the kitchen. She called after him.

'Caesar, please don't refer to your people in that tone.' She sighed. 'He seems to think he's better than everyone else,' she said to Charles.

At first Charles did not respond, but when they reached the front door he said, 'Well, threaten him with being sent to work in the fields if he speaks back.'

Emily had given Caesar the task of distributing cents to the children who now milled around the house to show off their clean hands. But as she went outside that afternoon, she was just in time to see Caesar slapping one of them across the face.

'Caesar, what did you do that for?' demanded Emily.

'He no clean him hands and he talk back,' said Caesar sullenly.

Emily seized his arm and spun him towards her. 'He's a child, Caesar. Don't ever hit anyone like that again. If one of the children hasn't washed then don't give them any money. And please hurry up, we're going out.'

'You gone walk, missis?'

'Now you're talking back to me. Shall I slap you too?'

Caesar shrugged. 'It what happens.'

Poor boy, she thought, how could he help but behave brutally in such a savage environment?

'I've had an idea, Caesar. Since I can't walk so far, we're going to canoe.'

He looked at her, panic-stricken. 'I don't swim.'

'We're not going to fall out of the canoe, child.'

'I don't know how to paddle.'

'Then stay here,' she said, losing patience with him.

But when she reappeared a few moments later with her shawl and her bonnet, he had dispatched all the children and had picked her a little posy of narcissi and myrtle. He presented them to her with a wide smile, but it was strangely bereft of warmth. Emily tucked the posy into her dress and chose a small canoe with *Dolphin* painted on the bow. She climbed in gingerly while Caesar held the craft against the jetty.

'So much of this island seems like water anyhow, we may as well take to it.'

'This island, him mud and you don't walk on it and you don't paddle over it,' said Caesar, climbing in after her. 'Master's niggers never run away. They starve to death or drown in them swamps.'

'Please don't refer to your fellows in that way,' said Emily again. She picked up the paddle nervously. She had not canoed since she was a child and it was much harder work than she remembered. It took them a long time to navigate through the reeds to flowing water and she could feel the strain on her back and chest muscles and the rise of blisters along the edge of her palms. They stopped shortly so that Emily could catch her breath. They were still only yards away from the shore, but it already felt like a release. They dug their paddles into the mud and held the canoe steady. In the distance, like a far-off mirage, was the boxy white house with the lines of orange trees leading to it. Nearby several egrets waded gingerly through the swamp taking no note of them; a pair of red-breasted merganser and some mallards pad-dled past. They were in a narrow creek, bordered by high marsh grasses.

'Which way to the sea?' asked Emily impatiently.

Caesar said, 'Frank know. He good on the water. Out there, that big river, him the Altamaha but I don't know where the sea.'

Emily sighed. 'Mr Brook said there was a beach on another island near St Simons. I should so love to see it. Can you fish, Caesar?'

He shook his head. 'Master's grandfather done keep fish. Catch them and keep them. In a stone tank next to the kitchen. He have fresh fish when him want.'

'Then we shall do that. Next time we come, we'll bring fishing rods. My mother taught me how to fish when I was your age.'

In spite of the ache in her back Emily couldn't bear to go back quite so soon. They paddled further. Caesar soon stopped splashing so much and they fell into a quiet rhythm. The stream joined a wider river but they were still hemmed in by acres of marsh. In the distance she could see a thick forest separated from them by reeds and water. Dark grey clouds seemed to meet the tops of the taller trees, which were shrouded with creepers. Two turkey vultures coasted above them, suspended in the thin thermals. Emily brought the canoe to a halt and listened.

There was a faint wind keening through the sedges but she could hear nothing else.

'What's that over there?' she asked.

'That Sugar Island. But him not an island. You walk there when the tide low. It where master grow sugar cane.'

'Another plantation?'

'Yes, missis. And more camps. We people live there.'

Emily suppressed a shudder. There was something secretive about it: a plantation on an island off an island, cut off from the main estate by the brackish tide. She could see nothing beyond the impenetrable forest, dark as jade.

'I think we should go back. Help me turn the canoe around,' she said.

But Caesar was even less adroit at steering than he was at paddling and Emily had to do it. The current was against them now and it was hard work. Emily realized that the tide must be turning and that she had no real way of finding the sheltered little stream they'd used to join the main river. Everything, with the reeds towering overhead, looked the same.

'We should just cut in here,' she said, when they found a break in the marsh. 'It might take us back to the stream we used to get out.'

Caesar said nothing until they were out of the main surge of the current. But as they continued, the marsh drew in until they could barely move the canoe forward.

'We must be quite near the shore,' said Emily, standing up. The canoe tipped alarmingly. She could see the tops of live oaks on the shore but she had no idea of the distance or how far the marsh extended.

'I wonder if we should just get out and walk.'

'No, missis,' said Caesar fearfully. 'Them's alligators. And we sink in the mud.'

She saw he was terrified that they were really lost and that he would get into trouble with Charles.

'Then we must turn back and try to keep going up the main river until we find the right stream. We can't go any further here.'

With difficulty they pushed the canoe away from the reeds and paddled backwards until there was room to turn it around. Travelling back along the stream was not hard; it was only when they faced the current again that they ran into problems. The canoe bucked and tipped. 'We must paddle hard and keep to the edge and we'll be fine,' said Emily, panting with the effort.

She was wondering whether they should just dig the canoe into the marsh and wait for the tidal current to subside, when a spasm made her double up in pain. Caesar was not strong enough to paddle the canoe alone and they began to drift backwards. Emily's mind went blank as she gritted her teeth against the pain. Caesar started to scream and shout and then, cutting through his noise, she heard something.

'Hush, listen,' she whispered.

He carried on shouting and she slapped him across the face. He looked at her in surprise. His expression turned sullen.

It was singing. A deep male baritone that was coming closer. Across the river a large canoe came into view with four men paddling and Frank at the helm, silently scanning the river. The men let out a great shout when they saw Emily and Caesar and swiftly paddled over to them.

'How you, missis?' asked Frank, as he grasped the canoe to stop it drifting further away.

'Fine, thank you, Frank. How did you know where we were?'

'Some of the people see you leave with Caesar and one tell me. Caesar don't swim and he don't paddle. When you don't come back, we try and find you.'

'Well, thank God you did.'

'Can you climb into this canoe? Montreal paddle Caesar back.'

With his help, Emily clambered awkwardly into the main canoe. She looked back at Caesar.

'Don't worry. You won't be in any trouble. It was my idea,' she said.

'It safe,' said Frank, after Montreal had taken her place and the men had turned the canoe around, 'only you have to know the tides and the creek.'

It was almost dark by the time they reached the jetty; the first stars were shimmering in the indigo sky and there was a faint trace of phosphorescence on the water. A thin, cold wind rattled through the rushes and the reeds and the frogs began to sing. The smell of the sea, of ozone and seaweed, drifted towards them. It was indeed a beautiful place, if you were there of your own free will, thought Emily. There was enough light to follow the gleam of shells beneath the orange trees and to see a glimmer of the white house in the distance where Charles, with his Madeira and his cigarettes, would be waiting for her.

Charles had, of course, remonstrated with her when she reached the house but flatly refused to allow her to take Frank with her in future. He was much too valuable, he said, to send him off on sailing expeditions with his wife.

Surely, thought Emily, I am your most valuable possession. But she said nothing, only commented that her future canoe trips with Caesar would have to be short ones, specifically for fishing. Charles said nothing more on the subject, but added off-handedly as she turned to go into the drawing room that Joel and Louisa Hall would be coming to luncheon the next day.

'The meat is better than when we arrived,' he said, frowning.

Emily smiled. 'Well, what did you expect? Your carpenter saws up the carcasses as if they're logs of wood. I've shown him how to carve proper joints so at least we'll get an approximation of ribs and rump steak.'

Charles laughed and for the few minutes before he disappeared into his office with Mr Stewart, she forgot she should be cross with him for inviting guests without asking her.

She called June in.

'Mr Brook has invited Mr and Mrs Hall for luncheon tomorrow. They'll be here at midday.'

June stood before her shyly, her eyes downcast. She looked tired, though this was not surprising. She spent all day preparing three meals and clearing up. It was late morning and she still had to do last night's dishes. 'We have oysters. Master shoot a wild turkey yesterday. I roast it and them's greens and cornbread.'

'Hmm,' said Emily, thinking how very uninspiring it was and how equally uninspiring to have to think of these things. 'And what about dessert?'

'Them's preserved peaches. Peach cobbler?'

'Oh, Lord,' said Emily. 'Well, I guess that'll have to do. Just do your best.'

At noon the following day, Joel and Louisa Hall's carriage came rolling up the drive right on time. Emily stood on the veranda in her best confinement dress that Virginie had let out, again. Her hair, which had been her glory in the north, was wilting, the curls limp in this strange, southern atmosphere. Louisa Hall stepped daintily out of the carriage. Charles rushed to help her and she curtsied and smiled up at him, then her large brown eyes darted swiftly around as if to take in any changes Emily might have made. She was quickly satisfied that there was none. Mr Hall followed her, more slowly and staidly.

As they entered the house, Emily saw it again through her guests' eyes. How bare it seemed with its rough-hewn pine furniture, all functionality and few aesthetics, in contrast to the Hall residence.

'Well, my dear, I'm guessing this is most certainly not

what you are accustomed to,' said Mrs Hall in a soft, southern drawl.

Now that she was closer to her Emily could see her eyes were a pale copper, like beech leaves in winter.

Virginie came in and poured them all a glass of wine.

Mrs Hall stared hard at the maid and then said, 'Such a shame you weren't able to procure a white nurse when you were in the north. Your little one is going to be raised by a darkie, like all the rest of us southerners.'

Emily took a careful sip of her wine, 'Virginie will help, but I'm planning to raise my own baby.'

Virginie paused fractionally and then left the room.

Charles said quietly, 'We were all raised by black nannies and it ain't done any of us any harm. The child might as well start off getting used to the situation.'

'Still,' said Mrs Hall, 'you'll have to find a wet nurse for her. I shudder when I think of it, but it has to be done. It should be easy enough, they have babies at the drop of a hat.'

Emily looked at her, astonished. 'Excuse me, Mrs Hall, Mr Hall, I'm just going to see how luncheon is progressing.'

She rose to her feet with difficulty, her cheeks burning, and walked through the house and leaned out of the door facing the kitchen. She called for June, who came rushing out, wiping her hands on her apron.

'The oyster stew ready, missis. I fetch Virginie to bring him in.'

Emily turned to find Mrs Hall standing behind her.

'Just thought I'd come and see if I could be of any assistance.'

'Thank you, Mrs Hall,' said Emily, 'but that won't be necessary. Virginie is about to serve, if you'd care to return to the dining room.'

'One word of advice, my dear,' said Mrs Hall, smiling at her. 'You want to watch her.'

'I beg your pardon?'

'I'm saying nothing,' said Mrs Hall, holding up her tiny, doll-like hands, 'but we all know how Mr Brook can be.' She turned to go back to the others.

At the least Emily had thought she'd have pleasant companionship from Charles's friends, if not the witty and erudite conversation she'd been used to in the north. But even before the oysters had been served she'd concluded that Mr Hall was ponderous and Mrs Hall shallow, spiteful and vacuous. She thought she might choke on the oysters. The turkey was dry, the greens overcooked and the cornbread crumbled in their fingers. The only good part of the meal was the gravy. They talked about cotton and the laziness of their involuntary servants, Charles more animated than he'd ever been in Boston. Emily was suddenly reminded of Penelope Bell: Charles regarded Mrs Hall with the same ardent, intense expression with which he had looked at Miss Bell not so very long ago.

With an effort, Emily turned her attention back to the conversation. She had drunk too much and eaten almost nothing. 'The thing is,' Mrs Hall was saying, 'they're just ungrateful!'

Emily opened her mouth to reply, but Mr Hall cut in.

'Mrs Brook, forgive me for pointing this out to you, but you ain't been here long enough to realize what a curse these people can be.'

'What do you mean, they are "ungrateful"?' said Emily angrily. 'You pay them nothing! Worse still, you deny them their very freedom, their right to choose. Look at our slaves – what little I've seen fills me with shame. They work all day for us and all they receive is cornmeal at midday and when they finish labouring. They have no clean water to drink or to bathe in. They have no soap to wash with. They have almost no clothes – two outfits per year – and as a result their clothes stink and are full of vermin, as ours would be if we had to wear them until they fell off our backs. Their houses are pitiful: they're crammed into those hovels like cattle and they have no furniture, not even a bed – moss and ragged blankets are their only comfort. And you expect them to be grateful?'

'Well, now,' said Mr Hall, 'it wouldn't be economical to give them more. We have to eat too. And when they finish work, they are at perfect liberty to hunt and fish and grow their own produce to supplement their diet. Many of them sell eggs and moss to the storekeeper in Darien. They could buy soap if they wished. The point is, they don't. They're naturally a dirty race.'

'"The first question to be proposed by a rational being is, not what is profitable, but what is Right,"' said Emily, quoting William Ellery Channing. '"To hope for happiness from wrong-doing is as insane as to seek health and prosperity by rebelling against the laws of nature."'

'We heard that you had radical views,' said Mrs Hall quietly.

'Radical? It's hardly radical to believe that a man has the right not to be treated as property. It's not radical to pay the people who work for you. And they're not naturally dirty. Anyone deprived of a livelihood, without access to clean water and unable to procure the very basics will descend into poverty and filth. Fleas do not discriminate on the basis of the colour of one's skin,' said Emily.

Across the table Charles's face was stiff with rage.

'It ain't ever worked before, bringing an outsider into the south,' said Mrs Hall softly, and she touched Charles's hand for one fleeting moment. 'Just a kindly piece of advice, Mrs Brook. We're your friends, so we won't take too much notice of your little outburst. But you're talking about our way of life, a way of life we've been practising for years. And I don't believe you realize how offensive and how dangerous what you're saying is. Men get lynched for less round here.'

'Excuse me,' Emily said and left the room.

Outside, she paused for a few moments to catch her breath and then noticed Caesar standing watching her.

'Go inside and fetch my shawl and bonnet and then meet me at the jetty with the fishing rods. Oh, and tell Joe to clean out the stone tank and fill it with water, ready for the fish we're going to catch.'

It was an overcast day: the sky and the river were oyster grey, but it was peaceful and calm on the water, with only the sounds of small waves lapping at the sides of the canoe and the call of wild birds. Caesar said almost nothing but cast sidelong glances at her and towards her rod to check he was doing the right thing. They did not go far, barely yards from the end of the jetty. It was enough though. After a few minutes, she had her first bite. She hauled the fish in to the edge of the boat and screamed when she saw it. It was a huge catfish with great barbs around its mouth. Caesar tried to grab the smooth, slimy creature and slide it into the bottom of the canoe. It hissed and spat at him and it took him several attempts. He put his foot across its head to hold it down while he pulled the hook from its mouth.

'I expect you don't want to eat him, missis. Him good for we people, not for white folks.'

'All right, Caesar, you can have it. You'd better kill it though,' she said, as the animal thrashed around wildly, making the boat sway.

It took Caesar several attempts, bashing it with his paddle, before it grew still. She looked at the dead fish. It was ugly, bony and mucus-covered with dark grey skin and a pale underbelly. She wondered how long she could prolong their fishing trip and how angry Charles would be on her return. She'd never seen him lose his temper before, but then, she thought, how little she had really known him before their marriage.

Their honeymoon had been their first real intimacy and,

in retrospect, it had been a triumph of his will over hers. They had not returned to England to visit her family; the tour of Europe had never happened; they had ended up in one villa in Italy for almost the entire trip and had barely ventured out to see the region or even Florence's many attractions; her *Baedeker* had remained practically unopened. And yet, once the larger picture was in place, as he wanted it, she was left free to choose how to spend their days so that she had the semblance of choice. He was delightfully compliant as to whether they should walk or ride, sit a while longer in the sun or visit the nearest *trattoria* so that at the time, save for the nagging ache at missing her family and the occasional twinge of annoyance at their lack of cultural activities, she had felt as if she were quite spoiled.

Why, she now thought, had she not seen this before? That Charles had loved her wild spirit and independent nature but once she was, as he saw it, his possession, he wanted nothing other than total obedience and submission.

Over the course of the afternoon, Caesar caught a minnow and she a couple of Altamaha shad, which Caesar said were very good to eat. But finally, as the sun began to sink, she could delay her return no longer.

As she walked in Charles said coldly, 'The Halls have left. I hope you're pleased with the impression you've made.'

'They were rude, Charles. And what I said is true. I've wanted to speak to you since we arrived: you keep your slaves in appalling conditions. The babies are left to scrap about in the dirt on their own and the elderly wither away with nothing. I met Mary, Charles. She worked for your grandfather and now she is crippled and dying in a hovel, cold, hungry, lonely and old. Is that your gratitude towards the people who have given their lives for you?'

Charles turned his back on her.

'I'm sorry for my outburst this afternoon. I realize I didn't make a favourable impression. But really, it's in your power to do something about this.'

Her husband picked up his wine and went into his office, slamming the door behind him. After a moment she tried the door but it was locked. She knocked and called his name but there was no reply.

Charles came to bed late that night, and when she touched his shoulder he turned away from her, and in the morning he was up and dressed before she woke. When she appeared at breakfast he was locked in his office again.

'This is so childish, Charles, please come out and talk to me,' she called through the door. There was no reply. Turning, Emily found Virginie standing behind her with a pot of freshly brewed coffee. Emily edged by her and went into the dining room.

Emily sat at the table alone with her coffee. As she was drinking it, she heard a commotion in front of the house and calls of 'Master, master!' Going into the hall, she saw Charles fling open his office door, his face blank, and go out to the veranda. Emily followed him and stood quietly in the doorway. A group of heavily pregnant women were standing among the narcissi, all speaking at once.

'Quiet,' said Charles authoritatively. He noticed Emily standing behind him and deliberately shut the door.

She stood at the window but she could only hear the rise and fall of the women's voices, not what they were saying. A few moments later they slowly turned towards the fields and Charles came back inside.

'What did they want?' asked Emily.

Charles shrugged. 'They don't want to work. They're being lazy.'

'Charles, some of them are as far along in their confinement as I am. You wouldn't expect me to go and work in the fields, would you? You complain when I even take a short walk or go out rowing in case I exert myself.'

'Please stop interfering, Emily,' he said, through gritted teeth.

He went into his office and fetched his gun, then pushed past her again and left the house.

Chapter 5

March 1860

They called her Clementine and she was the most beautiful thing Emily had ever seen. She had large pale blue eyes that would fade to grey and tufts of downy, blonde hair. Even Virginie smiled when she looked at Clementine, her haughty face momentarily warm. It had taken Emily by surprise how sharp and fierce and all-consuming her love for Clementine was. There was something primitive about it, as if just the smell of her baby's soft head had the power to slow her heart and still her quickening thoughts. Emily rested, sleeping when the baby slept, entranced by Clementine's scrunched-up face and out-of-focus gaze. Charles was delighted.

Shortly after the baby was born, a parcel with a foreign postmark arrived for Emily. She opened it carefully. Wrapped in layers of thin paper was a bird in flight, about the size of the palm of her hand, carved from white Carrera marble. The bird was balanced on a fine column of metal that stood on a matching base and it was perfectly smooth apart from one flaw near the wing where the marble looked as if, like sugar, it had melted in the heat. Charles said he'd commissioned it when they had had to leave Italy so abruptly. And when he kissed her on the forehead and cradled their baby in his arms she was reminded how passionately she'd felt about him during those first hot and heady weeks in Italy.

In the mornings the three of them would lie together for a precious few moments before Charles rose and she drifted off again. Seeing her fledgling family lying on the white sheets beneath the heavy rosewood canopy made Emily think of her own back in England and she sometimes woke to find her cheeks faintly coated with salt where she'd shed tears while she slept. Occasionally a fleeting expression on Clem's face, older than her inchoate features, reminded her of her father. When Clem cried inconsolably, Emily wished her mother was with her, wished for the comfort of a woman who had raised children herself, who knew and understood what to do and who would be familiar in this alien place.

It wasn't that there was no one to ask for advice – Dr Walker was all brisk reassurance – it was that there was no one to complain to: of her swollen breasts and sore groin and the bulge in her abdomen that remained even though the baby had gone. Not that she could have said a word of any of this to her brother, Will, had he been with her, but she could imagine his uncomplicated sympathy; how he would have strolled around the house with his hands in his pockets, laughing and whistling and making fun of her inability to stand without wincing or hold a conversation without becoming distracted. She wrote to her mother to tell her and Will about the baby and she read their letters eagerly but the act of writing merely made her feel more isolated.

'We're going to have to fetch more supplies soon,' Emily said to Charles.

It was almost two months since Clementine had been born, and every morning after Charles had left the house scores of children came creeping on to the veranda to show their clean hands and faces and to peek at the tiny, white child. Women started to drop in on her on their way back from the field to touch Clementine's smooth skin and to add a complaint and beg for something: soap, salt, flannel, meat. On this particular day Charles happened to arrive as she was in the middle of talking to some of their female slaves. Charles dispatched the women swiftly.

'The nearest store is in Darien. The men can canoe you there. But really, Emily, you ought not to give the women so much. They have sufficient.'

He had been very patient and gentle over the last few weeks of her confinement. Emily, perhaps because she'd just given birth, was more than unusually moved by the women's plight. She wiped away her tears.

'Did you see that woman? The one I was speaking to when you arrived? She's called Psyche. I believe she has rheumatism: she can hardly hold a hoe any more. She said the pain was insufferable. It keeps her awake at night. Charles, can't you—'

'Emily, for goodness sake,' he snapped, 'don't listen to them. They're all deuced liars. They're lazy and they know how weak-willed you are. Where's my baby girl?'

He picked up Clementine who had been asleep and now began to cry. He rocked her for a minute and then handed her to Emily.

Emily put the baby on her shoulder. She waited until her sobs had subsided a little and then said, 'I think I'm feeling strong enough to start going out again. Is there a horse I could ride?'

All their animals – the sheep, pigs and cattle – were at the inland end of the plantation and she had not had a chance to see if there were any horses.

Charles thought for a moment and then said, 'We've never really kept many. There's no point having horses to plough when we've got people to hoe. But I think there are a couple for pulling the wood wagon. From what I remember, they're not very good, certainly not the quality of horses you're accustomed to riding. They will not have been ridden for a considerable period of time either so they'll be impossible to handle. I doubt we even possess a lady's saddle.' He paused, irritated. 'What an infernal racket the baby's making! Call Virginie if you can't keep her quiet.'

He went into his study. Emily fed Clementine, who had eventually stopped crying, and then summoned Virginie.

'Go and tell Caesar to speak to whoever looks after the horses. I want them both ready and saddled tomorrow morning so I can choose the best one. And tell him to bring them to the house after Charles has left,' she added quietly.

The following morning was beautiful, warm and with a bright blue sky. Outside the house violets were blooming in profusion and irises grew in the nearby dykes. Some of the orange trees were covered with star-shaped white flowers. Caesar was waiting for her with a horse and an elderly man he introduced as Joshua.

'Them two horses, they pull the wagon, nobody ride them for years,' said Joshua. 'The other one a woman horse. She even more bad-tempered than this one.'

The horse was ugly and had not been cared for. His hooves were out of shape, his black and white coat shaggy. His long nose was pink with spots and his eyes were a curious mixture of blue and brown with yellow rings.

'Hard enough get the bridle and saddle on him,' grumbled Joshua. 'But I find this old thing and clean him up for you.'

It was a lady's saddle, the leather peeling and worn, stained with mould, the leg post rickety. It would do, she thought, until she had fully recovered from the birth and could use a normal saddle.

'Thank you, Joshua. Does he have a name?' asked Emily.

'No, missis.'

'Then I'll call him Oak, after my horse back in England, and hope that he is as sweet-natured.'

'Him ain't sweet-natured,' said Joshua. 'Missis, you no ride him. Him got a real bad temper.'

The horse snorted and rolled back his eyes and laid his ears flat. When Emily tried to stroke his nose, he pulled back his lips, exposing large yellowing teeth, and tried to bite her.

'Go and fetch some chunks of sugar, Caesar, and we'll see if we can soften him up a little.'

While she waited for Caesar to return, she stroked the animal's neck. He quivered and tensed. She leaned against the saddle and he swung round and bit her on the shoulder. She cried out and smacked him across the nose and he skittered sideways. Joshua struggled to hold him. She cupped her shoulder and could feel the indentation of teeth marks, swelling in her flesh. When Caesar returned she held out a piece of hard brown sugar on her palm and the horse snorted a couple of times, then took a step forward and snatched it from her.

'Good boy, now let's see how you do.'

She put one foot in the stirrup and swung herself up. Oak went rigid. Then he started to buck. Joshua held on to his reins and Emily gripped hard to the pommel of the saddle. Eventually the horse quieted.

'Let me have the reins.'

As soon as the horse felt the bridle go over his head, he neighed and reared and bucked again and this time Emily was thrown to the ground. Caesar came running over. Both he and Joshua looked petrified. Emily got to her feet, holding her ribs.

'I'm fine, just a little winded.'

She walked back to the horse again.

'No, missis, you hurt you self,' said Joshua, holding out his hand to stop her.

'I have to show him who's in charge,' she said. 'Hold him still.'

Joshua was almost pulled off his feet by the frantic horse, but Emily managed to swing herself on to his back. Oak started bucking again but this time more half-heartedly. Emily walked him in a circle round the house and then urged him into a trot. She jumped off and fed him another lump of sugar.

'That's enough for today. Bring him back tomorrow, Joshua, and make sure his coat's brushed and his hooves trimmed, will you?'

The following day, Oak eagerly took the sugar from her palm. He bridled and minced when she tried to mount him and tossed his head and rolled his eyes back but didn't try to throw her off. They set off at a brisk walk alongside the dyke. Emily was filled with excitement – she was at last going to be able to explore more than the narrowly subscribed walks she'd taken when she was pregnant.

Where the fields ended they came to a dense forest of live oaks. There, the sun shone through great grey curtains of moss; vivid green ferns and tiny olive-coloured orchids coated the branches and beneath grew a seemingly impenetrable thicket of saw palmetto, the palms' leaves razor-sharp. The horse fidgeted and danced along the edge of the wood until Emily found a path. Inside, a thick layer of dead leaves covered the ground and crunched beneath the horse's hooves. A small flock of Carolina chickadees called shrilly and darted through the trees in front of her. In between the oaks were red bay trees with dusty cinnamon-coloured bark that smelled of eucalyptus as Emily brushed past them and magnificent magnolias, their leaves like burnished metal plates, with gigantic creamy blossoms. Wild jasmine, thick with brilliant yellow flowers, clung to the tree trunks and a red and black woodpecker started his rattling drill, then gave a harsh alarm call and flew in an undulating path away from her. It was the most magical place Emily had seen. Even Oak grew quiet and walked easily.

Eventually the path through the wood led to the end of the island, the wood merging almost seamlessly with the shore, becoming reeds and rushes and sunken shrubs. A huge black and yellow striped butterfly flew lazily in front of them and alighted on a swamp privet. As they reached the edge of dry land, an alligator that was barely a couple of yards away from them, camouflaged against the mud, twisted swiftly and sank into the river, emerging a little way away from them, only its eyes and the scales of its back visible in the swamp. A treeful of herons took noisy flight; as she and the horse waited, they returned, one by one, and resumed their positions.

Emily tried to ride alongside the edge of the wood but the trail disappeared into a tangle of undergrowth and lethal saw palmettos. She would ask Caesar to round up a gang of boys to clear the paths for her for money. She thought of what she had so easily given up: a lucrative job and her independence. Once she'd paid for the funeral and sent enough money back to complete Will's education, and a little for her mother, Charles had appropriated the rest and, as he had made so clear, she was not at liberty to earn more for herself. Money had once meant little to her – it had been wonderful to have better clothes and be able to ride whenever she felt like it – but she had only worked for her father's sake. How far that money would go here, she thought: how many bars of soap and new clothes would it buy? How many slaves could she have freed? She sighed and Oak flicked his ears. She patted his neck and turned to head back the way they had come, but just then a deer exploded from behind a pine and bounded away, trailing moss in its antlers. Oak started and bolted, but instead of fighting him she urged him on and they galloped, with her leaning almost flat against his outstretched neck, through the wood, before bursting into the brilliant sunshine of the bare cotton fields.

Later that afternoon, Emily was in the drawing room, writing to Ely and Sarah and smiling to herself as she struggled to describe Clementine to them, when there was a knock at the door.

'Dr Walker – do come in! How nice to see you again,' said Emily. She turned to Virginie, who was standing in the doorway. 'Go and tell Bella to make us a pot of tea.'

'I thought I'd see how you were progressing,' said Dr Walker.

He sat down, smoothing out the creases in his trousers and folded one leg crisply over the other.

'I'm feeling considerably better, thank you.'

'Have you found a wet nurse for her?'

'Virginie gives her a bottle.'

'Let's have a look at her.' Dr Walker picked up Clementine out of her cradle, unwrapped the flannels she was in and inspected her. 'Hmm, all seems to be in order. Gaining weight. Good.'

He handed her to Virginie who tucked the baby away. Bella came in and poured them both tea. Emily noticed that Dr Walker was looking at the girl strangely.

'I was wondering, who is the doctor for the slaves?'

'I'm called out if there's a problem,' said Dr Walker, 'but only when it's a real emergency. No one wants to pay to have their involuntary servants treated.'

'I don't know how you stand it,' Emily remarked abruptly. 'You're a man of letters, an intelligent man, scientifically trained.'

'What do you mean, my dear? I'm not squeamish.'

'I didn't mean whether you minded treating them, I meant the whole issue of slavery. These people are kept here against their will and forced to work. Surely there is nothing more contrary to the human spirit or more ignoble than the enslavement of one man by another? Reverend William Ellery Channing said, "It is plain, that, if one man may be held as property, then every other man may be so held."'

Dr Walker took a sip of his tea. 'It has been mentioned to me that you have remarkable views.'

'No one could agree to that. No one. Our whole spirit rebels against the idea of being held as another man's possession,' Emily burst out. '"We cannot be owned as a tree or a brute."'

'Well, you have me there, my dear, there is nothing I can say to that argument. But leaving aside the bigger picture, the slaves here are kept well and treated with kindness. They have sufficient food, they have clothes and shelter and they are cared for when they are sick, if not by me, then at the infirmary on the plantation. Most of them are perfectly happy and would not know what to do with freedom if it presented itself to them.'

Emily started to reply but Dr Walker interrupted her and said with dignity, 'Please don't excite yourself, Mrs Brook. It's not good for you in your condition. Allow me to prescribe rest for you until you fully recover from being with child.'

Emily paused. Dr Walker had, she realized, conceded the major point. As for the minor ones, no one she had as yet met would agree to those.

'I do apologize, Dr Walker,' she said. 'I was an actress, you know, and we are quite passionate creatures by nature. I cannot say that I respect your views but we'll let them alone for the moment. Now, do tell me about Mr and Mrs Drummond. When I arrived I was far along my confinement and I only spoke to them briefly. I haven't yet felt sufficiently energetic to undertake a trip to the far end of St Simons.'

'I'd be delighted to,' said Dr Walker, passing his cup to Virginie to be refilled. 'By the way,' he added more softly, 'do you want to let me take a look at your other girl?'

'Bella? Why, what do you think ails her?' asked Emily.

'I rather think she's in the family way,' Dr Walker said dryly.

'Really? Oh my goodness, I've been so preoccupied with Clementine that I hadn't noticed . . .' Emily's voice trailed away and then she said quietly, 'She's so very young.'

'It can be a shock, how early the Negroes start.'

'Won't you stay for supper, Dr Walker? Perhaps you could contrive to speak to her yourself. I'm not sure Charles would countenance the extra expense of a proper examination.'

The doctor said he'd be delighted and in fact remained until late afternoon the following day.

When he had gone Emily turned to Virginie and said, 'I didn't know there was an infirmary here. Please take me there tomorrow.'

'Caesar show you,' said Virginie, not looking at her. 'I stay with the baby.'

'It far away,' said Caesar, looking anxiously at her. 'The infirmary at St Annie's – the other end of the plantation.'

'Well, how does everyone else get there?'

'They walk or the wood wagon pick them up if they too sick.'

'I'll ride,' said Emily, 'and you could ride the other horse.'

'We people don't know how,' said Caesar sullenly. 'Master don't have many horses because they cost more to keep than we.'

He held Oak for her while she mounted. They set off, Caesar walking alongside her, along the main road through the plantation that ran the length of the island.

'There another camp at St Annie's,' he said. 'Not so pleasant as this one.'

'Not as pleasant? Dear God.'

It was starting to grow warm, although the slaves still felt it was cool and complained to her about being cold in the mornings and in the evenings; their one set of clothes didn't allow them to wrap up warmly or cast off layers as the weather required. A couple of cardinals flew past and alighted on the cabbage palms, their plumage a vivid scarlet against the deep green fronds. The road led through the middle of a thick wood edged with saw palmetto, with curtains of jasmine trailing from the overhanging branches. A ditch along one side was choked with water lilies, their flowers opening pale pink. Emily thought suddenly of Undine, the nymph, the last part she had been about to play. She still couldn't quite reconcile herself with the contrast between then and her current situation. She, who had been only too eager to renounce acting, now felt that in doing so she had lost a part of herself. She thought she had understood the nymph but she realized that she had not; it was only here that she appreciated what it was like to live in the wrong element.

They'd been walking and riding for the best part of an hour when the horse started abruptly. A large snake, almost six feet in length, slid out of the ditch in front of them. Caesar gave a wild shout and ran behind Oak. Emily was a lot less frightened than she would have been had she not been on horseback and, in fact, was more concerned that Caesar might be kicked. She watched the snake, fascinated. It had two white stripes that ran the length of its face and diamond patterns along its sand and tan spine. At the tip of its tail was a set of pale chitinous rattles. Its muscular body slipped, as if oiled, across the road. In the middle it stopped and turned its head towards them, the black forked tongue flickering. Emily had to use all her strength to hold the dancing horse and Caesar, behind her, clung to the animal's rump. The snake shook its rattles at them; it was a dry sound, like corn being shaken in a metal canister, but there was something chillingly sinister about it. And now they could smell the snake too: a pungent, acrid odour that snagged at the back of the throat. The snake continued to glide over the road and slid into the undergrowth.

'A lot of good you'd be at protecting me if I was attacked,' Emily said with amusement, looking behind her.

'My mother bit by a snake. She ought to die but Edward chop her finger off. Them swamps full of snakes.' Caesar was still shaking.

Shortly afterwards he indicated a wide, muddy track that led off the road and through the woods. It grew distinctly marshy; the track was carried by a series of rotten wooden bridges and black pools of water glimmered between the trees. Emily started to get bitten. The wood opened up to reveal a couple of fields bordered by swamp and a line of tumbledown houses. Next to them was a larger, two-storey building made of the same shell and sand mixture with a wooden roof. Emily jumped down and handed Oak's reins to Caesar. She walked round the front of the camp. The conditions here were indeed 'not as pleasant'. The houses were much more dilapidated and a wave of fleas leapt up at her as she approached. When she peered inside one, three small children looked back at her, huddling by the embers of a dying fire, naked except for a filthy, ragged blanket. They had the distended stomachs and the glazed, shining eyes of the half-starved. The ground they crouched upon was damp, and thick with droppings from the ducks and hens that wandered in and out. Emily backed away.

'Caesar, tie up Oak and go and round up all the children here. Tell them about washing and how I'll pay them a cent a day to keep clean. Find the older children and make them rekindle that fire and keep all the poultry out of their houses.'

Caesar looked away and shrugged. 'Not gone make no difference, missis, that the only water,' and he indicated the swamp in front of them.

'Nevertheless, please do as I ask,' she said, her voice shaking, her legs already beginning to itch.

She walked into the infirmary and stood for a while in the doorway letting her eyes acclimatize. When she could see a little, she stepped forward. It was a scene she could not have imagined. There were windows, but most of them had no glass so they had been covered up with wood and sacking. A fire burned but it was almost heatless and the smoke shrouded the whole room. The place was filled with women, the majority of them lying directly on the mud floor with only a blanket wrapped around them. The stench was intolerable.

'Who is in charge here?' asked Emily, putting her hand in front of her mouth.

'Me, missis,' said a huge Negro woman, coming towards her through the gloom, stepping over the bodies. 'Dianna.'

'Well, for goodness' sake, take down these boards and bits of sack and let some light in. Get the fire going properly so it's not smoking all over the place.'

'No more wood, missis.'

'Then fetch some – we're surrounded by a forest. Tell Caesar – my boy – to help you. When the others come back this evening, make sure some of the men unblock the chimney.'

She walked round slowly, speaking to each woman. There were slaves who had just given birth and others who were about to. There was a young girl, maybe thirteen, whose flesh was being eaten away, joint by joint, by some malodorous disease. There were women who had just had a miscarriage, others who were burning with fever, some who were shaking with cold, several racked with rheumatism. Emily encouraged the ones who could stand to help sweep and tidy up the place and collect and wash the blankets that weren't being used.

'And what ails you?' asked Emily, crouching down next to a young woman clutching a tiny child.

'My name, it Rose. Me no feel well,' she whispered. 'Me have the fever and the child have it too.'

Emily felt their foreheads. They were both damp and hot

and the infant was trembling. 'The baby is so dirty, she will never get well if you don't try to keep her clean.'

'Oh, missis, we so tired. We start so early – when we not upon the hoe in them fields there, we have to walk three miles to them other cotton fields and we must get there by dawn. We work all day and then fetch we hominy and then walk all the way back to cook him. We too tired to do anything else but sleep. And missis can see the water here. We fear to clean our children in them swamp. Him full of mud and crabs. Him smell real bad.'

Emily sighed and turned to Dianna. 'You're going to have to boil water. When the men come back tonight, get them to set up a big fire so you'll have clean water to wash your patients tomorrow. I'll send some flannel you can use as rags. What's this you have on your legs?' she asked, turning to another slave.

'It a poultice made from the tulip tree leaves for we sores,' said the woman.

Emily left the women and climbed up the narrow, dark staircase to the next floor where she found the men. They too had a fire that was smoking heavily and although on this floor there was more glass in the windows, the panes were dark with grime. Emily fetched a rag and some water and began ineffectually to clean them herself. In the half-light, she looked around at the sick men who had, like the women, spent their health and strength labouring to put bread on her table. She thought of her honeymoon in Italy: the champagne she and Charles had drunk, the good coffees and fine meals, the villa with its beautiful roses, the trip to Florence, the ices and the art galleries. This was how it had been paid for.

The only person who had not spoken to her while she was in the infirmary was an elderly man who lay stretched out on his back, his head supported by a few twigs.

'What's the matter with him?' she asked.

'He old,' was the reply.

She crouched next to him. 'How are you feeling?' she asked softly.

For a long time, he said nothing. She waved away the flies that had gathered on his half-open eyes and lips. She wet his lips with a little water and wondered how pestilential it was. He moved his lips slightly and she bent forward to listen to him.

'I gone die,' he said simply.

Emily held his hand, and it was as dry as a desiccated leaf, the palm calloused. He took a couple of shuddering breaths and then stopped breathing. She looked at his face. It was completely still and almost grey in the dim light. The pulse at his wrist had ceased. She carefully put his hand on his body and covered his face with a blanket. And then she ran down the stairs and stumbled through the infirmary, bursting out into the light and fresh air. She untied the horse and mounted him. Sensing her agitation, Oak sidestepped and tossed his head.

'Caesar,' she said to the boy, 'do whatever Dianna asks of you and then return to Brook House.'

She spurred Oak into a canter and raced him all the way back. By the time she reached the house she was in a towering rage. Her muscles were sore from riding, her legs and arms itched from the flea and sandfly bites, her womb ached and her breasts felt swollen and the nipples chafed. There was no sign of either Charles or Mr Stewart, so she rode over to the nearest cotton field and asked a couple of the men. They said they hadn't seen either of them.

One of them said, 'Missis try Master Stewart's house? They sometimes go there in the day.'

Charles had said Mr Stewart lived near Jones' Creek, a part of the plantation she had not visited before. Emily had a vague idea where it was. She rode down the road in the direction of St Annie's, but before she reached the bridge she veered down a dirt track leading towards the woods. The grass here was thick and rank, sticky with burrs, its roots clotted with mud. There were a couple of misshapen fields in a loop of land trapped by the ox-bow of the river and a few pitiful cows tethered to posts. They'd trampled the ground to a fissured red mud; the river was clogged with a fetid ochre-coloured scum and gnats whined above it in a pulsating black cloud.

Mr Stewart's house was at the far end of the field, hemmed in on three sides by forest. It had once been white but the paint had blistered and peeled; the wood was blackened around the chimney stack, the rest coated in a powdery green film. Some of the roof shingles were loose, others had curled and cracked like wedges of hard cheese. Rusting pieces of metal littered the dirt yard. Emily dismounted and slowly climbed the tilting steps up to the veranda, stepping over the middle one, which had a gaping jagged hole in the centre. She knocked on the door. The wood felt soft beneath her knuckles. The door creaked open a little way. She pushed it and entered the small, dark sitting room. The window panes were encrusted in a green slime so that only a dim, underwater light penetrated.

Mr Stewart was asleep on the sofa, his feet on the arm-rest, which wept horsehair stuffing, his hat over his face. He was snoring. A half-empty bottle of whiskey lay on the floor. Bluebottles buzzed round the room before settling back on the stack of dirty plates congealed with food on the table.

'Mr Stewart?'

He jumped and pulled off his hat, then swung his legs to the floor and pinched his eyes together with one hand.

'I couldn't find you or my husband. The men said to come out here. Do you know where Mr Brook is?' she asked.

'I don't know, Mrs Brook. I think he's out hunting.'

There was a sweetish, rotten smell combined with the odour of feet. She said, 'I've just visited the infirmary. Have you been recently?'

'Why yes,' he said in his soft brogue. 'I go every day to check on them.' He looked up at her for the first time since she'd arrived, his squint more pronounced.

'Mr Stewart, how can you allow it? It's filthy, disgusting! They don't even have beds let alone medicine or clean water.'

'I know,' he said simply. 'I told the previous manager,

Evan St Clair, that something needed to be done when he started work here. But he said to leave it as it was.'

'How long ago was that?'

'Fifteen years, Mrs Brook.'

Emily walked round the room, taking deep breaths. She was shaking. The floorboards creaked and sagged beneath her feet.

'Today,' she said, as quietly as she could, 'I'd like you to let all the people who live at St Annie's camp finish work early. I'd like them to go and gather firewood for their homes and the infirmary. I want them to clean the place and wash the blankets and boil water to wash themselves and all the people who are sick and make sure there's enough clean water for the infirmary tomorrow. And I want them to gather moss and make mattresses. Then I want the carpenter to start making beds. Or at least pallets.'

'I'll make sure they finish early and do as you say, Mrs Brook,' said Mr Stewart, 'but I can't set Joe to work without Mr Brook's permission.'

'Don't worry, I'll speak to him myself,' replied Emily. 'And perhaps in future you could work the slaves a little less hard. One woman told me how they were so exhausted they didn't even have the strength to wash by the time they got to their huts at night.'

She backed out of the room and half ran, half staggered down the veranda steps. The door closed with the soft sound of mildewed wood behind her. She fumbled with Oak's reins as she tried to untie him. He picked up on her unease and tossed his head back and snorted. She mounted and spurred him into a canter, feeling as if her entire body might break out in hives.

Charles, when he returned home late that afternoon, was in fine form. He'd shot a brace of duck and a deer. Two of his slaves walked behind him, carrying it and the dead birds.

'Shall we get Joe to hack it up in chunks?' he said with a laugh as he came in.

He walked mud all the way through the house and leaned out of the door on the other side to give the men and June instructions about plucking and gutting and hanging. He reappeared and collapsed on the sofa, took off his boots and threw them across the floor.

'Bella,' he called, 'get in here and clean up. Such a beautiful day,' he said to Emily. 'How's my baby girl?'

'She's fine. She's sleeping,' said Emily, tight-lipped. 'Charles, I've just been to the infirmary.'

She launched into a description of the place and her conversation with Mr Stewart.

'That's enough,' said Charles. 'Get me a drink, would you,' he said to Bella. 'Why are you interfering, Emily? None of this is your deuced business.'

'I can't sit back and watch this kind of injustice without at least trying to do something about it. I can't believe you think it's acceptable to treat your slaves like this.'

'And I don't understand why you don't do as I ask,' he railed at her. 'You did everything your beloved father asked of you. You worked as an actress which you hated, and travelled to the other side of the world, leaving your family behind, simply because your father wanted you to. Yet you refuse to obey me.'

Emily looked at him with incredulity. 'You're being utterly ridiculous. John was my father. Of course I did what he asked of me.'

'Exactly,' shouted Charles. 'And I am your husband! You should do what *I* want you to do. You should obey *me*.'

There was silence as they stared at each other. Bella slowly poured Charles a large glass of Madeira and retreated.

'I was under the illusion that this was a partnership of equals,' said Emily quietly.

Charles snorted and tipped his head back and downed half of his wine in one gulp. She watched his Adam's apple poking sharply through the skin of his throat.

'So what do you think about the infirmary?' she persisted.

'Since you're so keen to be involved you can speak to Joe yourself,' he said bullishly, but as if the fight had left him. 'Get him to make pallets, not beds, and not until he's finished the repairs to the cotton gin. I don't ever want to hear another word on the subject.'

'Thank you, Charles,' she said gravely.

'What's for dinner?' he said roughly.

'You'll never guess,' she said, trying to make her voice light. 'We received a parcel this morning from the Drummonds.'

'I've been meaning to pay them a visit. Now your confinement is over and Dr Walker has given you a clear bill of health, we ought to call on them.'

'They sent shrimp but they're enormous, almost like lobster. And fresh peas – peas – at this time of year!'

'They have an enchanting garden,' said Charles. 'The steamer from Savannah goes past their property – that's where we were dropped off when we first arrived. When the wind's in the right direction, you can smell the scent of their roses. Why don't you write them a thank-you note and say we'd like to drop in? We'll take them some of my venison,' he said, suddenly almost childishly excited.

How impossible and unpredictable he was, Emily thought.

The following morning she spoke to Joe about the pallet beds and asked him to make new windows and shutters for the infirmary when he'd finished. She packed a bag with soap, flannel, sal volatile and laudanum and the leftover shrimp and ham from their dinner. As she set off on horseback to the infirmary, she startled a boat-tailed grackle, which burst out of a small bush, uttering shrill alarm calls. The bird was like an overgrown English blackbird with a fan-shaped tail and she was close enough to see the iridescent purple sheen of its feathers and the red ring around its eye. The sky was pale blue with long streaks of white cloud; an osprey flew low, close over her head, and out and away above the jetty and the marsh beyond. A thin, warm breeze brought with it the scent of salt and orange blossom. It would be the most beautiful place to live, she thought, if it were not for the reason why she was here.

As she approached the infirmary, she heard a woman

crying. She jumped off Oak and ran inside to find Rose naked, crouched on the ground weeping. Her baby, lying on the floor next to her, was also crying. Rose's back was red with blood, which slowly trickled down her hips and ribs and dripped on to the floor.

Emily stood in the doorway aghast and then ran over to Rose.

'What on earth has happened?' she asked, pulling Rose's clothes over her.

'Oh, missis,' cried Rose, 'Mr Stewart come in and asked who done tell tales on him. He say me tell you he work me so hard that me don't get no time to wash my baby and so he beat me.'

'He beat you? But your back is cut open. Lacerated,' she said.

'Him use a rawhide whip,' said Dianna, stepping towards them out of the gloom. 'It what the overseer always use.'

Emily took a deep breath and fought back tears. She looked around the infirmary. It was cleaner and tidier than yesterday, with a roaring fire and mounds of Spanish moss lined up neatly for mattresses. Piles of folded blankets lay on the ground and outside more were drying on a line.

'You've done well, Dianna,' said Emily.

She watched Dianna as she made up a poultice and pressed it into the wounds on Rose's back, then bound the whole lot with strips of the flannel Emily had brought. Emily warmed water and helped Rose, who winced with pain, to bath the baby. The child was literally encrusted with dirt. She gave the woman a few drops of laudanum and left the rest of her supplies with Dianna. She inspected the houses next, handing out cents to the vaguely clean children who begged her for meat. There had been some attempt at tidying but, in reality, Emily saw how futile it was and how, save for locking the shutters and keeping the doors closed at all times, there was no real way to stop the ducks and hens from wandering in and out as they liked. One of the older boys, who was about ten, asked her for a pig.

'A pig?' said Emily in surprise.

'We done have pigs but we no have permission now. Please ask master if we can keep pigs. Then we no have to ask missis for meat.'

'I will. I can't see why you wouldn't be able to have a pig. You'd have to ensure it didn't walk in and out of your huts like the hens though.'

When she arrived back at the house, Charles was there, eating cake and drinking coffee.

'That tyrant flogged a semi-naked sick woman in the infirmary.'

'I presume you mean Mr Stewart?' he said through a mouthful of cake. 'He's already told me about it. I keep telling you, Emily, but you're too stubborn to listen. The Negroes are liars. You simply cannot believe a word they say. If Rose had gone to work like Mr Stewart asked her to, none of this would have happened. As it was, she thought she could prey upon your sympathy even though she's too damned lazy even to look after her own baby, never mind do the job she's meant to be doing. It was entirely her fault she was beaten. You cannot overthrow the system. They have to be disciplined and I will not have you meddling in affairs you seem incapable of understanding.'

'It's unjust and unfair. You, as a lawyer, ought to know that better than anyone,' said Emily hotly.

'If they choose to spend their time complaining to you and making up all sorts of stories when they should be working, and you persist in coming to me or Mr Stewart repeating their lies, then you and they will have to live with the consequences.'

'They asked me if they could keep pigs,' she said, bursting into tears.

'For goodness' sake,' he said, starting to grow angry, 'they're not allowed to keep pigs because they can't afford to feed them. They don't have any damn money or food to spare! And you've seen for yourself what a disgusting state they allow their houses to degenerate into. Imagine how much worse that would be if they had pigs running in and out. My God, Emily, for an intelligent woman you can be so insufferably stupid.'

He banged his coffee cup down on the table so hard the liquid spilled and Clementine, who was in the corner being rocked by Virginie, began to wail. He grabbed his gun from where he'd left it propped up by the door and walked out.

'You look beautiful,' said Charles, leaning across and kissing Emily. 'That's a charming dress. I don't remember seeing it before.'

It was a week later and they were in one of the boats being rowed around the island to the Drummonds' in time for supper at five. The American habit of eating so early and so soon after the midday meal had never suited Emily but she had little choice in the matter. They had left Clementine with Virginie and the two of them were accompanied by four slaves.

'Thank you, it's new,' said Emily, smiling. 'I had it sent from my tailor in Boston.'

'Without asking me?'

Emily, not detecting the undertone in Charles's voice, laughed. 'Of course without asking you. It's a dress, Charles. It's not as if I were purchasing a horse.'

'I simply think it's needlessly extravagant,' he said in a pinched voice.

'Oh, for goodness' sake. I couldn't have bought it in Darien – they sell linen and flannel and homespun in that store. Besides, I literally have nothing to wear. My dresses for the confinement are too big and I still haven't lost the weight I gained when I had Clementine so I hardly fit into any of my old clothes. I've had to let out my riding habit but that's about the only thing that's bearable to put on.'

'Then I suggest the solution would be to eat less instead of needlessly purchasing a new wardrobe.'

'Charles,' said Emily, tears pricking her eyes, 'that's a most unkind thing to say.'

'I'm simply pointing out the obvious. You had a wonderful figure when I met you. Just because you're not on stage any more doesn't mean you have to let yourself go. Mrs Hall should be an example to you. A man could practically span her waist between his hands.'

He turned away and lit a cigarette. Emily started to cry. The two of them didn't speak a word until they rounded the end of the island and floated up to the Drummonds' jetty. They walked over the neatly clipped grass to a splendid avenue of live oaks, light glowing through the curtains of Spanish moss shrouding them. They followed the road up to a great white house festooned with wisteria and flanked by two tightly pruned bay trees. The air was sweet and spicy with the scent from hundreds of hyacinths blooming in pots evenly spaced along the veranda. One of the men, Israel, came with them, carrying the venison and an Altamaha shad Emily had caught and insisted on bringing in spite of Charles's ridicule. He'd said, 'For God's sake, other people's wives don't run about catching fish.'

The Drummonds came out to meet them. They were effusive about the fish, which they declared the best kind around these parts and were delighted that Emily had caught it herself. They waved away Emily's thanks for the giant shrimp they'd sent.

'You must be quite tired out. Or would you care to take a look around the gardens before we go inside?'

'I wouldn't miss them for the world,' said Emily, 'and of course we're not tired; after all, we've been sitting leadenly in the boat while our men have done all the hard work.'

'Ah,' said Mrs Drummond, looking at her sharply. She turned to Israel and said, 'Take the meat to the kitchen and get the cook to give you something to eat and drink for yourself and the others.'

'Thank you, missis,' said Israel.

'Please don't inconvenience yourself,' said Charles, frowning.

'Oh, it's no trouble,' said Mrs Drummond, taking Emily's arm. 'Now, I'd like to start by showing you my pride and joy.'

She led them to a glasshouse, made out of the same lime and shell combination as the slaves' huts, but with great sheets of glass along one wall. Inside it was warm and moist.

'I have all sorts of grand plans,' said Mrs Drummond, 'pineapples to begin with. But it does allow one to get fruit and vegetables growing that bit faster and earlier.'

'You've got a banana plant,' said Emily with surprise. 'I've only ever seen them in pictures.'

'They're almost ripe,' said Mrs Drummond, removing her glasses to peer up at the bunch of green fruit. 'I shall send you a couple when they are,' she added.

The Drummonds' garden was exquisite. In neat flower-beds bordered by a myrtle and oleander hedge, there were over a hundred different kinds of roses, some of which were already blooming. The orchard was no less impressive, full of orange, olive, date and mulberry trees. Hamish explained that he'd been employed by the government as an agricul-tural adviser. He had wanted the islanders to diversify into growing other crops – like dates and olives.

'My grandest plan, though, was for silk,' he said, still with a hint of his original Scottish accent.

'Silk?' asked Emily.

'Yes. I brought over several strains of mulberry from China together with the silkworms. It's the caterpillar one needs. Once it's spun its cocoon, you plunge it into boiling water to kill the grub and release the silk from the cocoon. Unfortunately, none of my plans ever caught on. But we have several magnificent mulberry trees of both kinds, with black and white berries. The fruit are delicious. We also have quince, peaches and plums, all flowering now, as you can see, and extensive raspberry and blackberry canes.'

'I've seen some trees blossoming in the woods. They look like wild plum.'

'They could well be escapees from here, or perhaps some of my earlier attempts to persuade the islanders to broaden their horizons,' said Mr Drummond.

The vegetable gardens were extensive too but Emily could only glimpse them. As the sun was setting, Mrs Drummond suggested they return to the house.

'I know this will sound somewhat strange to you but may we see where your people live?'

'Emily,' said Charles, with a warning frown. 'Really, Mrs Drummond, we don't wish to trouble you further.'

Mrs Drummond looked quizzically at Charles and then said to Emily, 'We can walk past the nearest camp. It's very close, just behind the vegetable gardens. Not that you'll see much, I'm afraid. It does get dark so quickly here.'

The Drummonds' slave huts were built to the same design and of the same material as the Brooks' but were in much better condition with well-finished doors and windows. Many of the slaves were crouched round a large fire, cooking their hominy. Mrs Drummond pointed out their own gardens and hens, ducks and hogs, all in pens.

'They sell me pigs, eggs and some of their poultry and I'm only too eager to buy whatever they can catch in the river,' she said. 'They try to sell firewood, moss and eggs to the store in Darien, but the man who owns it always cheats them. I found one of my women in tears because her husband had saved for months to buy her material for a new dress and as soon as she put it on, it ripped. It breaks my heart to hear how some people will take advantage of our darkies.'

One of the men picked up a burning branch and, without being asked, accompanied them back to the house, lighting their way.

They drank chilled white wine with their meal – Mr Drummond had had an ice house built in the garden – and ate dressed crab, followed by ham, chicken and an abundance of vegetables that Emily had not seen since their arrival: new potatoes, baby turnips, asparagus spears, green peas and celery, all steamed and dripping with fresh butter. The dessert was blackberries, preserved from last year's crop, and home-made vanilla ice cream. It was a revelation: what could be done with the land when they themselves did not even have a garden and their slaves had nothing.

As she and Charles walked back to the boat beneath the live oaks, the curtains of moss swaying above their heads, ethereal in the moonlight, he said, 'So, what was the matter? You didn't press them like you usually do.'

'I didn't need to. I could tell what they thought.'

'What do you mean?'

'The Drummonds are the benign face of slavery. They keep their people in much better conditions than you do and treat them more kindly and with more respect. But they are slaves nonetheless. They, like everyone here, agree with the system. Unfortunately, it's much more abhorrent in their case because they're Scottish. They haven't grown up with the custom as you have.'

'Ah,' said Charles, 'I thought that perhaps you had realized the error of your ways and decided not to be so consistently rude. But I see it's not good manners you're displaying, merely the insufferable arrogance of someone who assumes they know what everyone else thinks.'

They walked in silence the rest of the way to the boat. The slaves rowed them back, singing softly. The navy sky was streaked with plum and brilliant with stars. Phosphorescence dripped from the oars and swirled livid turquoise through the water. A water rail they disturbed in the reeds snorted like a small pig and Emily jumped and then burst out laughing. She reached out her hand to Charles, who took it like a thirsty man, pulling her towards him and wrapping his arms around her.

Chapter 6

May 1860

Clementine had a touch of colic and cried almost incessantly. When she finally stopped and fell asleep it was as if the tension in the whole household relaxed. It was May and Emily found the weather too warm for comfort. She was lying in their large, oppressive bed, supposedly taking a nap, but actually watching a nesting grackle in a cabbage palm. The male, who was attending to several females and nests, was working overtime, trying to feed them all and her female, the one in the palm, was growing increasingly impatient, calling out for food. Clementine started to cry again. Emily stiffened and stretched. She waited to see if Clementine, who was downstairs in the sitting room, would stop. There was a pause, a long moment of blessed silence, and then the baby began to wail, great raw shrieks that made Emily's heart constrict. She jumped out of bed and ran downstairs, still in her under-garments, her hair sliding out of its pins.

Caesar was in the front room, holding Clementine and

shaking her vigorously. His expression when he looked up and saw Emily was a mixture of guilt and fear.

'What are you doing? Take your hands off my baby,' screamed Emily, running across the room and seizing the child.

Caesar held Clementine out to her. 'Missis, she cry, I just—'

Emily slapped him across the face. 'Never touch her again. Never. Now get out.'

She hugged Clem to her and rocked her as Caesar slunk away. She turned to see June, Bella and Virginie watching her. Virginie's face was grey with tiredness.

'Missis, why not give her a little brandy, see if that make her quiet.'

'Yes, Virginie, we may as well try it.'

She unwrapped Clementine and inspected her carefully but the baby seemed to be fine. The brandy had a short-lived effect and Clem soon started to howl again.

'What on earth . . .' said Charles when he came in for lunch to find all four women crouched on the floor, soothing the baby, with Emily still not dressed.

'Charles, I cannot have Caesar as my boy any longer. You must tell him not to come near the house again.'

'Why not?'

'I found him shaking Clementine and she was screaming and screaming.'

'She's screaming now. I'm sure he was merely attempting to stop her.'

'He's not coming in the house again,' said Emily

obstinately. 'I've had a bad feeling about that boy since the day I met him. I don't want him near me.'

'Well, what do you expect him to do? He can't go and work in the fields.'

'I don't want him to work in the fields. I don't want any of them to work in the fields. But they're your slaves. You decide. And why can't he do the same work as the others anyhow?'

'Oh, Emily, don't be so ridiculous. Just look at the colour of his skin.'

'I fail to see what that has to do with anything.'

'For God's sake, stop being so obtuse. He's half white. He can't work in the fields like a common nigger.'

'So his black mother was good enough for some white man but none of them, not even the pale ones, is good enough to be treated as an equal.'

Charles stepped forward and for one moment she thought he was going to slap her but he stopped himself and turned away.

'Well, you'd better find another boy because I'm not having you riding and rowing around without someone to keep an eye on you,' he said after a moment.

'I've told you before, I want Frank. I want someone who can ride and paddle and won't hide when a snake appears. I don't want some belligerent child. I need a man who will actually protect me. Or else I might as well be on my own, which, frankly, is what I would prefer.'

'Dear God, Emily, you drive me to despair. I'll get you Frank. But Caesar must work in the kitchen with June. I'll tell him not to come into the house. And that's final. Now why is there no damn food on the table? And can one of you women shut that child up?' he shouted.

Emily went upstairs with Virginie and Clementine to get the baby out of Charles's way and so Virginie could help her dress. She sat in front of her looking-glass, rocking the baby in the cradle with her foot as Virginie brushed her hair. Her hands were cool.

'I should like to cut it all off, it's far too hot,' she said, shaking her mane of dark hair.

'I pin it up tightly, missis.'

As Virginie pulled and twisted and fastened her hair, Emily wondered if she'd over-reacted. She had never liked Caesar, with his odd looks and his sullen air of superiority, the way he lorded over other children when she asked him to hand out food or money to them, his careless condemnation of his own kind and his belief in his difference and his entitlement. Yet, she had to admit, his behaviour was no different than one would expect given the beliefs he was surrounded by and the brutality he had witnessed and been subjected to. He was, after all, still a child. A child I don't want around my own, Emily thought, and vowed not to think about it again. If she did, she knew she would start to feel sorry.

'Virginie, do you ever wish you were free?' she asked suddenly.

'All the time,' said Virginie tonelessly.

Emily grabbed her wrist. 'You know I don't believe you should be kept like this, don't you?' she said. 'If I had my wish, you'd all be free tomorrow.'

Virginie gave her a look of utter contempt and Emily felt her breath catch in her throat. Her maid went to fetch her dress, and when she turned back to her mistress her face was blank once more.

They were going to have a picnic on the beach at Sugar Island. It was pure, white sand and it faced the Atlantic, Frank had said. He knew the pattern of the tides and now that the water was at a low ebb they were going to travel across the thin spit of land linking St Simons to the smaller island. Emily climbed into the wood wagon and Virginie passed her Clementine and scrambled in after her. Frank walked, leading Oak. It was a beautiful day. The wide-open periwinkle-blue skies and the flood of clear light reminded her of Italy. They drove past the first camp and the children came running out after them, begging for rice and sugar. The causeway, at the far end of the island's most westerly tip, was a ridge of sand that rose above the marsh on either side.

'Master say he mean to build a bridge cross here, but he ain't done it yet,' said Frank.

Oak leaned into the harness as the wheels stuck in the sand. Gradually the sand grew damper and firmer and they moved more swiftly.

'We're in the middle now,' she said, looking out on either side to reeds, yellow with goldenrod and irises, and beyond them the river, brown and blue and gold.

'This Five Pound,' said Frank, when they reached the other side, 'master's sugar cane plantation.'

They drove around the edge of the fields. The slaves were weeding the slender, fresh green canes but the borders were a riot of wild flowers: pink cosmos, white and yellow daisies and golden black-eyed susans. At the far end, where the woods began, was another settlement and the sugar mill. Even though no sugar was being produced and the clay pots for setting the sugar were stacked in piles, drying in the sun, there was a strong smell of molasses. Emily passed Clem to Virginie and jumped out. She walked across the camp. It was the worst one she had seen, the houses little more than ruins. Glass panes were missing from the windows, the doors sagged and there were gaping holes in the walls and the roofs. In the centre Emily noticed a wooden construction and what she thought was a pile of rags. As she drew closer she saw it was a woman, her head bare in the baking sun, her arms outstretched and fastened in what Emily now realized were stocks. She ran over. The woman seemed barely alive, her eyes almost shut, her lips cracked and bleeding.

'Quick,' she shouted. 'Frank, bring water.'

Frank took out one of their bottles of water and came running over.

'Get her out of this,' said Emily, taking the stopper from the bottle.

'She there for punishment. Five Pound where we people get sent if a flogging ain't good enough,' said Frank reluctantly.

'I don't care. Please release her.'

As soon as Frank undid the screws and lifted up the top

153

section, the woman fell backwards on to the hard earth. Emily crouched down next to her and raised her head on to her lap and gave her a little water.

'What's your name?' asked Emily.

'It Charlotte, missis.'

Emily smoothed some ointment she was carrying for Clem on to the woman's lips and helped her drink a little more.

'Charlotte, why are you here?'

'Me live in camp four at Busson Hill. The previous manager, he force me.'

'You mean Mr St Clair?'

'Yes, and then he beat me when I resist him. So me run away. He send men and dogs and catch me. Same thing happen again. And again. The third time he catch me he send me here to work on Five Pound but the driver, Abraham, he force me too. Many times. Me ran into those woods there but he find me and put me here. That all, missis.'

Emily helped the woman to sit up and crouched in front of her. She'd thought she was about thirty, but now she saw that Charlotte was much younger, maybe a teenager, maybe in her early twenties. She had once been beautiful.

'And how long have you been here?'

'No know, missis. Maybe five days. Maybe a week.'

'Frank, would you help Charlotte into the shade. Charlotte, we'll take you to Busson Hill on our way back. You can tell Abraham what I said if he comes here and that I order him not to touch you.'

She left the bottle of water with the woman and a little food, believing that if she let her have too much at once, it might make her ill. Dispirited, she climbed back into the wagon next to Virginie. Frank led them a little further and then stopped.

'There no path through these woods to the beach, missis. I need to clear a way.'

He took out a machete and started to hack an opening amid the saw palmetto and pokeberry and laurel cherry. When he'd cleared some of the undergrowth he led the wagon into the wood. Inside, beneath the live oaks and cedars, it was cooler and fragrant but almost immediately they heard the high-pitched whine of mosquitoes. Emily wrapped up Clem and draped a muslin square over her face and her own but Frank, as he hacked away in front of them, pushing past trailing passion fruit vines with their grotesquely beautiful flowers, was soon black with sand flies and mosquitoes. After the third time he led the wagon forward, the wheels lodged in the sandy soil. The ground was no longer level but rose in front of them in a great ridge that extended on either side into the forest and dipped sharply down the other. The two women got out, but even so Oak struggled to heave the wagon up the side and Emily, who had climbed to the top, could see more ridges in front of them.

'Let's leave the wagon here,' she said. 'We can proceed on foot. I can carry Clem and you and Virginie can bring the food.'

Frank balanced what he could on Oak and led the

sweating horse. Emily was wondering if it was worth it; the day felt already quite spoiled by the encounter with Charlotte and now, all because she had had the whim of going on a picnic to the beach, they were in a forest, Frank drenched in sweat and being eaten alive and Virginie silent and grim. Only Clem was smiling up at her and that, she knew, would not last long as she was bound to be hungry soon and it would be a small torment for them all to stop and feed her here. As she was wondering whether they should turn back, her foot sank into a bog. She cried out and almost dropped Clem. She overbalanced and, since she couldn't use her arms to steady herself, she sat down, half in the swamp. Frank ran over to help her and pulled her out of the muddy morass. They walked round the side of it and Emily saw the gleam of water in front of them. She hastened towards it, pushing through swamp privet bushes. Before them lay a small lake, its surface plated with water lilies, purple water hyacinths growing in the shallows. On the far side a flock of spoonbills, their plumage the colour of peeled prawns, sifted the water with their comical beaks. The three of them stood mesmerized, watching the birds, which seemed unaware of them.

'We nearly there,' whispered Frank, 'just the other side of the lake.'

They traversed the boggy shores and came out on a sandy dune. Below them was the beach, the sand as white as sugar, and the sea.

'Finally,' said Emily.

There was a welcome breeze and she pulled the muslin

off herself and Clementine and scraped the mud from her boots and the bottom of her dress. They walked towards the ocean, through soft pink muhly grass and carpets of brilliant yellow and orange samphire, spreading like coral over the sand, the waves crashing on the shore in front of them.

'Here,' said Emily, pointing to the lee of a slight dune, 'let's have the picnic here.'

She handed the baby to Virginie so she could give Clem her bottle and wandered off down the beach. As she drew nearer the sea the sand was hard and flat and glazed with water as if it had been varnished; the suck of water created herringbone patterns in the sand. Tiny sanderlings dodged the spume, their legs ticking over in a flurry like mechanical toys. Oyster-catchers probed for worms with their brilliant red beaks and a flock of terns skimmed the waves, moving in synchrony like one living organism. Emily breathed in the sea air, heavy with salt, and felt, for the first time in a long time, as if she were free.

She looked back at the others: Frank crouched in a squat staring out to sea; Virginie, feeding Clem, looked bone-tired, the bronze sheen of her skin dulled, and then she suddenly noticed something. Perhaps it was because Virginie was tall and carried herself so well or maybe it was because she wasn't that far along, but it was only now, as she sat awkwardly in the sand, that Emily saw the hard, round swelling. She walked over to join them and as she ate the picnic, she plucked strange objects from the sand – the bleached bone-white discs of sand dollars and the fearsome casings of horseshoe crabs – like the leavings of creatures from another place and time.

Frank looked anxiously at the sun and said, 'Missis, it take longer to get here than I expect. I think we ought to go back or we may miss the tide.'

Emily sighed. 'I wouldn't mind being stranded,' and then she thought of the island, laced with creeks and swamps and ponds and the alligators that must live here.

The return journey was much easier. Emily rode Oak and held Clem, ducking under branches and lifting her legs out of the way of the thickest undergrowth; Virginie and Frank carried what was left of their lunch. Charlotte was waiting for them exactly where they had left her and Frank and Virginie helped her into the wagon. Emily recoiled from the smell of the poor woman and kept her muslin over her face as they traversed the causeway. Frank had been right to be worried: the river was now almost level with their path and small waves wet the horse's hooves.

'It's such a shame there isn't an easier way to the beach,' said Emily. 'I can't bear that again.'

'We can canoe there,' said Frank. 'Go right round Sugar Island, straight to the beach.'

'Really?' said Emily in astonishment. 'Why didn't you say? It would have been so much easier.'

'Missis say she want to see the island and go cross the causeway. So we take the wagon.'

My God, thought Emily, tears of frustration in her eyes, as they reached the grove of oranges leading to the Brook house, surely the price of despotism is steep. She looked down at Clem, sleeping in her arms. I will never, she swore fiercely, allow my little girl to grow up here with seven hundred slaves to command at her whim.

Dear Sarah and Ely,

I am puzzled as to why you haven't responded to any of my letters. I hope that I have not offended you in some way or that some terrible tragedy has not befallen you. Unless I hear otherwise from you, I will assume that we are still dear friends and will continue to write. Though what you will make of my letters after some time, I dread to think. It must read as a monotonous litany of degradation and beauty. I feel as if I have been subsumed into a special circle in Dante's Hell all of my very own. I have almost no society save a three-month-old baby (Charles, I now realize, only talked to me of poetry and plays when he was wooing me). I am surrounded by the most stunning skies, wonderful sunsets, unparalleled flora and fauna – and also by the evidence of daily neglect and casual brutality towards these people entrusted into . . .

Emily looked up from her letter-writing as a horrible screaming and crying grew louder. She ran to the door. Three women were outside, two supporting a third, who as they tried to lead her up the steps to the veranda, collapsed. Blood and dark jelly-like gouts of tissue pulsed over the wood as she convulsed and sobbed.

'What's all this? What's happened?'

'Oh, it the usual, missis,' said one of the women calmly. 'Jane go to work after she have her baby. Master only allow we three weeks' rest, and then we must go back to the fields.'

Emily shouted for Virginie to bring water and cloths and for Frank to fetch the wood wagon to take the girl to the infirmary.

'She bleed ever since she go back to work but Mr Stewart not let her rest. I think she not gone have any more babies.'

The woman told Emily her name was Sophy. When Virginie appeared with the water the two of them cleaned up the girl and made her a bandage out of flannel strips.

'Can you speak to master for we?' asked Sophy. 'How can we be strong if we go back to work so soon after the baby come? Do you know how many of our babies die?'

Emily said nothing.

'Most of them, missis, most of them. Master must buy new people if he not breed his own.'

Emily shuddered. 'Here's the wood wagon now. Go with Jane to the infirmary.'

The woman shook her head. 'Mr Stewart beat us if we not go back.' She and her companion started to walk away, then Sophy turned and looked at Emily. 'You have a child, missis, you know what it like. Please speak to master for we.'

Emily stood and watched the two women walk slowly back to the fields. Frank and the men who'd brought the wood wagon lifted Jane into it and drove her away. Behind her Bella scrubbed the steps, the pail of water gradually growing dark rust, but, even so, a stain remained. By the time Charles returned, Emily had played the argument with her husband in her head so many times she thought she knew what he would say.

Charles was in a foul mood. He rounded the side of the house and threw his hat on the ground and stamped his foot.

'These damn people. Someone has stolen my meat.'

'Your meat?' asked Emily stupidly, still staring out in the direction of the cotton fields where the women had rejoined their gang and were almost bent double, weeding between the young cotton plants.

'Yes, my meat,' shouted Charles. 'I shot a wild boar last week and it was hanging up in the meat safe and someone has stolen it. June said she locked the door but she can't have done. I'm going to have her flogged.'

'Wait, Charles!' She looked at him. 'You can't flog June. She wouldn't have taken it. Someone probably pilfered the key when she wasn't looking.'

'Then she should have been more careful.'

'Still! You can't beat someone because they weren't careful. It's not her fault if another one of your people stole the key and took your meat. What do you expect? You feed them hardly anything. We'd all be desperate for a morsel of pork if we lived off cornmeal mush every day of our lives.'

'Oh, not that again. For God's sake, Emily. The point is, they should know it's wrong.'

'Really? And how might they learn that?'

'From church. Where the rest of us learn what's right from wrong.'

'I thought they weren't allowed to go.'

'You're wrong,' he said coolly, 'they can attend once a month.'

'Then, by that argument, they'll steal four times as often as those of us who go every week,' said Emily.

He scowled and, picking up his hat, went inside.

June was timid enough to be bullied by anyone who came along wanting the key to the meat safe, and Emily thought of Caesar, working alongside their cook in the kitchen. As she turned to go inside, she caught sight of the bloodstain on the veranda steps. How would Jane feel when she recovered and realized she might never be able to have another child? The loss would be unbearable and yet perhaps it was a mercy. And she thought with a deep feeling of shame that she could not bring herself to raise the matter with her husband when she knew what his reaction would be.

'We're going to see Mr and Mrs Hall today,' Charles announced over breakfast. 'They've invited us for dinner. They want to see the baby. I know you don't care for them but you can at least make the effort.'

'I never said I didn't like them,' said Emily. She doubted Mrs Hall had the least inclination to see Clementine.

'You didn't have to,' said Charles, slathering peach preserve on to his brioche. 'It's obvious.'

They left mid afternoon in the wood wagon with Virginie and the baby and Joshua leading the horse. Frank had filled some sacks with moss and cotton to make it less uncomfortable.

'Why don't we have a carriage?' asked Emily as they bounced over the road out of the plantation.

'I think there was one once,' said Charles, lying back on the sacks, 'but it fell apart and St Clair never saw the need to repair it.'

'Are we going to get one?' asked Emily carefully.

'It depends on how long we stay here,' said Charles.

'What happened to Mr St Clair? Why did he leave?'

'He managed to save enough to buy his own plantation. It's a little further down the coast from here. He said he'd come and visit us once we'd settled in.'

Charles closed his eyes and put his hat over his face to preclude further conversation. It was like living in *Castle Rackrent*, thought Emily as she and Virginie were jolted against each other. By the time they arrived at the Halls' the two of them were covered with bits of sacking, cotton and moss, fragments of leaves and twigs, and Clem had been sick over Virginie.

'Next time I'm going to ride,' said Emily, jumping down.

'What, and leave Clementine at home? Never,' said Charles, taking the baby from Virginie. He strolled over to Mr and Mrs Hall.

Mrs Hall cooed over the baby. 'She's enchanting,' she said. 'You must be delighted.'

'Oh yes,' said Emily, stroking Clem's soft, blonde hair.

Emily had been right. Her interest exhausted, Mrs Hall promptly dispatched Clementine with Virginie to the kitchen without asking Emily. She then ushered her guests into the drawing room, which was filled with cream roses.

A Negro girl poured them gin cocktails. The girl, who was encrusted with dirt, finished serving their drinks and then stood over Mr Hall, fanning him. Emily felt ashamed and disgusted. She stood in front of the long windows, flanked by white drapes, sipping her drink and looked out on to the ocean. It was as if the sea had been tamed: flat waves curled and broke in miniature on the shore. A flock of willets with their zigzag banding of cream and suede parleyed across the sand, probing for shells.

Mrs Hall served crab soufflé with a glass of champagne, followed by trout fried in butter, wild turkey stuffed with walnuts and accompanied by steamed asparagus, green beans and boiled sweet potatoes with a dark red wine, heavy as blood. The talk was of cotton, rice and sugar and, naturally, the infernal slaves.

'Have you heard about the revolt?' asked Mrs Hall.

'No,' said Emily. 'Where was it?'

'The Broadfield plantation near Darien,' said Mr Hall. 'Not too many of them – maybe ten – and easily quelled.'

'Were they armed?' asked Charles.

Mr Hall shook his head. 'Just a bunch of men with pitchforks and hoes. They tried to kill the owners but fortunately Broadfield sleeps with his gun by his bed and he shot a couple of them. The rest escaped into the swamp but Broadfield rounded up the neighbours and they set the dogs on them and caught them.'

'What happened to them?' asked Emily.

'Far as I know, one was mauled by the dogs and died. The others were publicly flogged and hanged. It wasn't well thought through by any means but it shows they're thinking.'

'They're hardly thinking,' said Charles. 'It's the damned abolitionists in the north, spreading ideas down here.'

'At least it hasn't reached the island,' said Mrs Hall. 'Not that our slaves would dare.'

'You say that,' said Mr Hall, 'but Drummond caught a couple of his plotting. That was as far as it had got but these things have to be crushed.'

'You see,' said Charles, pointing his fork at Emily, 'you can't treat them too kindly and you can't believe a word they say.'

'And how did Mr Drummond crush it?' asked Emily.

'He sold them. I'd have taught them a lesson. They've got short memories, you see. That way, the darkies would see Quashie, or whoever it was who started it, every day and it would remind them of what might happen to them if they ever tried such a thing.'

The girl brought in dessert: orange sorbet and a cream cheesecake with orange liqueur and coffee.

'We make the liqueur,' said Mrs Hall, as if she really had made it herself. 'Our oranges aren't bitter.'

Charles's eyes had lit up at the sight of the pudding and Emily saw that this was what he really wanted in a wife: a beautiful woman who would serve him cake, care for the house and oversee the house slaves. He had as much as told her so when they first arrived but she had dismissed the notion. He did not want someone who would constantly question him. These people had grown up with slaves.

They'd been suckled by them as infants, raised by them, played with them before turning them into the fields and it had never occurred to them to challenge or change their situation. Why would they when it was so advantageous to them? Emily, like a cuckoo in their midst, was not one of their kind. There are no bonds as strong as family and here, where Charles had been born and raised, she saw that he was simply reverting to type. It was not that he had lied about being interested in the theatre and playing the flute; it was more that here he was at home, and at home he was coarse and unquestioning and uncultured. She pushed her dessert away.

The first weekend in June was hot and sultry. The cotton had started to flower and was a glorious golden against the louring, pigeon-breast-grey sky, the light as thick as honey. Emily had been thinking for some time that they ought to go to church; neither she nor Charles had been since they arrived, but it disturbed her that the slaves were deprived of the same rights. That Sunday was the one day in the month they were allowed to go. She snapped an earring into her ear. She and Charles were in their bedroom, getting ready. Emily looked out of the window. Streams of people were walking past the house and heading down the road through the plantation. They were in their Sunday best – garishly bright attire with feathers and combs in their hair, cast-off jackets and dress shirts and tattered dresses but not one of them had shoes. Some of the slaves, seeing her in the window, waved and called, 'How do, missis.'

'I'm almost ready,' she said.

'You're too early,' Charles said impatiently. 'Don't you realize that they are forbidden to attend our service?'

'Our service?'

'Yes,' he said curtly, 'their service is before ours.'

'Ah, the white people's.'

'You're wearing your riding habit,' said Charles coldly.

'Since we have no carriage I intend to ride.'

'People will think I am completely unable to control my wife,' said Charles, fastening his jacket.

'Well, then, you'll be pleased I'll be attending the service with our own people and not your sermon.'

She picked up her hat and riding whip and left him fuming. Joshua was waiting for her with Oak. The other horse was already harnessed to the wood wagon for Charles. Joshua had polished the bridle and the saddle until the leather gleamed like mahogany and he'd varnished Oak's hooves.

'Thank you, Joshua,' she said, taking the reins. 'He looks almost presentable.'

She gave the horse a chunk of sugar and pushed her Bible into the saddlebag. Joshua held the stirrup steady for her to mount. Purple martins wheeled and chattered around her as she rode along the road. The woods either side were lush and dense, fragrant with honeysuckle that hung in rafts from the trees' branches. Poison sumac and Cherokee roses bloomed pale as ivory in the margins. Most of the slaves waved or said hello and none of them made a single complaint or begged for anything as she passed them.

Christ Church was a slightly ramshackle white wooden building beneath giant live oaks. Emily, because she was on horseback, overtook the slaves and arrived at the church first. The preacher looked at her in consternation as she dismounted.

'I'm Mrs Emily Brook,' she said. 'I'm sorry to say that Mr Brook and I have not attended any of your services since we arrived on the island but we hope to rectify our omission.'

'Mrs Brook, I'm delighted to see you today but I'm afraid that you have been given the incorrect time for the service.'

'No, there's no mistake,' said Emily smiling at him. 'Excuse me while I attend to my horse.'

After she'd tied up Oak she wandered into the graveyard. It, like the church, was somewhat neglected, the graves overshadowed by dwarf palms and beautyberry bushes and rampantly spreading ferns. Inside the church it was hot: the wood was warm to the touch and dark, as little light, filtered first by the live oaks and then the stained-glass windows, was able to penetrate. The slaves filed in silently and took their places. There were far more of them than the church could accommodate and they sat on the floor, stood at the back and round the side of the pews or simply remained outside. With so many people pressed together it quickly grew warmer and smelled sweetish, of unwashed flesh and rotting cotton.

Emily thought the sermon prosaic and passionless but it hardly mattered what the preacher said; as she sat and fidgeted on the hard pew she was stunned at the utter hypocrisy of the situation. 'Love thy neighbour' and 'Do unto others what you would have done to you' were two of the simplest commandments that sprang to mind. This was where, according to Charles, his people were meant to learn right from wrong and yet the same morality taught them in this very building was denied them. Channing had written: 'The great teaching of Christianity is, that we must recognize and respect human nature in all its forms. To over-look this, on account of condition or colour, is to violate the great Christian law.' The longer she listened to the sermon, the angrier she felt.

At the end of the service, unable to contain herself, Emily did not stop to speak to the preacher, but fetched Oak. She had just mounted him when the Halls arrived in their carriage at the same time as Charles in the wood wagon. Emily waved at them, enjoying the stunned expression on Mrs Hall's face at seeing her leave a Negro sermon and sit astride a horse. She wheeled Oak round; at the junction between the roads, she turned left back towards the far end of the island and the Brook plantation, spurring Oak into a gallop.

Virginie had stayed behind with Clementine and when Emily arrived at the house, she sent her maid to fetch Bella.

'I would like something to eat. Some cold meat and bread and a glass of milk. But ask Bella to bring it, you could do with a rest.'

A few minutes later, Virginie returned with bread and ham and her drink.

'Where's Bella? You ought to lie down.'

'She not there, missis.'

'Oh, I thought she was too far gone to walk to church.'

'She not there,' said Virginie stubbornly.

Emily took a long drink of milk and then said slowly, 'Do you know where she is, Virginie?'

Her maid shook her head. 'No, missis.'

Emily looked out of the window. The weather had finally broken and it had just started to rain, long driving grey sheets blowing out towards the creek.

'Then we won't say anything about this to Charles until he asks for her,' she said.

Chapter 7

June 1860

*W*hen Emily woke there was a strong smell of burning. She jumped out of bed and ran to the window. In the distance she could see Sugar Island was on fire. Orange flames leapt into the air and the island was shrouded in thick, grey smoke that had started to blow towards St Simons. Emily grabbed her gown and ran downstairs. Charles, Mr Stewart and another man were calmly drinking coffee and eating cookies.

'It's the cane burning for the first harvest,' said Charles, looking at her with annoyance. 'Perhaps you'd care to dress and join us?'

'Who might you be?' asked Emily of the stranger.

'Evan St Clair,' said the man, rising. 'Delighted to meet you. I was Mr Brook's manager.'

She could hardly bring herself to take his proffered hand. He was not what she had imagined at all. Mr St Clair was a small, thickset man, all compact, dense muscle. His skin was very white, almost waxy, and marked with the scars of smallpox; his hair was jet black and his eyes were brilliant blue. He was good-looking in a feral kind of way. Emily wrapped her gown more tightly around her waist and helped herself to a cup of coffee.

'St Clair brought a horse for me,' said Charles. 'Those two old nags we have are quite unsuited to a gentleman.'

She looked outside to where a black stallion was tied up at the rail, fretting because of the fire. The smoke was clearly irritating him and his ears were pressed flat against his skull while his nostrils flared to reveal inflamed red skin. At first glance the horse was impressive but as Emily continued to examine him, she saw that he was ever so slightly knock-kneed and his hind quarters were weak. Charles couldn't even be trusted to buy a horse, she thought.

'St Clair arrived just in time,' continued Charles, taking another cookie and slapping the man's shoulder. 'Catching slaves is a speciality of his.'

Orange light from the flames flickered through the drawing room windows and she could feel a faint warmth from the fire. She closed the front door to try to keep the acrid smell out.

'And how does one embark upon finding runaway slaves?' asked Emily. Bella had been missing for the past two days.

'If they've been gone for a while, then we put an announcement in the paper with their description. When I lived here I would obtain some small item of theirs, a rag perhaps, and let the dogs smell it and then set the dogs on them. Usually ferrets them out. Of course, on an island surrounded by marshes and swamps, they ain't going to get far. There's nothing to eat and they're mortally terrified of snakes and alligators. And if they did, they haven't got any papers so they'd be picked up in town.'

'She's heavily pregnant,' said Emily. 'Releasing the dogs would be barbaric.'

'She ought to have thought of that before she ran away,' said Charles.

Mr St Clair was still looking at Emily. 'My guess would be that she'll come back. She can't walk far or fast. She'll starve and she'll fret about the baby. I say we wait a couple of days. Why tramp around getting bitten to blazes in those swamps?'

Emily watched Charles's expression. He looked mildly disappointed, as if he'd been deprived of a good day out. She could still feel those startling blue eyes on her. Clutching her gown, she said, 'I'm going to dress. Please send Virginie up to me.'

From the window she saw Charles and Mr St Clair head out across the fields with their guns and Mr St Clair's two pointers. When she went downstairs again she found Edward waiting patiently by the veranda.

'Good morning, Edward. You've just missed Mr Brook.'

'I come to see you, missis.'

'Well, what can I do for you?'

'I want to show you something. Will you come with me please? Just to the jetty.'

Emily picked up her bonnet and followed him. The

flames on Sugar Island were already dying down, leaving an angry red, smoke-filled glare above the sugar fields.

'It this,' said Edward, leading her out on to the jetty. Tied to the edge was a small canoe.

'It's beautiful,' she said, crouching down to touch it.

The canoe was slender yet sturdy, perfectly proportioned and smooth and silky to the touch, without a single snag or rough section.

'I make it,' said Edward.

'You made it,' repeated Emily. She had a vision of Edward working in the fields all day, coming home to his little house, tending his fowl and his small garden, cooking and eating and washing – all such laborious processes in this place – and then setting to work to make the canoe. And then rising at dawn the next day to begin all over again.

'You want to buy it?'

'How much is it?' asked Emily.

Edward named a price. It was steep and perhaps because he saw the expression on her face he said quietly, 'I make it well.'

'You're right. It is well made.'

A flock of seagulls flew past, screaming into the wind.

'You want to buy your freedom,' she said slowly.

'I do.'

'How much are you worth?' she asked and blushed for posing such a question.

'A fit, healthy man, well, he cost around a thousand dollars. Me, I the head driver. I worth more,' he said simply.

Emily thought of all the money she used to have: spent on hotel rooms and mediocre breakfasts, on champagne and oyster suppers and horses, on dresses she didn't need and bonnets bought on a whim. She thought of her jewellery: her necklaces and earrings and brooches wound through her mind in a tangled golden chain. Would they buy Edward's freedom? And how could one justify freeing one slave in seven hundred?

'I'm very sorry to say this to you but I don't have the money to buy your canoe, much as I should like to. You ought to ask Mr Brook. Perhaps you could persuade him to purchase it for me as a gift. Ask for more and maybe you'll receive the amount you should like.'

Edward looked out towards Sugar Island. When he turned back to Emily he said without rancour, 'He not gone buy it.'

Frank was waiting for her when she returned to the house to see what she would like to do that day.

'Perhaps we could take a turn in the *Dolphin*, although it'll be somewhat inferior to your father's canoe. Can you get us away from the smoke?'

Frank nodded. 'Yes, missis.'

They paddled through a choking pall of grey smoke that hung thickly above the water, heading down the Hampton River and towards the Atlantic. The smoke thinned into fine skeins the colour of raw silk and finally drifted away.

Emily took her handkerchief away from her mouth and said, 'Your father's canoe shows very fine workmanship.'

Frank glanced at her and nodded. He slowed his paddling and let the canoe drift with the current.

'Did he teach you how to make anything like that?'

Frank looked at the far shore and then said, 'When I a child he show me carpentry but him love to build boats. He say it my way out of here. I never understand him – I think he want me to sail away in my canoe.' He smiled sadly. 'When he work in the fields all day I make tiny canoes and float them on the dykes. He always please when they sail right. He say we gone build a big one.'

'And did you?'

She leaned over the side and trailed her fingers through the water. Behind Frank she could see an evil red flickering through the reeds around Sugar Island.

Frank shrugged. 'No, missis. Father stop teach me.'

'Why?' she asked, watching a small flock of seabirds as they flew past, low over the water.

'Mr St Clair get here. He make my father work much harder so he more tired when he come home. But there something else. A few years after Mr St Clair come, he start to beat my father. The manager don't usually flog the driver. And my mother and father, they get sadder. Like they lost. I keep asking, when we gone build the canoe? But then I stop because I can see it only make him look in pain. Father try to teach Caesar once but Caesar don't like that kind of thing.'

'I'm sorry, Frank,' said Emily.

She didn't know what else she could say.

*

'So did you find her?' Emily asked as they sat down to supper.

'No. But we didn't try terribly hard,' said Mr St Clair, looking at her with amusement. 'We went over to Sugar Island to check on the harvest.'

Emily tried to rid her mind of the image of Evan St Clair and Charlotte but found she was unable to do so. Other women had also told her of unspeakable things he'd done to them during his tyrannical reign. How many more slaves had he forced in his fifteen years on the plantation? And here he was, breaking bread with them and speaking to her in that soft voice of his. June had made a chicken pie filled with quail's eggs, served with potatoes and baby carrots and summer turnips. A bunch of roses and rosemary stood on the table, sent by Ann Drummond, along with some of her black cherry preserve, and a chocolate cake. There was nothing that Charles could complain about. Yet Evan St Clair still opened a little silver cask and liberally sprinkled his meal with dried chilli.

'I hear,' Mr St Clair said, as he helped himself to a second slice of cake, 'that you attended the Negro sermon last Sunday.'

'And I hear it was your decision to allow them to worship only once a month instead of every Sunday.'

'That's correct, Mrs Brook. And if I thought it should not have led to a revolt, I would have prevented them from attending church at all.'

'At all? These people are so religious they want their own church here on the plantation. May I ask why?'

'Well, first, I don't think they should mingle with slaves from other plantations. It sets them talking. They might learn things or incite each other into rising against their masters. At the least, they use the opportunity to barter for bits and pieces – usually our bits and pieces from the smithy or the carpenter's store.'

'And second?'

'I don't believe they should have any religious instruction.'

Emily took the coffee pot from Virginie and poured them all a cup.

'And why, may I ask?'

'If they actually listened to the sermons, it might make them think. And a thinking nigger is no good to us. Religion in the wrong hands can be an incendiary device. Mrs Brook, the preacher says we should be "just in all our dealings" and we should "treat all men as our equals". We tell them to abide by the Christian faith but we ourselves are not just in our dealings with them and we do not treat them as our equals.'

Emily laughed incredulously. 'You sound like an abolitionist, Mr St Clair.'

He took a sip of his coffee and said, 'This is the system and I use it as best I can and to my advantage. But it's a deucedly poor way of making a living, if you'll excuse my language, Mrs Brook. Right now we have myriad arguments to justify slavery, including the Bible – yes, I admit we do use the Bible to coerce them and sanction our actions. The day will come, though, when southerners will realize that it is more effective to pay a man for his labour and when that day comes, believe me, all those arguments, biblical or otherwise, will fade into thin air. Don't misunderstand me, Mrs Brook. I hate the creatures and I will make them work until they drop. As Mr Brook knows, I extract every ounce from them. But one day, we will be forced to pay them.'

'I hope that day will come long after I'm dead and buried,' said Charles. 'Virginie, where's the port?'

When Charles came to bed later that night he was drunk. He smelled of wood smoke and something else, lingering beneath the stronger odour of fire. She eased closer to him and slid her arm along his chest. He rolled away from her. But the imprint of the scent remained, a musky perfume that clung to his skin and impregnated the sheet beneath him.

She licked her lips and forced herself to say into the darkness, 'Did Edward show you his canoe?'

'He did.'

'And what did you think?'

'Very fine workmanship,' said Charles sleepily.

'Well? And shall you purchase it?'

'No. I've relieved him of his duties as head driver for a week or two and got him started on making me a canoe.'

Five days after Bella had run away four men carried her back. They had found her in the woods next to the causeway to Sugar Island. She was raving and hysterical and half starving. They put her on the veranda and ran back to work before they could be missed.

'Fetch warm water and cloths,' Emily said to Virginie, and rolled Bella on to a blanket. 'Bella, listen to me. Have your waters broken?'

'Yes, missis,' she gasped and then doubled up in agony as a contraction ripped through her.

Emily washed the girl as best she could and put a cool compress on her forehead and ordered camomile tea for her. She sent Frank to fetch Dianna and asked June to make the girl some gruel with plenty of sugar.

'Where were you, Bella?'

'I hide in the woods, missis. I so scared. And hungry. I have nothing to eat.'

'You're covered in bites, Bella. We'll put ointment on them otherwise they'll turn into sores.'

Bella started to scream again. The screaming went on and on. Emily held her hand and pressed a damp cloth to the girl's forehead. Bella gripped her hand so hard her fingers went white. Finally, as Dianna arrived in the wood wagon with Frank and Joshua leading the horse, the baby's head appeared between Bella's legs. After another half an hour, she cried out once more as the baby came out in a gush of blood and water and mucus. And then there was silence.

'It dead, missis,' said Dianna flatly and Bella began to sob.

Emily looked at the baby, lifeless in Dianna's arms, half cleared of its caul. Its skin was white and its hair was jet black.

'It's Mr St Clair's,' she said. 'It's Mr St Clair's baby, isn't it, Bella?'

Bella nodded, still crying and dripping with sweat. 'I hear he gone come back so I run away.'

'You won't have to see him again. I promise. Take her to the infirmary, Joshua.'

Dianna and Frank helped the girl into the wood wagon. Virginie and June started to clean the veranda.

'And the baby?' asked Virginie.

'Leave it there for the moment,' said Emily, and she paced in front of the house, waiting for Mr St Clair to return. She tried not to look at the child. The sight of its tiny, frozen, waxy, white hands made her quail.

At lunchtime Mr St Clair and Charles returned. Emily walked forward to meet them.

'Bella came back.'

'I knew she would,' said Mr St Clair, smiling.

'She had the baby. It was stillborn. It's there.' She pointed to the veranda.

'Dear God, Emily. You left a dead baby lying on the porch?' said Charles.

'I wanted you to see it. It's obvious it's Mr St Clair's. Look at it.'

The men glanced at it and Charles put his hand over his mouth and retched silently.

'It's a white baby born from a black girl.'

'That ain't proof,' said Mr St Clair, with a half smile.

'You raped her. Don't try to deny it.'

He stood in front of her, stocky and sure of himself as if there were no one else but the two of them.

'Don't you know that a nigger's word counts for

nothing?' he said quietly. 'I can do anything I like with complete impunity on my plantation.'

'It is not your plantation,' said Emily.

Something inside Charles snapped and he ran forward and seized Emily. 'Shut up,' he shouted into her face, 'shut up, shut up,' over and over again as he shook her violently.

Frank ran to one side of Charles and Mr St Clair took hold of him on the other and they pulled him away from Emily. Charles, when he'd regained his balance, struck Frank across the face, splitting open his lip and sending him sprawling. Emily went to help him up but Charles pushed her away, hissing, 'Don't touch him.'

'You,' said Mr St Clair, spotting Caesar, who had been hiding around the back of the house watching, 'get rid of that thing.'

'Yes, master. What I do with it?' asked Caesar, creeping towards them, holding on to the struts of the house as if they would support him.

'Her,' said Emily. 'Bury her in the graveyard.'

Virginie, who had been silently standing on the veranda, passed him a piece of cotton she'd been using to clean Clementine's face for him to wrap the baby in.

Charles gripped Caesar's arm as he approached and said, 'No. You do it,' to Frank and Caesar swiftly broke free and ran back to the kitchen.

Emily went inside and picked up Clem who had been asleep but had now woken and started screaming. She carried her upstairs to get away from the two men and sat on the bed crying and rocking the child backwards and forwards. Shortly afterwards she heard voices downstairs. Emily looked out of her bedroom window. She saw Charles and Mr St Clair run to the jetty and climb into one of the boats. Two slaves began to row them towards Sugar Island. She wiped away her tears and took several deep breaths. After a few minutes she went downstairs.

'You settle her, I can't,' said Emily, handing Clem to Virginie. 'What's happening outside?'

'They press the cane in the sugar mill and one of the men catch his arm in the roller,' said Virginie. 'Abraham cut his arm off to get him out. He gone bleed to death.'

'He's still alive? Have they sent for Dr Walker?'

'Yes,' said Virginie, swinging Clementine gently, 'but when he get here from Darien, it gone be too late.'

That evening Dr Walker, Mr St Clair and Charles came home in a state of high excitement and exhaustion. They were covered in dust and smelled of blood and the sugar cane's sweet green sap.

'How is he?' asked Emily, who was giving Clem her bottle.

'Dead,' said Charles shortly.

'I couldn't save him,' said Dr Walker, taking off his hat. 'He'd lost too much blood by the time I arrived.'

'The funeral is going to be tomorrow night. It's good for morale if we attend,' said Charles, giving her the briefest of glances.

The following afternoon Emily rode to the infirmary to see how Bella was progressing. It was another oppressive day, hot and humid with leaden skies. The sky and the creek were all one colour, the marsh a thin olive strip in between. It made Emily feel as if she were suffocating. Her skin prickled and itched. She rode through the woods along paths that Caesar and a gang of boys had cut for her. It was dark and still; hardly any birds sang. Oak's hooves rustled through tinder-dry leaves. There was the sharp, acrid smell of snake. She emerged from the wood just above the infirmary. The camp was unnaturally silent. In a bare patch of ground in front of the dilapidated building was an old, dead tree, blighted by lightning. Something was suspended from it, swaying gently. Emily urged her horse into a fast trot.

It was Bella. She was naked, hanging from a rope looped over the branch and bound round her thumbs. Only her toes touched the ground. Her back was cut open, covered in long, curling slashes. Blood ran in rivulets over her buttocks and traced lines in the dust clinging to her legs. Her bare feet and drops of blood had drawn cryptic patterns in the sand as she swung, pendulum-like.

Emily had nothing with her, no knife with which she could sever the rope and when she tried to untie her, Bella swung away from her and Oak sidestepped in the opposite direction, his ears pressed flat against his skull. She called for help and Dianna came running out of the infirmary.

'Hold her, will you,' Emily panted.

Dianna took Bella's weight. Emily fumbled with the knots, which were stiff and hard to undo, growing increasingly frustrated. Dianna was having trouble holding Bella. Eventually Emily managed to work one of the knots loose and the girl collapsed into Dianna's arms. The nurse lowered her, still unconscious, to the ground.

'Who did this?' she whispered, although she hardly needed to ask.

'Mr St Clair,' said Dianna.

'She's just a child, only a girl. How could he?' she said, sliding from Oak's back.

'They like them young, the buckra,' said Dianna with contempt.

'Oh, and I promised her she wouldn't have to see him again,' she said.

'Nothing you can do, missis,' said Dianna.

They half carried, half hauled the girl into the infirmary. She moaned. Dianna fetched water and a dirty rag to sponge the girl's back. Bella opened her eyes and began to cry. Emily sat next to them, holding Bella's hand. She could not remember a time when she had felt so utterly wretched and helpless.

It was dusk by the time Emily reached the house. Charles was sitting on the front steps, waiting for her, eating cold turkey and cornbread.

'How could you? How could you allow it? She'd been raped, she'd given birth to a dead baby. She was half starved and covered in sores. How could you let that animal near her?' she asked as she walked over to him.

'She shouldn't have run away. I keep telling you, you have to maintain discipline. There are seven hundred of them and three of us. What do you think would happen if we didn't stick to the rules?' He drew breath and then said more calmly, 'The funeral is about to start. Are you ready?'

Emily hesitated, trying to collect herself. She was finding it increasingly hard to cope with the capriciousness of his changing moods. But pushing Charles further at this stage would only lead to him losing his temper and could disrupt the slaves' ceremony.

'Yes. Do I have time to change?'

Charles snorted. 'Of course you don't need to change.'

'Well, since my riding habit is black anyhow I expect it'll have to do,' said Emily, almost in a whisper.

He held out the plate of meat to her but she shook her head. He put it on the veranda.

'That'll be gone by the time we get back,' he said, and strode out in front of her.

Edward was conducting the service for Jack, the dead man. When they reached Edward's house, he was outside praying. A number of men and women stood in a ring around him, Jack's coffin in the centre. They held torches made of pine that poured thick, black smoke into the darkening sky; the flames smelled sweet and resinous. Charles and Emily stood at the back. The slaves started to sing a hymn quietly. Four men picked up the coffin and carried it to the graveyard, followed by the others in a torch-lit procession. Emily and Charles walked behind them.

The slaves' graveyard was between the swamp and the wood near the causeway to Sugar Island on land that the Brook family had no use for. It was not fenced in and cows and chickens wandered freely through it. The men put the coffin on the ground and the people gathered around Edward once more. Edward spoke a few words about Jack, saying how hard-working he had been and kind. He exhorted the rest of the congregation to work hard for master and missis, to be good, kind and not to lie or steal. He concluded his short sermon with the words: 'Jesus said unto her, I am the resurrection, and the life: he that believeth in me, though he were dead, yet shall he live.'

He began the Lord's Prayer and the slaves joined in. Emily knelt with them in the fetid mud and prayed. Only Charles, of everyone there, remained standing, his head unbowed. Over the stench of the swamp, Emily could smell the dried blood on her hands. Her fingernails were black with it. After the final amen, the four coffin-bearers lifted the coffin and lowered it into the grave. Several of the men cried out and some of the women wept. The grave was half full of water. Emily felt her skirt growing damp as she continued to kneel, tears trickling down her cheeks. Charles turned on his heel and left. Emily remained kneeling and crying as the earth was dropped back into the grave and she didn't know what she was crying for most: the death of one man; the poignant, simple, moving ceremony; or Charles's coldness.

The next morning Emily rose later than usual hoping to avoid Mr St Clair but when she dressed and went downstairs he was still there, sitting on the veranda having coffee with Charles.

'June want to talk to you, missis,' said Virginie suddenly, putting the baby down and heading towards the door.

'She's always welcome to speak to me,' said Emily.

'She don't ask,' said Virginie over her shoulder. 'You have to call her.'

'Well, please tell her I'd like to speak to her then,' she said.

Virginie disappeared towards the kitchen. A moment later, June crept in. Her face had an ashen cast and was puffy, her eyes bloodshot.

'What's the matter?' asked Emily in alarm, taking the girl's hand. 'Are you unwell?'

'Missis, master sell me to Mr St Clair. He take me with him when he leave. And I never gone see my husband again.' She hid her face in her hands and burst into tears.

'There must be some mistake,' said Emily, passing the girl her handkerchief. 'What would we do without you? Who would cook our meals? I'll go and talk to Mr Brook. I'm sure you won't have to leave here.'

'Thank you, missis, thank you,' said June, wiping her eyes. 'What you want for breakfast?'

'Eggs, please, and some toast. Now stop crying. I'll speak to Mr Brook this minute.'

As June, still sniffing, left the room, Virginie came back in with a pot of coffee. She looked at Emily out of the corner of her eyes. She poured her a coffee and added cream and sugar and passed the cup over to her. Emily took it and went to join the men on the veranda.

Mr St Clair half rose. 'I trust Mrs Brook slept well last night.'

Emily half inclined her head, frowning at the impertinence of the man. There was something repugnantly intimate about an enquiry that from another man might have been merely polite.

'I hear you're planning to sell June to Mr St Clair,' she said, addressing Charles.

'He wants a house servant,' said Charles shortly, 'and I owe him some money.'

'For the horse?'

'No, not for the horse,' he snapped.

'She's upset, poor child. Mr St Clair, my husband may not have said, but June is married. She doesn't wish to leave her husband, Joe.'

'Joe the carpenter? I am aware that she's married.' He shrugged. 'These so-called marriages mean nothing. I'll find her a good man, you need have no fear, Mrs Brook. In a couple of months' time, she'll have forgotten all about Joe and she'll be as right as the bank.'

'How can you say that? She's devastated. As any woman would be who is about to be torn away from all she knows and her lawful husband.'

'They are simple people, Mrs Brook,' said Mr St Clair, smiling at her, 'they ain't got the ability to feel things the way we do.'

'Charles,' said Emily, turning to her husband, 'please don't sell June. You simply can't take her from her husband. And apart from that, how will we manage?'

'You'll find someone else. It's not as if June's cooking is terribly good.'

'She's growing better. Besides, you're always reminding me that I should be taking care of the house and supervising our meals. How can I do that when you sell the cook without even consulting me?'

Charles sighed and stood up. He looked at Mr St Clair. 'I can't bear this,' he said wearily. 'Choose someone else, will you?'

'Thank you, Charles,' said Emily.

Charles ignored her and walked down the steps, putting on his hat. Mr St Clair rose.

'Mrs Brook,' he said, and followed her husband.

Emily sat down and took a sip of her coffee. She realized that her hands were shaking and she felt a cold chill in spite of the heat. A few moments later Virginie came out with a plate of poached eggs and toast. She fetched Clem, who was in her baby seat, and placed her on the floor next to Emily.

'You can tell June she won't be sold,' said Emily, taking a bite of toast.

'Yes, missis,' said Virginie quietly.

Emily, rocking Clem with her foot, watched Virginie's tall, proud figure as she walked round the outside of the house to find June. It was too hot to stay outside for long so Emily retreated indoors with Clem. She sat in the window seat fanning herself and playing with the child, idly wondering whether to fetch Frank and go out in the canoe. It would be cooler on the water. A mockingbird called from one of the cabbage palms, and three scarlet cardinals flew through the orange trees. It was almost midday by the time she saw Charles and Mr St Clair return. Joshua had brought round Mr St Clair's wagon and his driver was standing by the horses, ready to take him further south.

'And we hope he never comes back, don't we?' she said, tickling Clem's tummy. The baby gurgled and flapped her arms.

Suddenly there was the sound of shouting and Clem jumped. Emily looked up. Two men were dragging Joe to the wagon. He was calling out, appealing to Charles who half turned so that his back was to Joe and the house. Mr St Clair, his whip tucked under his arm, personally manacled the carpenter's hands in iron shackles. June came running round the gable end of the house, crying and pleading. She clutched hold of Joe's shirt. The sounds, through the glass window pane, were muffled. Mr St Clair pushed June away and wound a rope around Joe's throat and dragged him to the front of the wagon. Joe slowly climbed up next to the driver. Mr St Clair passed another set of manacles up and the driver chained Joe's feet to the seat. June was now kneeling on the ground, her head resting in the dirt. Joe turned and looked directly at Emily.

Emily stood up as if in a daze. Virginie had come to stand silently by the window.

'He done sell the other one,' she said softly. She moved slightly, as if to block Emily's path. 'No use you gone out there. Nothing you can do,' she said.

Half an hour later Charles came in.

'Tell June she'd better have a meal on the table in the next few minutes,' he said to Virginie, kicking off his boots and propping his gun against the door. 'As for you,' he said to Emily, 'you've just cost me the carpenter. He was a lot more valuable than June. I owed St Clair more than she was worth and he'd have settled for her.'

Emily was crying. She blew her nose and said, 'How could you split them up? They were married, Charles.'

'And who is going to do the joinery round here now? I'm running a business not a goddamn charity.'

'Just think what he'd have done to a pretty girl like her,' she said.

'Don't start that again.'

Virginie reappeared carrying a tray of salad, boiled eggs, cold cuts and a loaf of bread.

'Tell Bella to get back to work. Virginie can't do all this and look after Clementine.'

Emily, who was still sobbing, said, 'She can't work. Haven't you seen what that man did to her?'

Charles rose and poured himself a glass of claret and then sat at the table and helped himself. Emily watched him eating and then she said abruptly, 'You don't believe they're human, do you?'

Charles said nothing, but continued to chew and scooped more salad on to his plate with his hands.

'You don't, do you?' she persisted, coming to the table and sitting down opposite him, drying her eyes.

He pushed a plate over towards her. 'If you want to know the honest truth, Emily, I never considered it for one moment before I met you and brought you here. You still fail to understand after all this time – this is how I grew up, this is how our family lived, how all southerners live.'

'And now that I'm here?'

'Now that you're here,' he said, smearing butter on a hunk of bread, 'now that you're here . . . God damn it, Emily, I don't like being pushed into a corner like this.' He scowled and said with difficulty, 'But I'd have to agree. They're not quite human. They're not animals, I admit. But they are a different race. A degraded race. They don't look like us. They don't smell like us. They don't think or feel like us. They ain't as smart as us and the best of them never will be.'

'Charles—'

'Emily, I'm talking,' he said fiercely, 'don't interrupt me. While we are on this subject, I never want to have this discussion with you again. I never want to hear or see you interfere with any of my niggers on this plantation again. I never want to listen to you say another word about any of them ever. I am sick and tired of you repeating all their damned lies. No more. That's the end of it. Do you understand?'

Emily said nothing.

'Do you understand?' he shouted, banging his fist on the table.

Emily jumped and Clementine started to cry. 'Yes,' she whispered. She picked up her daughter and held her tightly to her chest.

Charles bundled meat and salad on to the bread and

folded it up. 'We all got along just fine before you showed up,' he said, getting up and tossing his boots on to the veranda. 'Dear God,' he said. He went outside to put on his boots. A few moments later she heard the heavy tread of his feet on the porch steps and then he was gone.

Emily waited on the veranda for him in the afternoon but he didn't come home. There was no sign of Mr Stewart either. Eventually Emily ate, tough slices of beef in cold, congealing gravy, growing increasingly anxious, but there was still no word from him. She waited outside again, drinking a glass of gin, with his bottle of claret at hand, until the gnats became too bothersome and she had to retreat indoors. She sat in the parlour and embroidered, alert for every sound that might indicate he was on his way home.

Late that night she woke up. She lay in bed for a moment listening but could hear nothing save the customary croaking of frogs and a thin wind rattling through the palms. She stretched out her hand and ran it across the sheets but the bed was empty. She rose and went to the window, opening it a crack. Her hair felt thick and heavy on her back; the air was moist and mildly refreshing and she lifted her hair from her neck to cool herself. There was a half moon, like something broken in the sky; fragments glittered in the dark lines of the dykes. Below her stretched the cotton fields, black and silver in the half-dark, and, in the distance, the dense and tangled remnants of wood on the edge of the island. And then with a start she realized that Charles was standing below her. He was swaying slightly, as if he'd drunk too much, and he was looking straight up at her. His face, beneath the brim of his hat, was shadowed. For a long moment he stood still, staring. Eventually he walked towards the house, and as he disappeared from her view she heard him slowly mounting the wooden steps. She shivered and shut the window.

The days seemed long and leaden. Emily dragged herself through what she saw as her chores: visiting the slave camps with small gifts of sugar, salt, rice and flannel and looking in on the infirmary with parcels of soap, ointment and occasionally bottles of laudanum. The dirt and deprivation made her despair and she found it almost impossible to listen to the complaints of aches and sores and floggings; of hernias and dropped wombs and crippling rheumatism, knowing that there was nothing she could do. Before she had had the illusion of control – being able to speak to Mr Stewart or to Charles – but now she was faced with the reality of her own powerlessness.

One day she went to Darien with Frank, Virginie and Clementine to buy a bolt of cheap cloth to make new clothes for the slaves. Charles had grudgingly allowed it, as long as, he said, she bought the cheapest.

Frank waited outside the store for them. Inside it was dark and musty and smelled of hot wood, tar and sawdust. Motes of dust hung suspended in beams of sunlight. The store was full of worthless goods, mostly imported from the north, as well as a plethora of items peculiar to the south: rawhide whips, mantraps and shackles. Emily and

Virginie stood in front of a stack of bolts of cloth. She felt the least expensive one.

'That gone fall apart, no time at all,' observed Virginie, bouncing Clementine in her arms.

'What about this one?'

Emily pulled out the next bolt on the rack. Clouds of dust rose in the air, making her cough and Clem sneeze. It was coarsely woven, rough to the touch.

'That do it,' said Virginie reluctantly.

'Can I help you, m'am?' The store owner sauntered over, chewing a wodge of tobacco, the dark liquor swilling between his teeth. He had long, stringy grey hair and a bald pate. His eyes were so pale he looked as if he would be unable to see in the glare of the bright world outside his store. Emily disliked him. She knew he cheated the Negroes who brought him moss and eggs to sell. She also now knew he had sent a message to Charles to inform him of the bills she was running up purchasing extra rice, soap and home-spun for the slaves.

'I'd like to buy this cloth, please.'

'May I ask what you need it for, m'am?'

'Clothes for our slaves,' said Emily shortly.

The man raised his grizzled eyebrows. 'Mighty fine stuff for slaves, m'am,' he said, making no move to extract the cloth.

'Please charge it to our account. I'll send my boy in to pick it up.'

The man shrugged and spat on the floor. Emily walked round the pool of saliva and out into the blinding sunshine.

'Frank, would you pick up the cloth and take it to the canoe,' she murmured, as she passed him. 'While we're here we might as well buy an ice,' she added, hoping this small pleasure would help alleviate the general despondency that clung to her like a malaise. 'You'd like that, wouldn't you?' she said, turning to Virginie.

Clem was wriggling and the maid was struggling to hold her. Virginie said nothing. They walked across the baking sandy road to the inn and sat on the veranda. A woman came out and half-heartedly wiped the table with a dirty rag. Emily ordered two ices.

'She can't sit here,' said the woman, cutting her eyes at Virginie.

'She's holding my baby,' said Emily.

'She can't sit here,' the woman repeated.

Virginie picked up one of the chairs and lifted it over the veranda rail, setting it down in the road. Then she walked down the steps to the front of the inn and manoeuvred the chair into the thin sliver of shade created by the veranda railings and sat down, settling Clem on her lap. The barmaid frowned. A few moments later she returned and banged the two ices on to the table. Emily leaned over the railings and handed one to Virginie. Virginie gave a spoonful to Clem whose mouth puckered at the unexpected cold sensation. Emily sipped her ice, crunching the crystals between her teeth. Virginie's head was almost level with her feet; she could smell the oil in her hair. The ice was flavoured with orange and quickly melted into an overly sweet syrup at the bottom of the glass. Emily retrieved

Clem from Virginie to try to keep the child in the shade, and pushed herself back against the wall of the inn, which smelled of peeling paint and old tar.

A couple of men staggered out of the inn past her. They were in navy with grey coats slung over their shoulders and carried rusting rifles. Another three followed them. All of them were drunk. One was pushing a pack of cards into his trouser pocket. They stumbled into the street and halted in front of Virginie.

'What have we here?' asked one. He had long, greasy black hair curling over his shirt collar. 'Nigger thinks she's a lady.'

'Ought to teach her some manners,' said another, spitting into the sand. He swiped at her ice and knocked the glass to the ground. Emily jumped to her feet and stepped forward into the blazing sun.

'She's my maid. Please let her alone,' she said with as much dignity as she could.

The first soldier touched his hand to his cap and swayed. 'Beg your pardon, m'am, but it ain't right for her to be sitting in front of an inn eating an ice.'

'You steal the money for it, you black bitch?' said the second, who had short ginger hair and prominent, bulging eyes.

'I bought it for her,' said Emily.

'Didn't you hear me? I was talking to you,' said the ginger-haired man, leaning down and leering into Virginie's face.

Emily looked around desperately and caught the eye of

the barmaid, who was lolling in the doorway with a smirk on her face. As soon as she felt Emily's gaze she disappeared inside.

'I say we teach her a lesson,' said the dark-haired man.

'She's mine,' said Emily. 'Don't touch her.' Clem burst into great gulping wails.

'Then you'll be grateful to us for showing your nigger how to mind her manners,' said the dark-haired one. He looked up at her and she saw that his pupils had disappeared to pin-pricks. He lashed out and struck Virginie so hard that she fell off the chair and landed in the dirt at his feet.

The five of them cheered. The ginger-haired soldier undid his belt and slid the leather from his trouser loops, wrapping the end round his fist, leaving the buckle free.

'What's going on out here?' cut in a man's voice above the jeers of the soldiers and Clem's crying.

Emily turned and stared. Charles was standing at the entrance to the inn, Joel Hall behind him. He smelled of brandy and his eyes were bloodshot.

'Just telling this uppity nigger to mind her place,' said the ginger-haired man, grinning up at him.

Charles stepped forward and looked down at Virginie lying at the soldiers' feet. A muscle worked in his jaw.

'That there's my property,' he roared at them, stabbing one finger towards the girl. 'Get your filthy hands off her or I'll charge the lot of you for damages.'

The soldiers backed off, their expressions ugly. Virginie slowly got to her feet and dusted the dirt from her dress.

Her lip was split open and the blood running down her face was matted with sand. She silently looked up at Charles who passed her his handkerchief.

'Charles, what are you doing here?' asked Emily.

'This is no place for a lady,' said Mr Hall, touching his hat brim to her.

'Get back home, Emily,' said Charles tightly, still not looking at her.

Virginie took Clem from her and soothed the child into quiet. The street was strangely empty. As they walked towards the dock they saw no sign of the soldiers or of Frank. But when they reached the dock they found him lying in the bottom of the canoe, a red weal on his cheek-bone, one eye black and swollen shut, his blood splattered across the bolt of homespun. Virginie handed him Charles's handkerchief without a word.

They cut the ruined section of cloth off the roll to use for rags and over the next few days Emily and Virginie cut out simple dresses for the women and children and lent them needles and thread so they could sew the tunics themselves. Once Charles came in and stood over them. As she knelt on the floorboards, the wood grain pressing into her flesh, the homespun stretched around her in an oatmeal-coloured puddle, Emily realized that she was afraid. Not only that she was afraid but that this had come to be her normal state when Charles was near her. She could feel the chill that characterized this sensation creeping through her veins, sharp as frostbite. Charles said nothing and left shortly afterwards.

She wished over and over again that her education had been more practical. Here her French and Latin were useless. She wrote long, increasingly frantic letters to Ely and Sarah, even though she had yet to receive any reply, and kept her diary more assiduously.

The summer became increasingly hot and humid. She went to bed early so that she did not have to sit with Charles as he drank in the evenings. She started to rise early too, getting up before he was awake, so that she could ride Oak when it was still cool. She normally rode through the woods as the early morning sunlight filtered through the clouds of Spanish moss, the pale blue wash of a bird's egg. She would stop by the edge of the sea amid the sweet grass and watch the sun's rays gild the tips of the waves as if they'd been chiselled and polished, startling the egrets that gathered at the shore and stalked through the reeds. And then the day would start to close in oppressively as she returned to Brook House, the sky growing increasingly bland, then dark, until it rained in the afternoon and, for a brief interval afterwards, the world was as new.

One morning when she arrived at the infirmary it was to find it packed and the air foul.

'It the flux,' said Dianna as Emily stood on the threshold, her hand over her mouth.

Emily walked among the patients, many of whom were shivering with fever. Every so often one of the slaves would stagger to their feet and rush outside, clutching their stomach and moaning.

'It gone get worse, missis. More and more folks gone fall

sick,' said Dianna, who followed her with a damp rag, wiping some of the patients' foreheads.

'And what can you do for them?' asked Emily.

'Nothing, missis.'

Emily felt like crying. She decided to visit the Drummonds and ask their advice. It was still early enough in the morning for the heat to be bearable so she mounted Oak and left straight away.

Ann Drummond was sitting at the table in her dining room wearing a white linen dress with a pearl necklace like a string of humming bird eggs, arranging cream roses in a porcelain vase. The muslin curtains blowing gently in a faint sea breeze stirred languorously across the floor. It felt like another place entirely. Emily was hot and dusty, sweating and uncomfortable in her heavy black riding habit. Her tears had turned to anger on the ride to Orange Hall.

'My dear,' Mrs Drummond exclaimed when she saw her, 'what terrible heat to be out in.'

She spoke briefly to one of the house servants and led Emily into the drawing room. The maid brought in a jug of lemonade and a plate of fresh figs.

'You are looking a little wan,' observed Mrs Drummond, pouring her a glass. 'I'd recommend taking some iron drops in camomile flower tea three times a day. Around eight drops and only half a tumbler of tea.'

'I'm quite well,' said Emily, 'only too hot. The heat simply doesn't agree with me.' She bit into a fig and its warm, swollen flesh burst against her teeth. 'It's the people,' she continued. 'They're sick. Dianna, who runs the infirmary, says they've got the flux.'

'I can see you are not used to them. You find the people hard to deal with,' said Mrs Drummond, looking at her keenly. 'You will stay to luncheon, won't you?'

Emily was about to say no and then realized that she was exhausted. She couldn't bear the idea of going back out into the heat again.

'Yes,' she said, 'I will. Thank you.'

'It's the weather – our involuntary servants always come down with something when the weather changes. And the bad marsh air. We are saved from most of the effects of it here since we're right on the coast. The marsh is so much more extensive at the Brook plantation and the air that much worse. And then, of course, there's the water. I don't believe you have wells on your plantation.'

'Only for our own water,' said Emily. 'The slaves drink it from the river. Or the swamps.'

'Then it's not surprising that they are ill,' said Mrs Drummond dryly.

'But what can I do?'

'Nothing,' said Mrs Drummond, 'there is nothing you can do. It would be too expensive to bleed them all and your husband wouldn't agree to it. You'll have to leave them to it. Some of them will die. And, Emily, I cannot stress this enough. You must stay away. The flux is so much worse for a white woman.'

They ate a salad with crisp slices of cucumbers and radish, home-made mayonnaise and lobster. It reminded

Emily of Ely Crawford and the day they had gathered ungainly crustaceans from the shore. She wondered why he had not written for so long.

'The food here is so delicious,' said Emily with a sigh.

Mr Drummond smiled but Mrs Drummond only looked at her with concern.

'How is the little one?' she asked.

'Clementine is doing very well. She copes with the heat far better than me.'

'She doesn't ride around the country in the middle of the day,' Mrs Drummond observed.

The maid brought in a bowl of raspberries and another of brandy oranges with cream in a silver jug.

'Your husband is a very stubborn man,' said Mr Drummond.

Emily looked over at him in alarm. He'd hardly spoken throughout the meal. She wondered if he thought it improper that she had arrived on her own and unannounced.

'He persists in growing cotton.'

'Oh,' said Emily, 'but I thought that was a good thing.'

'It was once,' said Mr Drummond. 'Sea island cotton is the finest cotton you can buy, it has such long, strong and silky staples. It used to fetch a high price on the market. But it no longer does. All the rest of us now prefer rice. The island is ideally suited to it – it needs to be irrigated, to grow with its feet wet. And if there's one thing we do have in abundance here, it's water.'

'Oh,' said Emily again. 'I've never considered it. But if it fetches a higher price, why doesn't he grow rice?'

'Well, it takes money to change from growing one crop to another and rice is complex. You have to have a system of sluice gates to flood the fields. The water needs to be controlled. He'd need to hire an overseer or buy a driver who knew what he was doing. So the initial expense is considerable. And then he has other theories.'

'Really? And what are they?' asked Emily. She had never once had a conversation with Charles about cotton, only about the slaves who grew it.

'Charles believes, as do we all, that war is imminent. But he thinks that cotton will save us. He thinks when war breaks out and the north is no longer willing to trade with us that he will sell his cotton to the English; it'll command a high price then and our rice will not. His cotton, he says, will win us the war. It'll make the south solvent and keep us supplied with arms.'

Emily thought for a moment. 'Then if cotton is not worth as much as rice at the moment, he's gambling on war. He *needs* war.'

'That's right, my dear,' said Mrs Drummond, 'and, in the meantime, he's losing money. His crop is also at risk from disease. Perhaps you could try talking some sense into him.'

'I'm not sure Charles respects my opinion on cotton,' said Emily carefully.

'Well, at least you also have Sugar Island,' said Mrs Drummond. 'Not that sugar is fetching high prices at the moment either.'

Emily rode home in the late afternoon, comfortably full

from the Drummonds' delicious meal and with a parcel of vegetables fresh from the garden, some live crabs in a basket and a musk melon filling her saddlebag with the sweet smell of sun-warmed honey. Charles was sitting on the veranda, his feet on the table, drinking a glass of claret when she arrived back at the house. She wiped the sweat and dirt from her face and placed the melon, the crabs and the parcel on the table. She unwrapped the brown paper to show Charles.

'And that,' she announced, 'is my last meal.'

'Do you expect me to ask why?' he queried, taking a sip of his ruby-coloured drink.

'Because everything here is bought at the cost of slave labour. I live idly and eat and drink my fill while I'm surrounded by your pitiful chattels and it is their untiring work in your fields that puts the food on our table. I refuse to accept this injustice or my hypocrisy any more. "Have we yet to learn that 'it profits us nothing to gain the whole world, and lose our souls?'"'

'You and your deuced Channing.' Charles shrugged. 'The Drummonds' vegetables were grown by slaves too. And no doubt these fine crabs were caught by their people as well.'

Emily hesitated. She picked up the melon and inhaled its scent deeply. 'Then I won't eat them either,' she said and she tipped up the basket of crabs and shook them on to the ground. The crabs raised their claws and skittered sideways into the grass.

*

The following morning Emily woke with her stomach growling. She got up quickly and put on her riding habit. The ride, she thought, would take her mind off her hunger. She drank a glass of cold water and went outside. There was still dew on the ground and the air smelled sweet and salty. Oak was already tied to the fence, waiting for her. He nickered when he saw her and looked at her with his wild blue, brown and yellow eyes. She gave him a lump of sugar and patted his neck and he pushed at her hip, looking for more.

Her ride was exhilarating. She cantered as much as possible, startling deer and wild boar, the babies striped the colour of muscovado sugar and syrup, but when she returned to the house she was ravenous and trembling slightly as she hadn't eaten since lunchtime the day before. Charles was having breakfast on the veranda. As she walked up the steps, the smell of freshly brewed coffee, hot bread straight from the oven and thick, crisp slices of bacon grew stronger.

'Shall I fetch June to make you some breakfast?' asked Charles.

'No. Thank you,' she said, and marched past him.

For the rest of the day Emily was plagued by hunger and her stomach rumbled and gurgled. She had a headache and felt irritable. Clem's crying set her teeth on edge. As the day wore on she felt light-headed and her vision and hearing would black out if she stood up suddenly. In the late afternoon she went to bed and slept fitfully, fighting with the hot, damp sheets.

At dusk Charles came into their room and sat on the bed. He took her hand.

'Won't you join me for supper?' he asked.

'I told you I wouldn't,' she said fiercely. She half sat up and took a sip of water. The air in the room smelled stale and her temples were throbbing.

'I caught the crabs after you let them go,' he said. 'June's cooked them with the peas, beans and carrots from the Drummonds. They will be delicious. And it's lonely without you.' He brushed the hair out of her eyes clumsily. His fingers felt thick and stubby against her skin.

'I said no,' she said and turned away from him.

He stood up immediately and looked down at her. 'Well, perhaps it ain't such a bad thing. Eating a little less might help you regain your figure.'

She heard him leave the room and regretted her words. She'd pushed him into lashing out at her and, really, all she wanted was for Charles to climb into bed with her and hold her tenderly. She could still go downstairs and take his hand and bring him back. It was not too late. She loved him, she knew she did, but here that love was slowly being poisoned. She got up and walked to the window and opened it. The air felt cool against her skin and the first stars were glowing in the evening sky.

There was a passage in Channing's book that had upset her dreadfully the first time she'd come across it and now she kept returning to it. He had written: 'Slavery upheld for gain is a great crime. The cry of the oppressed, unheard on earth, is heard in heaven. God is just, and if justice reign, then the unjust must terribly suffer. No being can profit by evil-doing.'

It was wicked, even evil, how Charles lived his life. And how dreadful to love someone who sinned so flagrantly; to be forced to share the sin alongside him. For their marriage to survive they would have to leave here. But then, even if they did leave, he would still keep the plantation. How could she lie next to him knowing what she knew?

That night Charles climbed into bed quietly so that he wouldn't wake her and turned away from her. She slid her hands across his back and round his chest and he rolled towards her. He held her tightly, so hard it was almost painful, as if he were losing her, as if this were his only way of telling her so.

In the morning when she came downstairs, Charles kissed her on the forehead and passed her Clem to hold, who was smiling and laughing. He poured her a cup of coffee himself.

'I don't want it,' she said weakly.

'For God's sake, Emily,' he said quietly, a muscle working in his jaw, 'you're not behaving rationally. Look around you. Everything you see is owned by me and has been paid for by this crop of cotton, by the work of those people out there. The house you're living in, the clothes on your back, the furniture – that infernal horse you ride. You can't even lie naked in the mud outside. Every inch of the land on this island belongs to a plantation owner.'

When she didn't respond he said, 'I know how you feel. I don't understand you but I do know, you've told me so damned often. Besides,' he added, waving Virginie away, 'you've got to look after your child. You won't be able to do that by starving yourself. You're behaving churlishly, Emily. Do you think a single one of these people would understand your refusal to eat meat and drink milk? Do you think they would understand you tipping out crabs and tossing away melons?'

Emily collapsed on the sofa and started to cry. Charles stared at her stonily and then, losing patience, he shut himself in his study. Emily cried until Clementine began to wail. She dried her eyes and rocked the child. She eventually quietened. Then Emily sat down and drank the coffee Charles had poured for her. It was, by now, slightly cold. Even so, it was the best cup of coffee she could remember drinking.

Chapter 8

August 1860

There was a storm coming. They could see it in the distance, a dark purple bruise to the east of Sugar Island, crackling with lightning. There was the faint bass note of thunder. Flocks of gulls flew over their heads, moving away from the storm, their pterodactyl shape sharp white against the darkening sky. The wind had picked up and was rustling through the cabbage palms, making the saw palmettos rattle like sabres and trembling the waxen fruit and flowers of the orange trees.

Emily felt almost excited as she watched it. She and Charles were sitting on the veranda drinking gin with slices of orange from their own trees that added an extra astringency. The previous month had been calm, almost as if they had both accepted an uneasy truce. Charles had been kinder, more solicitous. Emily had taken to wearing a white shirt and a pair of cream breeches from Charles's wardrobe and found this attire much cooler and less restrictive when she was riding. She knew Charles objected but didn't want to fight with her and was likely to continue to ignore her outfit as long as she only wore it on their own land. Clementine could just about sit up if she was supported and had started taking a little bit of solid food and Emily felt that at last the little girl was starting to become a person.

Just before she went to bed Emily looked out of the window. The storm had reached Sugar Island and seemed to have grown in strength; the thunder vibrated in her core and she could hear the waves pounding against the levy, the faint lowing of frightened cows. The wind made the palm leaves stream like jellyfish tentacles and thrashed the orange trees' foliage. The rain lashing against the windows and pounding on the roof made it hard to sleep. Clementine cried and Emily got up to comfort her but when the baby woke again she left Virginie to soothe her. The storm felt right on top of them. The house shook as if it were frail and insubstantial, while the thunder cracked and rolled above their heads. The lightning lit up the whole room with an alien glow. At one point she found herself holding Charles's hand.

Some time in the early hours of the morning the storm blew itself out and she fell asleep. She woke later than normal to find Charles swearing at the window. He pulled on his trousers over his nightshirt and ran downstairs. She rubbed her eyes groggily and walked over to the window, then gasped in shock. The river was now barely yards away. During the night the whole end portion of the island had been engulfed. The water was almost level with the nearest slave camp. And Sugar Island was an island, cut off completely from the mainland. She pulled on Charles's shirt and trousers and followed her husband.

She couldn't see him but she assumed he was inspecting the cotton and the animals. In her bare feet she walked gingerly across the wet grass, water glistening in small pools and puddles. The ground was littered with leaves and branches and a liberal portion of the shingles from the roof of their house. It was a beautiful day, faintly warm, the sky edged with rose and buttermilk, the water's surface smooth and glassy. She walked a little way to the river's edge where the driveway abruptly ended.

She looked into the water. Below her were the drowned orange trees. She could see the deep green leaves, the white stars of the flowers, the lime-green unripe fruit still attached to the branches, waving gently in the faintest of currents. The trees looked ethereal, like a dream in a fairy tale. Yet she shivered and backed away from the sandy edge. The whole island, with its watery dykes, its marshes and swamps, its fragile causeways and catacomb of rivers and streams, suddenly seemed insubstantial. She turned to see Virginie standing on the veranda, holding Clem and watching her. Clem, sitting on Virginie's hip, was pulling the woman's dress taut around her expanding abdomen.

'I need to go to the camp to see if the people are all right,' Emily said as she walked back towards her maid, picking her way through jagged bits of bark from the palm trees.

Virginie said nothing but turned to go inside.

*

St Annie's camp and the infirmary had not been badly affected since they were on the sheltered side of the island and the swamp had absorbed the impact of the rising water levels. A number of trees had fallen during the storm but Emily expected they would be sawn up quickly for firewood. The people in the nearest camp to the house were cold and frightened but unharmed. The huge live oak above them had not come crashing down on top of the huts as they had feared and the water had stopped just short of washing them away. She and Frank canoed over to Sugar Island. The place was deserted. The slaves had already left. Frank told her that his father, Edward, had taken them to the main part of the plantation in the flat-bottomed boats to work in the cotton fields. She and Frank walked round the cabins. They had been devastated. Already in the worst condition of any of those on the island, their roofs and parts of the walls had been blown away or crumbled like sugar in the relentless rain.

'What will happen to them?' she asked Frank.

He shrugged. 'Build them over again. Them's plenty oyster shells and wood.'

'Do you think Mr Brook will let them stop work so that they have time to repair their homes?'

'No, missis,' said Frank, not looking at her and scuffing the raw red earth with his bare foot.

She looked around her. It was like being in a twisted version of paradise. In front of her was the deep, green verdant forest, richly festooned with honeysuckle and a scarlet-blossomed creeper. Giant black and yellow butterflies flew past with slow wing flaps. Frogs sang a thin, reedy chorus; a white eagle soared overhead; the second crop of sugar cane was a vibrant emerald lawn bordered by jewel-coloured wild flowers. All around her was limitless sky, the river as blue as the heavens above, the Atlantic stretching into infinity. And yet here, in the midst of this beautiful arcane wilderness, was the squalid evidence of an enslaved people, the filthy cesspools, the dirty, muddy hovels open to the skies through whose interior scrawny, scrofulous fowl pecked.

Frank paddled them back, aiming for the jetty that was swiftly being erected at the new coastline. Emily was leaning over the side, watching the canoe's passage as its bottom brushed the tips of the orange trees. She saw Frank's paddle catch in the branches but instead of pulling it out, he left it there and the boat halted. She looked up at him.

'Missis,' he said, 'missis, can you teach me to read?'

'Why, of course, Frank.'

'It against the law to teach us folks to read.'

'But your father can read.'

He nodded. 'He say he pick it up.'

'Picked it up?' said Emily. 'You can't just pick up reading the way you might catch a cough.'

'He can't say who teach him,' said Frank, adding, 'and he don't teach me.'

'Why not?'

Frank said nothing for a long time. He looked out to sea and down at his toes, resting in the brackish water at the bottom of the canoe and then finally he said, 'My father say it no use. I got no prospects.'

'Of course I'll teach you, Frank. It will be our secret,' said Emily softly.

Louisa Hall was wearing a green silk dress as iridescent as a butterfly's wing with an emerald necklace like a net of gems cast around her throat. She stood on the steps to the front porch of her house, which was as stolid and glowing as a giant, crystalline cube of sugar, and she herself was radiant. It was the day after the storm. Emily was cross and hot and tired. She objected to having to put on one of her best dresses, which was still too small for her. Charles had not allowed her to ride and so they'd spent the last hour being jolted over to their neighbours' in the wood wagon. There was little sign of the storm here. Their end of the island had absorbed the brunt of the bad weather with its network of tidal lagoons and myriad marshes; under Mrs Hall's strict guidance, her people had already cleared the litter of branches from the flowing lawns and fixed the loose shingles on their house. She noticed that even the beach had been tidied of flotsam and driftwood.

Emily drank a crisp white wine in Mrs Hall's drawing room. Mr and Mrs Hall and Charles were talking animatedly about cotton and rice, arguing the pros and cons. The Halls had changed their crop several years ago and clearly seemed to be benefiting financially.

'How did it fare in the storm?' asked Charles of the rice crop.

'It withstood,' said Mr Hall. 'That's the beauty of the

system. When the water levels rose, the fields flooded and then we drained it away through the sluices. Rice is perfect for South Georgia, as I keep telling you, but you're too deuced stubborn to listen.'

'How is the cotton?' asked Mrs Hall quietly.

'I've lost half a field – completely disappeared underwater. The rest of it has been battered by the wind and the rain. It's a little early to start the harvest but I think I'm going to have to otherwise I might lose everything. Plenty of broken branches and snapped stems – the bolls on them ain't going to get any bigger now,' said Charles.

'Well, you might be in luck, should have a spell of good, clear skies for a few days now,' said Mr Hall, 'but I have to warn you, the price of cotton is not high.'

'I'm going to keep it. Stockpile it,' said Charles.

'Stockpile it? For what? You think there's going to be a shortage of cotton?' said Mr Hall.

He was such a leaden lump of a man, thought Emily. How could Mrs Hall not be exasperated?

'Oh, I think there will be a great demand for it. When war breaks out, the first thing that'll happen is that the north will stop trading with the south. So then those of us that are ready and have goods that are in demand – like cotton and sugar – will trade with England,' said Charles, smiling triumphantly.

'So you truly think it will come to that? You really believe there'll be a war?' asked Mrs Hall.

'I do,' said Charles. 'All the signs of it are there. And not only will I be paid in hard cash, I expect the English will bring us decent guns for once. That's how we'll defeat the Yankees.'

The three of them stared at him. Emily was appalled. Charles seemed to have taken leave of his senses. She looked at the other two. There was a grudging admiration in Mr Hall's face and Mrs Hall was smiling at him.

'Trust you, Charles Brook,' she said breathily.

Mr Hall's expression hardened. 'Still, you have to eat today not tomorrow. How's the horse?'

'Oh, he's fine and dandy, thank you kindly.'

'And any idea when you might be able to pay me back?'

'Pay you back? For what?' asked Emily.

'For the horse, Emily,' said Charles irritably. 'Mr Hall lent me the money to buy the horse.'

'Well, it's not just that, is it?' Mr Hall drawled. 'There's the—'

'I don't think this is a suitable topic for discussion in front of the ladies, do you?' said Charles harshly.

'Why do you need to borrow money from Mr Hall?' asked Emily.

There was a long silence and then Charles said, 'As I said, not a suitable dinner party conversation,' and his grey eyes, when he stared at her, were as hard as shale.

'Perhaps after dinner we could play a game or two and you might win some of it back,' said Mr Hall, smiling wolfishly.

Charles inclined his head but she could tell he was still angry.

When the dishes were cleared away Emily hoped that they could leave. They hadn't even looked at the rice fields, which was why she thought they'd come. Instead, Joel Hall pulled out a pack of cards and started to deal. To her surprise, he dealt to his wife too. Emily wandered over to look at the bookshelves, such as they were. She picked a couple of books at random and sat down in one of the armchairs. Every so often she glanced over at the three of them. Charles and Mr Hall were drunk. They were looking bullishly at each other and Mrs Hall sat opposite them, poised and delicate like an exotic bloom waiting to be plucked by the highest bidder.

Emily slipped outside. The tide was in and the sea was almost up to the edge of the grass. She took off her boots and walked along the thin, firm strip of sand that was left, the sea whispering at her feet. The stars were bright and there was a misshapen moon. The line of palm trees along the shore rustled in the breeze. She wondered if there really would be a war and what would happen to them. She'd never expected to be living on the plantation for long and if war broke out they could be trapped on the island.

She looked back at the bright tableau inside, at the three of them leaning over the table and their cards. As she watched, Mr Hall rose heavily to his feet and left the room. For a long moment Charles and Mrs Hall stared at each other and then Charles said something and ran one finger down Louisa Hall's cheek. Emily stood stock-still. A stray wave washed over her feet and she jumped at the chill water. She looked down at her toes, sinking in the damp sand, marbled with foam. She ran along the shore to where she had left her boots, picked them up and then ran around the side of the house, the coarse grass pricking her feet. She climbed into the wood wagon and lay down among the bags of Spanish moss, looking up at the brilliant constellations, waiting for Charles to join her.

And Charles, when he finally staggered over to the wagon, had lost more money and was sour with rage. He refused to speak to her.

A few days later Emily and Virginie were on the veranda. Emily was drinking tea and Virginie was kneeling on the floor changing Clem's nappy. Emily had felt a kind of nausea for the past few days. She'd put it down to general unease: the closeness of the river and the fragility of the land made her nervous.

'Are you going to tell me who the father is?' she asked.

Virginie glanced up at her and set her jaw. She turned back to the baby without saying anything.

'Do you wish to be married?'

Virginie only snorted.

Emily sipped her tea and looked out towards Sugar Island. A small flock of gulls cawed more incessantly than usual, as if there were a boat coming in. And a few minutes later, a boat appeared. Standing upright with his hands behind his back was a tall, thin man. Emily stared, trying to make out who it was. The boat turned and made for their jetty. He was most properly attired in a linen suit and a wide-brimmed canvas hat. His glasses glinted in the sun. From a distance it looked like Ely Crawford. Surely it couldn't be him?

Emily ran to the jetty, arriving just as he stepped off the boat and the Negro who had been rowing handed up his luggage.

'Mr Crawford,' she called, holding out her hand to him.

'I decided to come and see for myself how you are. We hadn't heard from you for so long.'

His hand was warm and firm in her own.

'But I wrote, ever so many times. I thought you had forgotten me,' she said and smiled. 'You don't know how pleased I am to see you. You have no idea how isolated it is here.'

'I think I have some idea,' he said dryly. 'It has taken me a considerable amount of time to reach the Brook household.'

'Leave this,' she said, indicating his luggage. 'Someone will bring them over.' Emily led Ely Crawford towards the house. 'Come and have some tea. Are you hungry? Thirsty? What can I get you? This is Clementine and my maid, Virginie,' she said as they reached the veranda.

'She's enchanting,' said Ely. 'She looks like you.'

'Well, her eyes are grey like Charles's and her hair is blonde like his too. Perhaps she'll grow more like me. Virginie, go and fetch Mr Crawford something to eat and another pot of tea. And ask June to make us some lemonade,' she said. 'Are you exhausted?' she asked Ely.

'A little tired but I had plenty of rest yesterday at Mrs Baker's boarding house. A most hospitable hostess.'

'Yes,' said Emily, remembering the kindness Mrs Baker had shown her when she'd arrived in Savannah.

'Mrs Brook,' Ely began awkwardly, 'Mrs Baker told me about your – your situation. The plantation. We had no idea. I would have come earlier had I known.'

'It was a shock to me too,' said Emily quietly. 'But tell me, how is Sarah? And your father? And you?'

'We are all well. Living very quietly. Sarah is her normal self – preoccupied with writing another novel. We have to force her to seek society. And Father is also in good health, working tirelessly as usual. And I, well, I am also the same. I'm writing another pamphlet on slavery. Now I see that I am unexpectedly to have first-hand experience.'

'Oh, Mr Crawford,' said Emily, her eyes filling with tears, 'it is far worse than you can imagine. And I'm told that this is not the worst of it. There are crueller masters and harsher places.'

'Ah,' said Ely, putting his fingertips together to form a steeple. 'Then you have had no influence over Mr Brook?'

'None whatsoever. He refuses to listen to anything I have to say on behalf of these poor people.'

Virginie arrived and bent stiffly over their table. She laid out a fresh pot of tea, cups and saucers, a jug of fresh lemonade, glasses, a plate of bread, butter and blackberry preserve and a bowl of fresh peaches with a small, sharp knife.

'Thank you, Virginie,' said Emily. 'Please can you take Clementine inside so that we can talk in peace.'

When the woman had gone indoors, Emily turned back to Ely, frowning. 'I don't understand why you did not receive any of my letters – and why I never heard anything from you.'

'No,' he said slowly, 'it is most odd. Sarah and I both wrote.' He hesitated and then said, 'When, may I ask, will Mr Brook return?'

'I don't know,' Emily said. 'He's probably out inspecting the harvest with our overseer, Mr Stewart. The cotton is being brought in at the moment. Mr Crawford, do you really believe there will be a war?'

She poured him a cup of tea and he stirred in some milk. 'I think,' he said carefully, 'there may well be. But we need as much ammunition as possible before men will fight on behalf of their fellow men to free them.'

'So you need war,' she said sadly.

'No one wants war,' he said gently, 'but it might end up being the only way these people can be released from their chains,' and he gestured in the general direction of the fields.

'I think that as soon as you are rested and refreshed, I will take you on a tour of the plantation this afternoon and you can see how things are for yourself,' said Emily.

After Ely had finished his tea, Emily had Oak and the mare saddled up. The mare was reasonably well behaved nowadays: Emily had had Joshua get her accustomed to wearing a saddle and bridle again just in case anything happened to Oak. They rode first to the nearest camp and then to the cotton gin, through the fields where men and women were bent double picking cotton and the woods to St Annie's and the infirmary. Emily felt that over the months she'd been living at the Brook plantation her heart had inevitably hardened, particularly since Charles would no longer even listen to her complaints. There had been some slight improvements thanks to her stay: the children were cleaner and many of them wore the simple tunics she'd had made; the houses were a little neater and tidier and some of the camps had made an effort to keep the fowl out of their homes. The infirmary was slightly more sanitary, the windows washed, a fire burning in the grate and with a plentiful supply of blankets and towels. But that was the extent of the changes she had wrought.

Thirty-one slaves had died of the flux and Emily had been unable to do anything to alleviate their suffering. The women were still sent into the fields three weeks after giving birth. They were still flogged if they spoke back, complained to her, didn't work hard enough or fast enough or finish on time. The food was pitiful – cornmeal every day – with the slaves eating their first meal at midday after working in the fields since sunrise. There were no medical supplies to speak of, save for the poultices Dianna made and the strange concoctions and tisanes she brewed from native shrubs. They lived in overcrowded hovels with barely a stick of furniture, infested with fleas and sand flies. The clothes they wore were dirty and rent with holes and were literally falling off their backs. There was no fresh water and their only latrines were the dykes that filled and emptied with the tide. Charles still only allowed his people to visit the church service for Negroes once a month.

Emily saw it all afresh at Ely's side. She suspected that he did not take in the sunlight slanting through the live oaks, the majestic magnolias with their burnished leaves, fuchsia-pink water lilies blooming in the ditches, wild roses and honeysuckle, extravagant orchids, clouds of butterflies and flocks of birds as bright as precious stones, the glorious sunset, crimson and gold, the light like molten metal. They rode back in silence. Ely, she could see, was both distressed and angry. Just before they reached the house, Ely halted his horse.

'Mrs Brook,' he said.

'I know. And it is so much worse than this – what you have witnessed is the brute experience of everyday life. But some of the things that I have heard and seen . . .'

'Have you kept a diary?' he asked quietly.

'Yes.'

'Then you should publish it. There is no more vital time than now. There is no one else in your position – who has had first-hand experience of slave-holding but who is not a southern sympathizer. My God, what power your words would have! And as a woman too. You must have had access to sights that no female slave would speak of to a man.'

'Let's talk about this later,' she said. 'Tomorrow I'll take you over to Sugar Island. That camp is worse than either of the ones you have seen today. The Negro driver is a bar-barian. And now they are marooned. Unless our head driver, Edward, rows over there, they are cut off without food. Charles is home,' she added, seeing his horse tied to the rail.

Charles had quite clearly not been supervising the harvest. He was covered with mud and stank of the swamp. A brace of wild turkey hung from the veranda, their tiny eyes screwed shut, blood dripping from their beaks. He shook Ely's hand and looked at him narrowly and then at Emily and back at the abolitionist. A muscle worked in his sharp jaw. He did not look particularly pleased to see her old friend.

'And what brings you here, Mr Crawford?' he asked, pouring himself a glass of Madeira before offering one to Ely almost as an afterthought.

'I came to see Mrs Brook, and you, of course, Mr Brook,' Ely said politely. 'We miss her very much.'

'And sniff around some slaves, no doubt.'

'I had no idea that you were a plantation owner until I arrived in Savannah,' said Ely. 'We were all under the impression that you were a lawyer and I assumed that you were continuing to practise in the south when I received your address from your old law firm in New York.'

Charles said nothing and then shouted for Virginie to bring him some hot water. He ran up the stairs, taking them two at a time. Emily watched Virginie climb the stairs slowly, carrying a basin of hot water. At what point did it become cruel to make her continue to work?

Over supper Charles asked Ely what his plans were, shovelling venison into his mouth as he spoke.

'We'll go on a tour of the plantation tomorrow,' said Emily. 'I'll show him all the paths I've had the boys cut through the woods.'

Charles put down his fork and looked at her. 'I forbid you to take him to Sugar Island,' he said.

'Why?' asked Emily. 'The beach is magnificent.'

'I don't believe that is why you wish to visit the island,' he said, picking up his fork and pointing it at her. 'And if you try, I'll burn your canoe.' As she stared at him in shock, he hurriedly downed his wine and stood up. 'I'm going out,' he said. He shrugged on his coat and left the room, slamming the door behind him.

There was silence. Ashamed, Emily looked down at her plate. Ely coughed.

'Well,' he said after a moment, as if nothing had happened, 'I came all this way to see how you are and I have omitted to ask you.'

'You can see that I am well,' she said, trying to smile at him. 'I want for decent company and stimulating conversation, that is all. But otherwise I am healthy and fit. I get plenty of exercise what with all my canoeing and riding about the place.'

'Yes,' he said. 'I can see that.'

The following morning Emily suggested that they ride over to Fort Frederica. It was a colony, she told Ely, established by General James Oglethorpe in 1736 to protect the southern boundary of Georgia against Spanish invaders. The general won a victory over the Spanish on St Simons Island and peace led to the colony being disbanded.

'I've never been. I thought it might be most interesting to see it – a town that has lain dormant for a hundred years.'

A few settlers had remained but they too finally left when there was a fire in 1758 that burned the town to the ground, she added.

'I'd like to visit Sugar Island,' said Ely firmly, mounting the mare and following her.

'I can't risk my canoe being burned,' Emily said, 'but perhaps tomorrow we could venture a trip to the beach? It would mean boating round Sugar Island and you would see enough, I'm sure.'

'Your maid's child must be due soon,' he said suddenly.

'Yes. She won't tell me who the father is.'

'She's not married?'

'No. Many of them have been forced – by white over-seers or managers or even their own people. But I don't believe she was.'

'No woman is ever utterly safe,' said Ely. 'But in any case your maid should have lighter duties.'

'I doubt that Virginie will receive any special dispensation,' said Emily shortly.

They rode down the road that ran like the island's spine through its centre until they reached Christ Church, shaded by live oaks and palms, its roof carpeted in resurrection ferns that were shrivelling and blackening in the heat, and turned along a track through the woods.

'Your diary,' said Ely, 'would be invaluable.'

'It's intimate.'

'But you might rewrite it. Take out the more personal elements,' he persisted.

'What do you think would happen to Charles if I published something like that?'

Ely said nothing.

'Perhaps,' she said slowly, 'I could do something more modest. Use it to write a pamphlet anonymously, but still based on my own experiences. And we could see how that was received.'

'That would serve our purposes,' agreed Ely. 'And you could publish the diary later to a public whose appetite you have whetted.'

She smiled at him. It would be good to work again and for a proper reason after all this time.

'I'm sorry Charles put a stop to your book about your travels. I was looking forward to reading your views on Italy,' said Ely.

'What do you mean, Charles put a stop to it?' she asked, frowning.

"I'm sorry,' said Ely awkwardly, 'I thought you knew. You and I share the same publisher,' he explained, 'and they told me that Charles had paid them more than your original advance on the condition that they would never publish your work.'

Emily looked at him with astonishment. On her return to America she had received a letter from her publishers saying that they did not want the book after all. In spite of her promise to Charles not to publish her Italian diary, she had cried quietly to herself and burned the letter. Had he been behind it all along?

'I'll speak to them,' said Ely quickly. 'I'm sure they would be delighted to publish something written by you on such a controversial topic. In any case, there are plenty more publishers out there.'

Emily said nothing. She needed to think about the implications of Ely's unsettling revelation on her own. For now, she resolved to push it to the back of her mind. The path led towards the coast and they followed it through the dark and tangled woods, the undergrowth crackling beneath the horses' hooves. Emily realized that they were riding along what had once been the central street in the town.

'I feel like the prince in *Sleeping Beauty*,' she said, 'hacking my way through briars to find an entombed city.'

She jumped off and tied up Oak and the mare. The closer they looked, the more they saw the hidden remnants of the town. On either side of them stood the remains of ruined houses, now choked by creepers, with figs and peaches, cherries and bitter oranges growing between the cracked bricks. They found a lime kiln and a pile of greenish oyster shells for making the walls of the buildings. A few garden plants had gone native: wild rocket and sage, lemongrass and rosemary grown dry and woody. Emily found a wine bottle made of thick green glass and a broken clay pipe sticking out of the soil like a piece of bone. And finally, where the wood met the river, they came across the crumbling fort, its rusted cannons staring sightlessly out towards the marsh.

'It's a ghost town,' she said. 'It's hard to believe that a thousand people lived here.'

'It's hard to believe there were a thousand people on this God-forsaken island at all,' said Ely.

Emily thought of the people who had lived here: tending their crops, building houses, creating new lives for themselves in this virgin soil, struggling with petty jealousies and minor hatreds, falling in love, forming friendships; of all the richness of human emotions that had once existed. How insignificant we are, she thought, looking around. In a hundred years from now what would remain save weeds and wilderness?

They sat on a grassy mound overlooking the fort with their backs to a live oak weeping moss into the water. Ely opened a bottle of wine and they ate peaches that had grown hot and soft in their saddlebags. In the pale light filtering through the leaves, she noticed afresh the lines on his face, the threads of grey in his hair. He had aged since she had last seen him.

'May I ask, Mr Crawford, why you have never married? I can understand Sarah's reasons, she does not wish to give up her freedom as a writer, but as a man you are at liberty to do what you will.'

Ely glanced at her and then away.

'Forgive me, I have been too impertinent,' she said.

'I was engaged,' he said. 'I was in my early twenties. She was eighteen and very beautiful. Gentle. Kind. We agreed to wait until she was twenty-one.'

'Did she break off the engagement?'

'In a manner of speaking,' said Ely. 'She died of consumption.'

'I'm so very sorry, Mr Crawford.'

Ely finished his wine and turned to her. 'Mrs Brook, it's

dangerous to stay here,' he said. 'What if war breaks out? You'd be safer in the north. You and Clementine could come and stay with us.'

'And Charles?'

'Do you think he would care to leave? His law practice in New York quite clearly holds little attraction for him.'

She sighed. 'Doubtless you are right. He thinks that when the war begins he'll sell his cotton to England for arms. I imagine he would want to stay and fight.'

'He seems,' said Ely slowly, 'altered. Even his accent is stronger.'

'This is who he truly is,' said Emily. 'He was different when he was in the north, away from his family and all that he was familiar with. He'll fight to the death to protect his right to keep slaves.'

'Then you cannot stay here with him. It's against all that you believe in. Come with me,' he said. 'Come back with me.'

They returned to the Brook plantation in the late afternoon. Unusually, Charles was home. He was sitting on the porch steps with his head in his hands. When she approached him he glanced up at her. He looked as if he'd been sitting too near a fire: his grey eyes were bloodshot and his skin was puckered and red. She realized with a shock that he'd been crying. Instinctively she stretched out her hand to him and he grabbed hold of her and pulled her towards him. She knelt on the ground at his feet.

'What's happened?' she asked.

'The cotton,' he said, wiping his eyes with his free hand. 'It's got boll worm.' He let go of her hand and she sat on the step next to him. 'It's caused by a moth. The caterpillars eat the cotton bolls from the inside out,' he said.

Ely turned away from them and loosened the horses' girths.

'We're just about ruined, Emily,' Charles added.

'There's still the sugar cane.'

'Yes, there'll be another harvest later this year and we haven't sold the first one yet.' He looked slightly more cheerful but then added, 'We don't have much though and it's not bringing in a high price.'

'What will you do?'

He shrugged. 'Borrow more. Emmanuel will lend us money. Hope that the harvest is better next year.' He suddenly put his arm around her and pulled her tightly against his chest.

'You don't wish to sell the estate then?'

'No,' he said, letting go of her and a jeering note entered his voice. 'Though I know that's what you should like me to do. Lose everything. Not even have the chance to make the plantation pay.'

'I'm simply considering the possibility that there might be a war. And our safety. The safety of our daughter,' she said, trying to keep her voice as calm as she could.

'We'll be safe enough here,' he said confidently.

As Emily washed and dressed for dinner, she wondered about the boll worm. A moth had a short life cycle but, still, there would have been a time lag between the caterpillars hatching and the crop being completely ruined. A few days? A couple of weeks? She had no idea what one would do if one found an infestation early – if there was anything that could be done – but surely Charles would have had some warning? She thought of all those times when Charles had been out for the whole day, when he hadn't been hunting, and she had thought he'd been in the fields, tending to his cotton.

'When are you leaving, Mr Crawford?' Charles asked Ely abruptly just as they were taking their seats at the dining table.

'Charles,' Emily exclaimed, 'you can't ask our guest that. He can stay as long as he likes.'

'He damn well can't. This is my house and I did not invite him.'

'I shall depart tomorrow morning, Mr Brook,' said Ely stiffly.

They ate their meal in silence. After they had finished their main course, Virginie came in carrying a tray of coffee, cream and sugar with cups and saucers, a sponge cake, plates and cutlery. Charles banged his fist on the table and stood up, his face suffused with rage. Virginie put the tray on the table and stepped back.

'Can't you see,' yelled Charles, turning on Emily, spit gathering at the corners of his mouth, 'can't you damn well see that she's with child? She shouldn't be carrying anything. Bella should be here, doing Virginie's job. Can you not manage the simplest of things?'

Emily looked at her hands, gripping the edge of the table, the fingernails white and drained of blood.

'Look here, Mr Brook,' said Ely, rising.

'You can keep your damn mouth shut,' roared Charles, pointing his finger threateningly at Ely.

As Virginie left the room the two men slowly sat down, breathing heavily, still staring at one another. Above her, Emily heard the creak of the floorboards as her maid walked into her daughter's bedroom.

It was drizzling. Mist swirled through the marshes. The sky and the river were granite grey, melded into one. Ely stood next to the jetty, his linen suit darkening in the rain, his luggage on the ground next to him. He thrust out his hand and shook Charles's stiffly.

'Goodbye, Mr Brook,' he said.

'Give my love to Sarah and your father and travel safely,' said Emily.

Ely turned to her. 'Please bear in mind what I said, Mrs Brook,' he said.

He touched his hat to Charles who nodded. Israel picked up Ely's cases and loaded them into the boat, then helped Ely in. As soon as the boat cast off, Charles strode away. Emily remained where she was, watching until Ely was swallowed up by the fog. She turned back to the house. Frank was crouched in front of one of the wooden struts supporting the veranda, waiting. It was time for his reading lesson. She sighed. She was tired.

'Come inside, Frank,' she said.

He hesitated at the steps as he always did. 'Missis, shall we . . .'

'No, Frank. Please come in and sit at the table.'

Frank preferred to have the reading lessons in the canoe where no one could see them, but now that he was learning to write he needed the solidity of a desk. She took out paper, a pen and ink and a board she'd made up with the letters of the alphabet. Frank, his bare toes curled beneath his soles and his hands hooked into his armpits, looked uncomfortable.

Emily pointed to each of the letters in turn and he said what they were. After almost a month he was able to read the alphabet and had started to write the letters. She wrote out a list of words for him to copy, before realizing their inappropriateness. They were English school words – cat, mat, rat – so she scribbled them out and wrote: sugar, cotton, boll, palm, mockingbird. He leaned forward to watch, his whole body relaxing as he focused on what she was doing.

'How do you spell the letters?' asked Frank.

'What do you mean? You just say how the letters sound and then you write them down.'

His face grew still as it sometimes did when he'd been told off or thought she disapproved. It was a way of silencing his emotions and she suddenly recognized it as the feeling she had as she made herself grow small and quiet inside when Charles was on the verge of losing his temper.

'Go on. Please explain what you mean,' she said more kindly.

'Suppose you say the letter A or B, what you write for how that sounds?' he asked slowly.

'Well, normally you simply write the letter. But I see what you mean. You might try: aay, bee, sea, dee, gee, instead,' she said, writing the words as she said them.

'Sea for C,' he said quietly.

'It's only a guess. You might do it differently,' she said gently.

She passed him the list of words relating to St Simons and the pen so he could copy them. He began to form the S for sugar and then immediately looked up again.

'What is it, Frank?'

'Why don't you go with Mr Crawford?'

'Why didn't I go,' she corrected. 'What do you mean?'

'Why didn't you go with him? Go from all this.' He made a small gesture towards the palms dripping with rain, the sea, grey as infinity in the windows and so terrifyingly close, a half bottle of rum on the sideboard.

She was about to berate him for his impertinence and then she looked at him, really looked at him for the first time in weeks. She could see fear at the back of his eyes, a fear that was always present, but also the beginnings of trust. He was looking openly at her. He wanted to know the answer. She understood that he cared what she was going to say when no one else on this island did. When, she wondered, had she stopped thinking of the slaves as individuals and started to think of them as a category, not quite a race apart, but a type of person requiring rules about how one behaved with them? And was that way of thinking so very different from the code of conduct that governed slavery?

Frank looked down at the piece of paper and neatly wrote out the rest of 'sugar', his copy marred only by a minor ink splat at the end.

'I been thinking what the true difference is between we and you, you white folk,' he said tremulously, his voice gradually growing in strength, 'and now I think I know. It not that we have nothing because some white folks, they got nothing either. The difference is we have no hope. But that change when you come. Not because you can free us. I know you can't. Not because you can make our lives better because you can't if Mr Brook don't let you. But because the way you think is different. Make we sadder, this hope.'

'Why are you telling me this?' she asked, gripping the table.

'You in danger of losing your hope,' he said, and then added quietly, almost as an afterthought, 'missis.'

That afternoon she saddled up Oak and went in search of Charles. She eventually found him past the camp at Jones' Creek. The slaves were picking cotton and he was inspecting some of their baskets, crumbling the empty grey bolls to dust between his fingers. When she called his name his look was wild and unfocused.

'Charles, may I speak with you?' she asked, sliding off the animal.

'What do you want?' he asked hoarsely.

She leaned against her hot horse, her arm around his neck as if he would give her support.

'Shall we walk a little way?' she asked, indicating the proximity of the Negroes and wanting some privacy.

'I'm busy. What is it?'

She stroked Oak's damp neck and said quietly, almost timidly, 'Would you let me and Clementine go?'

'Go where?'

'Go north.'

'To live with those abolitionist scum?'

'To stay with Sarah, to begin with. I don't believe it is safe for us here. If war breaks out, we'll be trapped. And I can't bear seeing this misery around us and being unable to do anything. I can't bear seeing you a part of it.'

'Ah, so that's the real reason. Nothing to do with protecting your daughter. Well, we're here and you will just have to bear it. I can't leave and you're not going without me.'

'Please, Charles. What good will it do to keep us here? You're endangering your daughter's life.'

'You don't know what you're talking about,' he said fiercely. 'You know nothing of the political situation and understand less. I am not putting Clementine in danger.'

'Why do you even want me here, Charles? Surely it would be so much easier for you if I left.'

'Because you're my wife. Your place is here. At my side.'

She gripped Oak's mane, struggling not to cry, her throat tight and constricted.

'And Louisa Hall?' she asked.

239

'What about her?' His eyes had narrowed to slits and his face was rigid with such a hatred it took her breath away.

She stuck her foot in the stirrup and swung herself on to Oak's back. She wheeled the horse around and urged him into a canter. When she reached the house, she instructed Bella to make up a bed in the spare room and then the two of them carried her clothes and jewellery into the new room. It was only when the move was finally complete and Bella had left her that she allowed herself to lie back on the freshly laundered bed and cry.

Chapter 9

*B*y the stables a bush bloomed. It had giant trumpet-shaped flowers that were a delicate waxy pink with yellow stamens. One evening as Emily was canoeing with Frank she saw a pod of porpoises, arcing out of the water, their bellies rosy-hued, the late afternoon sunshine creating golden highlights on their flanks. The reading lessons were going well and Frank was picking up words and simple sentences quickly. Clementine had started to crawl and her fleeting expressions were endlessly fascinating. Emily tried to hold on to little blessings like these, roll them in her mind and shake them in her palm, clinking them together as if they were marbles. She reread her diary and set to work on the pamphlet for Ely.

One morning after Charles had left for the day Frank came to see her.

'Abraham want to see you, missis,' he said.

'The driver on Sugar Island? Why?'

'He say he rather talk to you, not master.'

They canoed over to the island. It was a calm day, the water gently rippling, and it was hard to believe that a storm of such magnitude had ripped through the island not so long ago. Abraham had seen them and was waiting at the jetty. As Frank tied up the canoe, he helped her out.

'Thank you, missis,' he said.

'Why did you wish to see me?'

'Please come with me,' he said and started to walk towards the sugar cane fields.

To Emily's untrained eye it looked as if the young cane had grown too fast. Thin and straggly, it had folded in on itself. Abraham took hold of one of the broken stems and hacked it off at the base with a machete. He made a cut down the centre of the stalk and peeled it back with his thumbs. His fingernails were thick and yellow, the nail bed the colour of sepia. He held the cane out to Emily. The pith inside was dark red with rotten white patches.

'It looks diseased,' said Emily.

'It red rot,' he said. 'Not good for sugar.'

'And why are you showing this to me?'

Abraham dropped the cane on the ground. 'You think master will be pleased to hear this news? This White Transparent, best cane of them all, now it sick. He count on it when the cotton gone rotten.'

'He'll be angry and he might blame you – so you want me to tell him.'

Abraham nodded.

Emily sighed. 'He'll be angry whoever tells him, Abraham. But it's not your fault. I'll tell him that.'

'Thank you, missis,' he said, revealing gaps where he'd lost teeth.

Now that she was standing face to face with him he no longer seemed like a man capable of forcing and flogging a woman, only sad and broken like all the rest of them.

He held out his hand to her. As she shook it, she felt his calluses against her palm.

She and Frank canoed back to St Simons in silence.

While Frank went to fetch her horse, Emily entered Charles's study. She wondered if he might have any information about red rot, a way of treating it perhaps. Anything that would let her know how badly he was going to take the destruction of his only other crop. And she also wanted to know how serious it was going to be for them. She doubted that he would have written down all his debts in a ledger but she wanted to look just in case. The study was a mess. There were papers all over the desk, with an empty glass, a dried-up ink well, and a bottle of whiskey on top of them. There were pitifully few books but she found an old one on sugar cane, the cover mildew-stained and battered. The bureau itself was locked but Emily didn't think Charles would have hidden the key very thoroughly. She searched through the open drawers and finally found it, underneath a heap of yellowing bills and a dried peach pit.

She opened the bureau and took out the ledger. Emily didn't have a particularly good head for figures and she had to force herself to look at the cramped writing, smeared with the dead bodies of insects and ink splats. Even a cursory glance, though, showed her that the situation was not good. They owed far more than she had ever imagined. As she put the ledger back, she saw a pile of cream envelopes wedged into a compartment of the bureau. She hesitated, wondering if they were love letters, and then, feeling slightly sick, she pulled them out. She immediately saw that the writing was her own. These were the letters she had written to Ely and Sarah and there were several from the Crawfords addressed to her. She held the bundle to her chest and took several deep breaths trying to still her racing heart. If there was anything good that could be said of this betrayal, it was that Charles had not opened any of the letters, simply not posted hers and hidden them all. She locked the bureau and replaced the key, then ran upstairs and stuffed the letters beneath the mattress in her room to read later.

She took the book on sugar cane and put it into the saddlebag, then rode off in search of Charles. She found him by the cotton gin, standing grimly next to piles of his ruined crop as his slaves knelt in front of him, trying to salvage any healthy cotton.

'I'm sorry, Charles,' she said, dismounting, 'I have some bad news.'

He looked stonily at her.

'It's the sugar cane. It's got red rot.'

'And how would you know that?'

'One of your people told me.' She could see questions forming on his lips that had nothing to do with the actual disease and had everything to do with power. 'I brought over your book on sugar cane, just in case there is anything about red rot in it.' She held it out to him.

He refused to take it. 'How ridiculous, Emily,' he said, scowling at her. 'As if I'm going to read a book standing out here by the cotton gin.'

And then the magnitude of what had happened hit him. He started to swear and kicked over one of the baskets of cotton directly into the face of a young girl who had been filling it with healthy cotton. Emily felt herself turn ice-cold in spite of the heat of the day. Charles's rage was frightening to behold. The girl cowered in front of him and began to pick up the scattered white balls. Emily dropped the book on the dusty ground and swung herself on to Oak. His back felt like the only safe place to be. Her instinct was to ride away as fast as possible but she controlled herself and merely urged the horse into a trot. After all, where was there to go?

For a few days after Emily had moved into the spare bedroom, she'd heard Charles's footsteps on the landing outside and her heart had begun to pound. He'd hesitated outside her door and had then gone back to his own. And then he'd stopped. He'd said nothing. During the day he barely spoke to her. He drank even more than before and openly rode to the Halls' to gamble. One night in mid September when Charles was still out, Emily woke to hear moans coming from Clementine's room. She lay in bed half asleep. She'd left the shutters open a crack and shafts of moonlight were stretched across the room. For a moment, as the curtains skated across the floor, whispering through the cold blue light, she thought she was on stage, the chorus of frogs the bars of some unearthly music, the cries of someone in pain an inexplicable part of the next scene. She sat up in bed. She was damp with perspiration. She wiped her face with the end of her nightgown and, grabbing a shawl, ran into the next-door room.

Virginie was lying on the floor clutching her naked stomach. The skin was stretched taut and there was a darker line running from her navel. Her lips were pulled back to reveal her teeth, gleaming white, almost in a snarl, and the whites of her eyes glowed.

'You'll wake Clem,' she whispered. 'Come into my room.'

She couldn't understand why she felt so little sympathy for the maid but it had something to do with Virginie's rather cold demeanour. When Emily had reduced Virginie's duties she had reacted with undisguised relish, and while it was only natural she should be resting Emily felt there was something repugnant about her attitude. She helped Virginie on to her own bed.

'Have your waters broken?' she asked.

'Yes, missis,' Virginie answered and groaned.

Emily gave her a drink of water and, having poured a little on to her handkerchief, wiped her brow. She went downstairs and walked across the lawn. The shadows of the palms were black and surreal stretched across the grass, which shone eerily in the stellar light. She banged on the kitchen door and June immediately rose from where she was sleeping on the floor, looking frightened.

'Go and fetch one of the men. We need Dianna. Virginie

has gone into labour. Then boil some water and bring it and some sheets and towels to my room,' she whispered. She ran back upstairs to see if Virginie needed anything and changed into the riding breeches and shirt she'd appropriated from Charles.

At some point during the night Charles returned home. He leaned against the doorway to Emily's bedroom, breathing an acidic fug of alcoholic fumes and looking slightly cross-eyed at Virginie.

'This no place for master,' said Dianna, waving him away. He staggered and grasped the banisters and half fell into his own room. A short while later, in between Virginie's screams, Emily heard him snoring.

Some time in the early hours of the morning, just before dawn, Virginie gave birth.

'A baby girl,' said Dianna, picking up the child and wiping away the slick of blood from her face. Dianna pinched her nostrils and she started to cry.

Emily, so tired she could barely keep her eyes open, brought her lamp over to look more closely at the little thing. She was so tiny and wizened, creased from her long confinement, her hands clenched, her black hair matted with mucus. Emily put down the lamp and slapped Virginie across the face. The child was almost white.

Virginie, exhausted and wet with sweat, hissed at her, 'You think I want him? You think I want him any more than you? But I ain't got no other room to go to. You so wrapped up in being in this new place with all us niggers to look upon, he think you ain't interested in him any more. He say you too fat when you with child. Even after your baby born, he say you lost what he love you for.'

It was the most Virginie had ever said to her before. Emily moved carefully to the door, feeling the women, Dianna, June, Bella and Virginie, all watching her. She opened it and stepped into the corridor, closing the door quietly behind her. She walked outside as the first rays of sun pierced the lower leaves of the live oaks, the reedy sound of the dawn chorus swelling with the light. And she suddenly thought of Caesar with his skin the colour of milky coffee, his hard grey eyes and frizzy blond hair – and the dimple – such a distinctive dimple in the centre of his chin. How could she not have realized? He looked nothing like his brother Frank. His half-brother Frank. He was Emmanuel's son.

Emily had begun her pamphlet with the words: 'I can testify with the experience of an eye-witness, having been a resident in the southern states, and had opportunities of observation such as no one who had not lived in a slave estate can have.' It was now finished and she wrote out the whole thing neatly, concluding:

The principle of the whole is unmitigated abominable evil;
moreover the principle being invariably bad beyond the power
of the best man acting under it to alter its execrable injustice,
the goodness of the detail is a matter absolutely dependent upon
the will of each individual slave-holder, so that though the best
cannot make the system in the smallest particular better, the bad

can make every practical detail of it as atrocious as the principle
itself. It is in short a monstrous iniquity.

It was late afternoon and she felt tired and cross. Virginie's baby kept her awake most nights. She'd moved Clementine in to her room so that her little girl wouldn't be woken too, but the walls were thin and they both now slept fitfully and woke early. Virginie had decided to call her daughter Sugar. Emily had snorted when she told her but Charles had smiled and said what a lovely name it was. Emily ineffectually wiped the ink stains on her hands and rubbed her eyes. It was an intolerable situation. She didn't know what was worse, the betrayal or the hypocrisy of the three of them and Charles's two children all living under one roof. If she hadn't needed Virginie to look after Clem she would have tried to send her away. As it was, she spent most of the time feeling furious: furious every time the child cried, every time Virginie calmly took out her breast to feed her, every time Charles surreptitiously watched her, or when his face lit up as he looked at Sugar. And yet she dared say nothing to him.

She would post the fair copy of the pamphlet to Ely but what if Charles found the original? It might be better to hide it, she thought. But where? Frank was the only one she could trust, but if Charles found out Frank would be the first person he'd approach and the first place he would search would be the house where Frank lived with Edward and Molly. No, she would have to hide it somewhere much cleverer than that, she thought. In fact, better if it was hidden with someone she didn't like or trust. Mr Stewart and his dilapidated house by the creek sprang into her mind. What if she hid it in his house? She looked at the clock on the mantelpiece. If she was quick, she could get there before him.

She folded up the pamphlet, wrapping it first in brown paper and then in oilskin. It would take too long to get someone to fetch Joshua and Oak so she set off on foot. She had not been back to Mr Stewart's house since the day she'd first gone there and spoken to him about the infirmary. Now, as she walked through the coarse grass and past the bony cattle towards his house, it loomed above her, larger than she remembered, the colour of a cabbage-white butterfly's wing. In the early evening, surrounded by the dark hedge of forest thicket, it felt cool. She walked round the house once, looking through the algal-glazed windows. She called Mr Stewart's name a couple of times and then knocked on the front door. There was no reply. The door was shut firmly, swollen closed. She pushed hard until it opened. She went into the sitting room, the wooden floorboards creaking. There was no one there. The room was dark. An empty gin bottle stood by the remains of a fire beside a plate piled high with a stack of gnawed bones, ribs and drumsticks. Apart from the broken sofa, the table and a couple of chairs, there was almost no other furniture in the room. The kitchen, as it was in their house, was across the back yard. She climbed the stairs to the first floor.

Mr Stewart's bedroom faced the front of the house. The

sheets were rumpled and dark with dirt and there was a foul smell like stale sweat and fetid fruit. She looked in the one other room in the house, which faced the woods and was darker than the other but also cleaner and neater. Something lying across the bed shimmered in the deep green light. She stepped closer. It was a silk sheet. Its crumpled folds had the metallic gleam of mint soaked in milk. She shuddered. There was something terribly wrong about such luxury in these surroundings. The room held a faint trace of an intangible scent, a delicate sweetness found nowhere else in the house. She walked round slowly. There was an old rosewood dresser with an upholstered stool, the stuffing bursting from the faded satin cover, and a mirror, the glass marbled with flaws, held fast by bronze lion-like paws. In front of the mirror lay a wooden hairbrush, an empty glass perfume bottle and a photo in a silver frame. She picked it up, leaving a shiny patch of wood amid the dust where the photo had stood.

The photo was taken in front of their own house, its white veranda clearly visible, orange trees on either side, their leaves rich and glossy, the branches pin-pricked with star-shaped white flowers. In the centre of the photo were two children, a boy and a girl. They were smiling and holding hands. She hadn't realized that Mr Stewart had spent his life on the plantation. She was about to put it back and open one of the drawers when she stopped. She looked at the photograph more closely. The child on the left had a sharp chin and pale eyes. He had curly blond hair and his head was tilted back. It was, she suddenly thought, Charles, when he was a little boy. Why on earth would Mr Stewart have a photo of him in his house? she wondered. She turned her attention to the girl. She was enchanting, with long blonde hair and large, dark eyes. She was wearing a pale dress with a sash around her waist. Even as a child she was impossibly slender and her beauty was marred by an expression of intense cunning. It was Louisa Hall. Emily quickly replaced the frame on the dresser, leaving finger marks trailing through the dust.

She walked quickly back to Mr Stewart's bedroom. She peered out of the window. The clouds had turned dark and the cerulean blue of the sky was fast fading to dark plum. Mr Stewart was walking down the dirt path through the field directly towards his house. Emily pulled back from the window, her heart racing, and clutched the pamphlet to her chest. Then she ran down the stairs and out of the back door, startling two chickens, who clucked and fled. She ran across the dirt yard and through the long grass at the back, burrs and seeds snagging her dress, cicadas whirring around her and leaping into the air as she passed. She plunged into the silence of the wood. Her plan, if she had seen Mr Stewart, had been to tell him she was looking for Charles, but instead of calmly walking out of the front door and waiting for him on the veranda, she had panicked. And now, she thought, she would have to see it through.

She stood just inside the wood, her breath ragged, and waited. After a few minutes a ball of light appeared, glowing greenly through the dirty windows. Mr Stewart must have lit an oil lamp. She shifted slightly and dry leaves crunched underfoot. She would walk round the edge of the field, just inside the wood, she thought, until she was out of his sight, and then she could cross through the cotton fields and back on to the road. It was only when she was about to move that she saw the child. In the twilight she was barely more than a silhouette in a moth-pale ragged dress. Her hair was cropped short and her knees were too big for her brittle legs. She had her arms folded and she leaned against the kitchen wall, watching Emily. She must have run right past her. Emily held her breath. She didn't know what to do, whether to go back and speak to the girl, find out what she had seen. But after a few moments the girl turned away. She pushed herself upright and slowly, slowly, she walked to the house and let herself in the back door.

Emily retreated back further into the wood but found that it was hard to move through such a tangled thicket. Thorns caught at her clothes and dry sticks snapped beneath her feet or poked her in the face. She managed a few yards before giving up and crashing back into the field. She hoped that in her black dress at the edge of the wood she would not be visible if Mr Stewart should look out. She skirted the field, sticking as close to the wood as she could, stumbling and tripping over tree roots and clods of earth, until she came to a cotton field. With one glance back at the dark house, she plunged into the field.

She followed the hard, mud path worn by the slaves' feet at the edge of the field. The night air was cool against her skin. She brushed past the cotton bushes as she ran; many of the leaves were dead and dry and rattled against the branches and her skirts. The hard ground beneath the bushes was littered with grey, diseased bolls. As the night deepened, the stars shone, giving her enough light to see by. Emily reached the main road through the plantation and followed it back towards the house. But she stopped a little way away. It was an eerie sensation standing outside and looking in, as anyone else who lived on the plantation or who passed by might do. The parlour was brilliant with light and she could see Bella and June moving around, carrying crockery. Something sparkled – crystal or silver-ware perhaps. Virginie was upstairs, no doubt, with Clementine. There was no sign of Charles and his horse was not tied to the veranda. The door to the kitchen was open and soft candle- and firelight spilled out on to the grass. She could smell meat being seared.

She walked across to the newly erected jetty where the barge and a number of their smaller boats and canoes were moored. As she made her way over the jetty, the water sliding jet-black and winking with light beneath her feet, a couple of men turned round.

'How do, missis,' one said quietly.

They were sitting on the end, dangling their feet over the side, shucking oysters and a pile of shells had built up between them, the inner surfaces glistening with pearlescence.

'Can you take me over to Sugar Island?' she asked.

'On your own?' said one.

'I won't be on my own. I'll be with you.'

The two men looked at one another. She saw the swift flash of teeth.

'Not many white women do that. Get in a boat with a slave on they own,' he replied.

They helped her into a canoe and pushed off. Emily sat in the middle, holding her pamphlet tightly. Their paddles bit into the water, which glittered from the blades in obsidian-smooth droplets. Reeds whispered against the sides until they reached the beginning of the central open stretch of sea. A stiff breeze curled the tips of the waves into a frothing cream and she could feel the pull as the men had to work harder to steer a straight course. The wind was warm and smelled of something rotten, of old fish and swamp mud.

At her request one of the men led her to Abraham's hut. It was set away from the others on the edge of the wood and even by starlight she could see it was almost as decrepit as the rest of the hovels. The roof was broken and the walls were cracked and bowed. Abraham was sitting outside on the ground, staring at his feet. A little further away the rest of the camp were crowded round a miserable fire, almost burned back to charred embers. The air was thick with wood smoke. Abraham looked up and when he realized who it was he scrambled to his feet in haste. She held out her hands to reassure him.

'Hello, Abraham.'

'Missis,' he said, swallowing with difficulty. He took a step backwards.

'Abraham, I was wondering if you might do me a favour.'

In the faint light from the fire she saw his shoulders relax. 'Anything, missis,' he said.

'Would you be able to hide this for me, please?' She held out the pamphlet.

He scratched his head and looked at the sleek oilskin package.

'One moment, missis,' he said, and disappeared into the darkness of his hut. He returned with a flat, rusting metal box. 'I put it in here and then hide it up there.' He pointed to the roof.

The roof looked as if it might tumble down at any minute.

'I hide it good,' he said. 'Tell no one.'

'Thank you,' she said, and reluctantly handed him her manuscript. 'Thank you, Abraham.'

He and the other slave who'd been waiting a few yards away walked her back to the canoe. Abraham stood on the broken jetty and watched until the canoe was swallowed up in the darkness. When they reached the shore, Emily walked over shells that glistened in the stellar light and crunched beneath her feet, past their one remaining orange tree. Just as she was about to cross the grass to the veranda, she saw a figure approaching, weaving along the road. His shadow was long and dark, spilling across the glacially bright dirt track and he himself was in darkness. The man stopped walking and stood swaying. She wondered how well he could see her. She was dressed in black standing in front of a white house on a brightly lit night. She resisted her first impulse, which had been to run past the palms and enter the house through the back door. Slowly she climbed the steps to their front door and went inside to wait for Charles.

*

The following morning she rose early and after breakfast she and Frank canoed to Darien. The craft slid through the water, pushing past reeds that towered above them. The salt-sweet smell of the marshes became more cloying as the day grew hotter. Small creatures stirred in the swamp: catfish and crabs and shrimp-like crustaceans. Egrets and herons and water rails stalked and rustled through the rushes.

When they reached the town Emily left Frank with the canoe and walked down the sandy street to the general store.

'What can I do for you, m'am?' asked the proprietor, coming out of his room round the back, wiping grease from his mouth.

The smell of hot grits and burned coffee followed him.

'I wish to post this letter please,' she said, passing over her pamphlet, which was addressed to Ely.

She looked around for a while longer and bought soap, thread and candles – all items that Charles had agreed she could have – and then stepped out into the brilliance and heat of the day. She couldn't bear to go back to St Simons just yet so she walked down the street a little way and stopped at the inn. She sat in the shade on the veranda and sipped a small glass of sherry. Two men were sitting at the far end with their boots propped up on the wooden rail drinking whiskey and smoking. Their dark grey coats were draped over the back of their chairs, and they wore navy trousers, their shirts open at the throat. At first she thought they were brothers and then she realized that they were Confederate soldiers and she shuddered, thinking of the last time she had seen men like that here.

Her thoughts turned to her predicament. She couldn't bear to think of her father: how humiliated he would be if he'd lived to see her like this. What, she wondered, would he advise? She thought of Will with a pang. He would cheerfully tell her to leave Charles and come home. She smiled as she thought of his freckled face, his gap-toothed grin and his easy demeanour. But she couldn't bring herself to think of leaving her marriage. She and Charles had been wed such a short time – even if he had been with at least two women during their relationship. She had stood at the altar in her silk dress the colour of a shell and promised to be with him for better or for worse. That as she spoke those words she had no conception of what the worst might be was no excuse. In Emily's experience of life so far, every problem could be solved through hard work and she saw no reason why her marriage should be any different.

The soldiers had noticed her and were openly staring. She shifted in her seat to angle herself away from them and as she did so she saw a wagon draw up to the store. A man got out and went in. There was something about his stolid back that looked familiar. She watched closely, waiting for him to leave. A few minutes later he reappeared, tucking his bill fold back into his jacket and carrying a brown paper parcel. The brim of his hat shaded part of his face but she recognized him. It was Emmanuel Brook. She stood up and walked across the road. Emmanuel half turned and tipped his hat. He was about to jump into the wagon when he stopped and wheeled around.

'Mrs Brook?'

'Mr Brook. How are you?'

'What on earth are you doing here on your own?'

'I'm not on my own,' she said, indicating Frank standing waiting for her at the end of the street by Darien's rudimentary dock.

'You're here on your own with one Negro?' he said incredulously.

'I was not aware that you were about to pay us a visit.'

'Did Charles not mention it?' he said coolly. 'I'm going to look at some land and thought I'd call in. I'm only staying for a day.' He scanned the boats in front of them. 'Charles said he would send the barge but I ain't seen it.'

'It doesn't look as if it's here,' she agreed. 'I'm heading back to the plantation so I'll make sure it's on its way. I'll tell them to look for you at the inn. Good day, Mr Brook. I'll see you very shortly.'

'Wait,' he said, putting out one hand to detain her.

Emily stepped back so that he would not touch her and she saw his pale grey eyes grow hard.

'You ain't going on your own. Wait here with me, Mrs Brook. The barge will be along soon.'

'Thank you, Mr Brook, but I'll be quite safe.'

She inclined her head and walked towards Frank whose face was tight with nerves.

*

259

There was nothing special to offer Emmanuel. June was preparing steak, ham, potatoes, gravy and cornbread. Emily walked into the house from the kitchen to find Charles and Emmanuel sitting side by side, each with a few sheets of paper in their hands. Their expressions were ugly. Charles stood up.

'Would you care to explain the meaning of this?'

He was holding her pamphlet.

'Where did you get that?' she asked.

'Never mind,' said Emmanuel. 'You just answer the question your husband put to you.'

'You took it from the store-keeper!' Emily said, turning to Emmanuel. 'And you, Charles, had told him to give you my mail. That's why none of my letters to the Crawfords reached them and I never received any of theirs. How could you?'

'It's not appropriate for a wife of mine to be corresponding with abolitionists. Crawford should never have come here and put ideas in your head. This nonsense is seditious.' Charles waved the wad of paper at her.

'Ain't you realized yet what this could do?' said Emmanuel, his grey eyes as cold as water. 'This could have your husband – my deuced brother – lynched if anyone believed even a quarter of all your lies.'

'I've been very careful to keep it anonymous,' said Emily. 'There is no mention of Charles nor any members of his family or even where the plantation is. And there is not a single untruth: I have witnessed everything I wrote of firsthand. I've been living here for almost ten months. One would have sufficed to see the full horror.'

Charles snatched the papers from his brother and threw them all in the fire. Emily gave a cry and stepped forward to rescue them but Emmanuel barred her way and she shrank from physical contact with him. She had seen that narrow, contemptuous expression on his son's face too.

'I forbid you,' said Charles, his anger increasing to frightening proportions, 'ever to write anything like that again.'

'Charles, I would like to leave. I have asked you before, but I'm begging you now. Please let me and Clementine go.'

'You're not leaving,' he roared. 'I've damn well told you already. And if you should even attempt to desert me, I swear on my mother's grave that you will never see your daughter again.'

She looked at him, stunned. 'You can't stop me from seeing Clementine! It's a mother's right to be with her child. She needs a woman's love. Charles, she's only a baby.'

'You still don't appear to understand,' he said, standing menacingly over her. 'I own you. I own Clementine. Believe me, if you leave, there's not a lawyer in the land who won't support my right to keep a hold of my own property. Emmanuel here is my witness.'

Emily backed away from him and then turned and ran upstairs. In the darkness on the landing Virginie was standing silently rocking Sugar and watching. She slipped back into her room as Emily approached.

Emmanuel left as he said he would the following morning. Emily had stayed in bed and heard the wagon being brought round. She couldn't see from the window so went into her old bedroom and looked out. To her horror, Oak and the mare were tethered to the back of the wagon. She ran downstairs.

'Your wife is a disgrace to the Brook family,' Emmanuel said.

Charles's expression turned sour as he saw her standing in front of the house wearing his trousers and shirt.

'What are you doing with my horse?' shouted Emily.

'He's not your horse,' said Charles, 'he's mine. And I've sold them both to Emmanuel.'

'To pay off your debts?' she said. 'Does your brother know how much you owe? How much you've gambled away?'

'You should keep your mouth shut, Mrs Brook,' said Emmanuel tightly. 'My brother's sold me these horses to stop you running off on 'em.' He held out his hand to shake Charles's.

'Wait, I could buy him from you.'

Emmanuel merely pushed his hat further on his head and walked towards the jetty.

'At least let me say goodbye to him,' she said, but Charles seized her arm and held her.

Emmanuel's wagon driver led the horses over to the barge where it was being held flush with the bank by Charles's slaves. It was only when the horses and Emmanuel were on board and the slaves had picked up the oars and started to row, that Charles allowed her to twist out of his grasp. She rubbed her arm where he had grasped her and knew that, should she care to look, a black ring of finger-prints would bloom on her pale flesh.

After Charles had ridden away on his own horse, the only one left on the plantation, Emily ran indoors to find Virginie.

'Quick, pack a couple of bags for Clementine and myself,' she said.

'You think that wise?' said the maid, who was rocking Clem in her baby chair with her foot and feeding Sugar.

'Please just do it,' said Emily.

She ran back out to find Frank. 'We need to go to Sugar Island right now,' she said.

The two of them took the canoe and started to paddle. Once they'd landed on Sugar Island they walked across to Abraham's house. As Emily stepped inside a tide of fleas rose and fell with each of her footfalls.

'It's a thin box, somewhere up there,' she said to Frank, pointing to the roof.

When he reached up to retrieve the box several bats exploded out of the rafters and brushed past her face. Emily opened the stiff catch. Inside was a dollar, a few cents and a worn copy of the Bible. She took out her pamphlet and handed the box back to Frank.

'Frank,' she said, 'I'm going back to the house and then I'm going to need you to be ready to take me somewhere.'

He dipped his head, his features almost in darkness. 'Yes, missis.'

The front door of Brook House was open. Inside there was silence. There was no sign of Virginie. Emily ran up the stairs two at a time and burst into her room. Virginie was calmly packing a carpet bag. Her baby was lying in the centre of Emily's bed.

'Where's Clementine?'

'He took her.'

'Charles?'

Virginie nodded. 'Yes, missis.'

'And where did he take her?'

'He don't say.'

'Did you tell him I was going to leave?'

She realized she was starting to sound hysterical. Virginie said nothing. Emily gripped the door frame, feeling a surge of anger rip through her. She tried to breathe more deeply to calm herself and stop herself from grabbing hold of the woman and shaking her. She wanted to break her bones.

'I think he take her to Mrs Hall,' said Virginie in a rush, looking up at her with her large, almond-shaped eyes.

'Thank you, Virginie,' she said. She stuffed the dress and shawl that Virginie had laid out into the bag, picked it up and ran downstairs.

'How do we get to the Halls' plantation?' Emily asked Frank as she climbed into the canoe. 'Mr Brook sold my horse.'

Frank held the boat steady and looked up at the sky as if the answer lay there. 'Could go down Hampton River and join the ocean but them currents make it hard and they see us come. Best thing is down past the Drummond plantation and walk over. Take longer but it a better route.'

Emily nodded. 'Be as quick as you can, Frank.'

She took the pins out of her hair and shook it out, pulled it as straight as she was able to without a brush and pinned it into a tight bun. Then she picked up her paddle and wielded it as fast as she could. She had never paddled as far or as hard before. Soon her shoulders, back and arms started to ache and she could feel blisters beginning to form on her hands.

After a while Frank looked at her with concern and said, 'I can do it on my own, missis. Rest a while.'

She was about to contradict him but then pulled up the paddle out of the water and laid it on her lap. She stretched her back and rubbed the balls of flesh at the base of her fingers. After she had rested for a few minutes she began to paddle again, struggling to keep up with Frank's strenuous pace.

They rounded the corner of the island and paddled level with the Drummond plantation where the Brunswick River met the Atlantic Ocean. The water had a thick, sluggish undertow and Emily could feel the cross-currents dancing across the bow. She looked longingly at the Drummond estate, so serene with its avenue of live oaks, pristine lawns stretching to the edge of the island and that large and gracious garden.

Frank dug in his paddle and they drifted towards the shore. 'It hard to get back if we go any further,' he explained, helping her out.

They were on the border between the Drummond and the Hall plantations.

'Wait here,' she said, 'I'll be back soon.'

Frank shook his head stubbornly. 'I come with you. It too dangerous on your own.'

Emily, whose only thought on the entire journey had been of Clementine and trying to banish the hateful image of Louisa Hall holding her daughter, looked at Frank afresh. It was the first time he had contradicted her. He finished tying the canoe to a tree root and splashed through the reeds to reach the bank. They walked along a raised path above the rice paddies. The water had been drained away after the harvest and the damp denuded fields smelled like a dead thing left to rot in the sun. To her right the ocean was preternaturally calm. A flock of gulls flew overhead; their shadows slid over the algal-glazed mud.

When they reached the house, Emily murmured, 'Wait here for me.'

She climbed the steps to the porch and was about to push open the great front door when it swung open.

'I thought it might be you,' said Mrs Hall acidly.

'Where's Clementine?'

'Sleeping in my bedroom,' said Mrs Hall.

'I want to see her,' said Emily, trying to step past her.

Mrs Hall suddenly pushed her hard so that she stumbled back and nearly fell. She moved forward and closed the door behind her.

'I think you'd better leave,' Mrs Hall said. 'Charles is here and I know he doesn't care to see you.'

'I want to see my daughter.'

'You've forfeited any rights you had. She's staying here with us.'

'And how are you going to explain that to Mr Hall when he comes home?'

'I'll tell him the truth. That Charles's wife has been trying to stir up trouble by publishing a collection of lies in the hope that a Yankee mob will lynch him and that she's threatened to run away taking his only child with her. He'll invite Charles and Clem to stay here, as I have done.'

'So you're not planning to tell him about your indiscretion?'

Mrs Hall took a step towards her and slapped her across the face. Emily put a hand to her burning cheek.

'I want my daughter,' said Emily, pushing past her.

'If you don't get off my property, I'm going to set the dogs on you. You and your nigger lover.' She tossed her chin in Frank's direction.

'Look,' said Emily, her eyes filling with tears, 'please, just let me see Clem and then I promise I'll leave. Even though you don't have children of your own you must be able to understand how I feel.'

Louisa Hall gave her a long, cold look out of her fox-brown eyes. Then she whistled. Two dogs and their handlers came round the corner of the house. The dogs, shifty-looking mongrels whose ribs showed, were snarling and salivating; one was the colour of liver, the other grey.

'I'm going to count to ten and then I'm going to let them go.'

Emily looked at her in horror.

'One . . .'

'You can't do that. Where's Charles? Let me speak to him.'

'Two . . .'

'Missis,' screamed Frank.

'Three . . . four,' said Mrs Hall.

Emily jumped down the steps of the porch and ran towards Frank. They started down the long driveway, Emily stumbling and tripping over tree roots and stones. Frank ran with grace and ease. His speed was astonishing. Emily quickly started to struggle to breathe. She felt as if her limbs were made of lead and she was running through molasses.

'Ten,' shouted Louisa Hall triumphantly and behind them came a dreadful baying as the men released the hounds.

'Head for the Drummonds'. I fetch help,' shouted Frank, and he took off even faster than before. She watched his pink soles flashing.

The driveway seemed never-ending. She could hardly draw another breath; it was as if her heart might burst. But she could hear the dogs approaching. She reached the end of the drive and climbed over the fence. The dogs were not far behind. At any moment they would appear. She took a huge shuddering breath. She didn't think she could go any further.

There were shouts and Frank and a gang of men armed with sticks came running towards her from the slave quarters, followed by Hamish Drummond carrying a whip. The slaves surrounded her just in time. She collapsed on the ground, half sobbing, gasping for breath. Behind her she could hear the dogs barking and the sickening thud of wood on flesh. Then Mr Drummond was there, cracking his whip and the dogs howled and fled. He grasped her arm and helped her to her feet.

'Mrs Brook, can you walk?'

She nodded. He kept his hand firmly about her arm and led her back to the house.

'Why on earth were Mrs Hall's dogs chasing you? She seems unable to control them at all.'

'I beg to differ,' said Emily, still trying to catch her breath. 'I think she has exemplary control over them. Mr Drummond, would you mind sending your men with Frank? We have left the canoe and my bag on the edge of the Halls' plantation.'

He spoke briefly to his men.

'Oh, my child, what has happened to you?' said Mrs Drummond, throwing up her hands when she saw her.

Emily could only imagine how dishevelled her hair must look but she could see that her clothes – men's clothes at that – were damp with sweat and covered with dirt. Mrs Drummond bustled her into the house and had one servant fill a bath while another brought her lemonade, a tot of brandy and a cold turkey sandwich. Emily ate ravenously. She hadn't realized how hungry she was. When her bag arrived at the house, she bathed and changed into a linen travelling gown and brushed her hair.

'You look almost human,' said Mrs Drummond, frowning at her. 'Let's have a look at those hands.'

Emily laid her hands on Mrs Drummond's cool palms. The older woman smoothed ointment into her blisters and bound them with strips of muslin.

'Now,' she said, taking off her glasses, 'perhaps you could tell me what has been happening?'

'I was planning on leaving Charles. I think war will break out soon and I don't want my daughter to be here – it's too dangerous – but Charles won't let us go. This morning he sold my horse and then took Clementine to Mrs Hall. She set the dogs on me when I tried to see Clem.'

Emily started to cry. She could feel the Drummonds glance at each other.

'He's having a liaison with that deuced woman,' said Mr Drummond gruffly.

'Yes, dear. It's been going on for some time,' said his wife quietly.

'You knew?' said Emily, wiping away her tears.

Mrs Drummond squeezed her hand. 'Our people will row you over to Savannah, to Mrs Baker's boarding house. She'll take care of you. I'll speak to your husband and see if we can come to some arrangement about Clementine. It's certainly not proper for a baby to be without its mother and it's foolish of Mr Brook to try to detain you both here with war so imminent.'

'The boys will bring round the boat,' said Mr Drummond.

'I can't leave without Clem,' said Emily.

'You will have to,' said Mrs Drummond. 'Everyone's temper must cool down. I'll go and see Mrs Hall myself this afternoon and we'll fetch that maid of yours to look after

Clementine. You'll be reunited with your daughter before you know it.'

At the jetty Emily shed more tears.

'I can't thank you enough for what you've done,' she said.

'Nonsense,' said Mr Drummond awkwardly.

Mrs Drummond smiled. 'We'll speak very shortly,' she said.

It was late afternoon as the men pushed the boat off the jetty and started to row up the Brunswick River, the light a golden slick on the water. Emily waved to the Drummonds and, as they turned to go back to the house, their slaves burst into another of their bittersweet songs.

'Mrs Brook,' said Caroline Wyatt Baker when she opened the door, as if it had not been ten months since she'd last seen Emily. 'Now how many of these boys are staying?'

'Just Frank,' Emily said.

The men placed her carpet bag and provisions that the Drummonds had given her on the veranda.

'Thank you,' said Emily.

'Bye, missis,' one said and then they silently disappeared into the night.

'You'll have to sleep out back,' said Mrs Baker to Frank, 'but you'll be comfortable enough. Now help us in with these things. I got just the room for you,' she said to Emily.

Mrs Baker led her to a room on the first floor and lit the oil lamp. She fetched hot water and a rum toddy and did not ask where her husband was.

'Now you sleep well and tomorrow morning, I'll bring you the best breakfast in Savannah,' she said as she left.

Emily, although she was exhausted, tossed and turned, disturbed by the gas light outside the window. It was almost dawn when she finally fell asleep and it felt as if it were the middle of the night when the maid pushed the door open and brought in breakfast.

After she had left, Emily sent Frank down to the dock to see if he could spot either one of Charles's men or the Drummonds'. She spent the whole day sitting on the veranda with a book on her lap, pretending to read, waiting for a message. But none came.

At the end of the second day Emily confided in Mrs Baker. The landlady listened quietly but Emily suspected that she had known all along about her situation.

'I can't stay here any longer,' she said. 'I must return to St Simons to fetch Clementine.'

It was evening and they were sitting in the guests' lounge. Mrs Baker had brought in a pot of mint tea.

'And how are you aiming to do that?' asked Mrs Baker. 'Mr Brook ain't going to let go of her. I know Ann Drummond and I know she'll have tried to get those two to see reason. If she'd gotten your baby girl back, you'd have heard all right.'

'But I can't sit here and do nothing,' cried Emily, jumping to her feet and starting to pace in front of the windows. 'And I can't run away to the north and leave my child here.'

'Tomorrow morning we'll send someone to take a

message over to the Drummonds. You could hire a boat and Frank could go. You mustn't go, Mrs Brook,' she said, seeing the expression on Emily's face. 'Now, I suggest you get a good night's rest and we'll sort this out first thing.'

Emily continued to pace and fret. It was only as it grew light that she finally fell asleep.

She awoke with a start. Mrs Baker was standing by the bed.

'I got the maid here waiting for you. I think you should get up right away, there's someone to see you,' she said, shaking Emily by the shoulder.

'Who?' asked Emily, staggering out of bed and wrapping her shawl around her.

Mrs Baker said, 'It ain't anyone you were thinking of but it is someone who'll help you.'

When she was dressed and her hair pinned up, Emily went downstairs and into the lounge. A man was sitting upright at the table by the window, looking outside, the early morning light blurring his sharp features. When he heard her step he rose eagerly and turned towards her, still clasping his hat in his hands. It was Ely Crawford.

'Mr Crawford, what in the world are you doing here?' asked Emily. 'There's nothing wrong with your father or sister, I hope?'

Ely Crawford shook his head, put his hat on the chair next to his and sat down again. 'I made a mistake,' he said. 'I left you on St Simons. I came back for you and Clementine. It's too dangerous for someone like you and for such a young child.'

'Oh, Mr Crawford, what could you have done? It's my fault. I wasn't ready to leave.'

Mrs Baker came in at that moment with a plate of ham and grits.

'I arrived last night and was planning to catch the steamer to St Simons but Mrs Baker kindly told me that you were here.'

'I told him what happened,' Mrs Baker said to Emily. 'The steamer leaves this afternoon for St Simons. I thought you might make a better emissary than Frank, Mr Crawford, and could talk directly to the Drummonds.'

Ely nodded. 'I'll try. And tomorrow I'll catch the steamer back with your daughter, God willing, Mrs Brook.'

After Mrs Baker left, Emily passed Ely a copy of her pamphlet. She'd written another version to help pass the time the day before. She explained the arrangement Charles had made with the general store.

Ely immediately started to read it, letting his breakfast grow cold.

'This is truly remarkable,' he said, pushing his glasses back up his nose. 'Harrowing but exactly right. It's beautifully written and cogently argued.' He put down the papers. 'It's just what we need. The majority of people in the north are against slavery but are not willing to go up against the south in support of their ideals.'

'But I don't want my little treatise to be used to help start a war,' said Emily. 'Remember what Channing called it? "An unholy interference". Much as he believed in the liberty of the slaves, he wrote: "Better were it for us to bare our own breasts to the knife of the slave, than to arm him with it against his master."'

'You should go on the stage,' said Ely, then realizing that he had inadvertently made a joke, added, 'Mrs Brook – Emily, if I may – with your voice and looks and passion you could win the cause for us through oration alone. I sincerely hope it won't come to war. But in the event that it does, we need to ensure you are as far away from here as possible. Mr Brook is bound to have told others what you have written and it must be general knowledge what your views are. As you said yourself once, it would be shocking in an Englishwoman not to be prejudiced against slavery, and people here are bound to have reached that same conclusion.' He rose, leaving his half-eaten breakfast. 'I'm going to book my passage on the steamer and also our tickets on the train north. It's imperative that we leave as soon as I return tomorrow. I'll send a telegram to my sister to let her know that you are safe and to expect us soon.'

'Thank you, Ely,' said Emily, her eyes filling with tears. 'You've been so very kind.'

The following afternoon Emily stood at the docks with Frank waiting for Ely. She had packed the small number of belongings she had back into the carpet bag along with the jars of preserves and cured ham Ann had given her. The train to the north departed that evening. The time since Ely left had passed agonizingly slowly. Savannah's port was small but crammed with boats of different sizes, shapes and descriptions. A shrimping vessel set sail, casting out its nets as it reached the open water, and seagulls screamed around it and lined up on the rigging. There was the smell of the sea and seaweed, horses and rotting vegetation.

A fishing boat arrived and the men landed their catch on the wharf in baskets piled with glistening flounder, bass and catfish. They unloaded a creel of trout and a couple of small sharks, and giant shrimp and crabs which scuttled over each other. Emily, distracted, bent over one of the sharks and stared into its sightless eyes, dark as grapes, its tiny white teeth fearsomely serrated. A constant procession of people came and went, haggling for fish, booking passages, heading out on fishing expeditions. In contrast to their industry, small groups of Confederate soldiers hung idly round the docks too, eyeing the women, drinking and smoking. Their homespun clothes were mismatched and their general appearance slovenly.

'You know, Frank,' she said, turning to the slave, 'if Ely brings Clementine back, we're going to head north to Boston. I can't ask you to come with me. You'll have to return to Mr Brook. I'm afraid of what he'll do to you for coming with me. Nevertheless, it would be so much worse if you ran away, as he would perceive it, to Boston. But I promise that one day I'll find a way to buy you from Charles and grant you your freedom.'

Frank said, 'Thank you, missis.' His face fell a little and he said, 'Missis, what do I do when I free?'

'Whatever you choose. Perhaps the Crawfords could help you find a trade.'

Frank's smile was so wide Emily couldn't help smiling back. And then his smile faded.

'What is it, Frank?' she asked gently.

'Freedom,' he said, 'what will it mean? You say that you want us all to be free. But how can that be when white men hate us? Not just the southern men, look like they want to lynch us, but the northern men. They think we people should be free but they don't like us no more than any other white man. They don't like to look us in the eye, they don't want to touch us, they don't want to work with us. I see how Mr Crawford looks at me, no matter what he write in them pamphlets.

'So, missis, I ask you, what gone happen to us? You gone ship us back to Africa? Because we gone so long it not our country any more. You gone to give us some place in the hills to live where the water tastes foul and the land is full of rocks and no white man want it because it ain't worth a dime? Because I don't see how we can work alongside you, as men, as equals, as brothers. What happen if Mr Crawford marry and has a daughter and I ask to marry his daughter? You see,' he said sadly, for Emily had given a tiny, involuntary shudder, 'underneath it all, you no different to the rest.'

Emily looked at him, appalled. After a moment she took a deep breath and said carefully, 'What was done to you was the greatest wrong ever inflicted – to steal men from their homes and turn them into chattels. It's immoral and unjust to treat a man as property. But how you undo such a great wrong – that I don't know. I don't believe in giving you arms and telling you to wreak revenge. Before I came here I thought it was simply a matter of education: educate the white southerner to believe in equality with the black man; educate the black man so that he could seize his freedom with both hands and use it wisely and well. I can see now that there are no easy answers, Frank.'

She turned away from him so he couldn't see her expression.

They stood in silence and then Frank said softly, 'Sorry, Mrs Brook. You the only person ever been kind to me.'

At last in the distance they saw the steamer approaching, the sun glinting from its white decks, the paddles churning the sluggish brown river water into coffee-coloured spume. It trailed a wake of gulls like streamers. She hastened down the quay and clasped her hands tightly together. She felt cold even though the sun was still high in the sky. As the ship approached she scanned the decks nervously and then saw Ely. He was leaning against the railing on the upper deck wearing his cream linen suit. He took off his hat and waved it at her. He was on his own. Emily burst into tears.

As soon as the ship docked he came straight over to her and she could see from his face that it had not gone well. She wiped her eyes with her handkerchief.

'I'm sorry, Emily,' he said. 'I spoke to the Drummonds and the Halls but there was little I could do.'

She blew her nose. 'What happened?'

'I'm afraid,' he said, 'that Mr Brook has already had a

lawyer draw up a contract. On the grounds that you deserted him, Clementine will remain with him.'

'But I didn't desert him. I only left after—'

'I know. But he told the lawyer that you said you wanted to leave, that he had to sell your horse to prevent you, that you had packed a bag for yourself and the child without his permission.'

'Did you see her?'

He shook his head. 'Charles has taken her back to Brook House. At least she'll be with Virginie and in her own home. Mrs Drummond saw her and said she was well.' He hesitated. 'She said that Clementine was upset but to reassure you that the child will settle once she reaches familiar surroundings. My suggestion is that we try to fight this from Boston. When we are in the north, we can hire the best legal advice there is.'

'I can't leave,' said Emily, 'I can't abandon my child.'

'Why don't we return to Mrs Baker's and we can discuss it further?' said Ely gently. He took her arm and they walked slowly and silently back to the boarding house.

Mrs Baker must have seen them heading down the street because she brought a bottle of sherry out to the veranda when they arrived. Emily saw her and Ely exchange glances as she poured them out a measure. As soon as she'd finished her glass, Mrs Baker topped it up and then she spoke.

'Mrs Brook, I've known Mr Brook a long time, longer than you. I think we both know what an intractable gentleman he can be. You pestering him now to change his mind ain't going to help one little bit. He'll realize soon enough that your little girl needs a mother. And don't think you'll get anywhere staying here. I know his lawyer too and it won't help you none. Mr Brook will come to his senses. But in the meantime, I'd do as Mr Crawford says. If the worst comes to the worst, you can surely hire a better lawyer in Boston.'

Out of the corner of her eye Emily saw Ely glance at his pocket watch. She finished her sherry and stood, her head swimming.

'Mrs Baker, perhaps you'd be so kind as to fetch my bag for me? I believe it's time to leave.'

Chapter 10

The flocks of terns and oyster-catchers reminded Emily of the beach on the far side of Sugar Island. Here too the sand was white and crystalline and the ocean savage. Along the shoreline was a dense pine forest, such a deep green it was nearly black, with drops of resin like semi-precious jewels oozing from the trees. She was the only person walking along the beach and the emptiness and desolation served to heighten her feeling of isolation.

It was 2 April. It was cool but the sky was a perfect blue and the garden around the Crawfords' house was clotted with daffodils poking through green-gold moss. She had thought the change in the weather would lift her mood but it had not. In her pocket was the letter from Charles she always carried with her. His spiky, barely legible hand had faded and the paper was worn as soft as new leather and had become as fragile as tissue. It was the only letter she had received from him since she'd travelled north to Cape Cod with Ely. Charles had written that as she had deserted her husband and her only child, Clementine would remain with him. She would, in due course, receive a copy of his lawyer's contract proving beyond doubt that the law lay on his side. There was nothing about Clementine, how she was faring, whether she could stand by herself, how many teeth she had. Charles concluded by hoping that she, Emily, had recognized her mistakes and would soon return to her position by his side as his wife.

In tears she'd shown the letter to Ely and Sarah. Ely had frowned. Sarah had held her hand and said, 'Don't even consider returning to him. We'll find a way to bring Clem here.'

Yet the months had passed and there had been no response to any of her letters. Theodore Crawford had hired a lawyer but the sole correspondence they had received from the south was a letter from Charles's lawyer stating that he had received no further instructions from his client. A couple of weeks ago she'd sent Clementine a birthday card, a tiny, black wooden horse and a white cotton lace-trimmed dress with pantaloons but she had heard nothing.

Ely had allowed a respectful interval to elapse before he asked Emily about the pamphlet and whether she was ready to publish. She had answered that she was not. She said that its publication might endanger Charles's life and thus that of her daughter. Moreover, Charles would see the pamphlet as an indication that she had finally terminated their relationship and it might prevent her from ever seeing Clem again. Ely had accepted her opinion but she sometimes caught him looking at her, a mixture of fondness and frustration warring over his fine features.

Once, walking slowly through the Crawfords' house, wondering what to do with herself, how to get through the days when every waking moment she ached for her child, she noticed a photograph hanging on the wall of the hall. It was of Ely and a girl, a very young girl. She had dark hair and a round face and large, kind eyes. Ely, looking so much younger, without harsh angles or the air of quiet dignity he now possessed, radiated happiness. She looked at the picture for a long time. She wondered how he could bear it.

She picked up shells as she walked, tapping the sand from the best of them and chinking them in her hand. She felt that she had lost so much, her joie de vivre certainly, but something far greater than that. Only a year and a half ago she'd been a successful actress, she'd been rich, much loved and fêted in the major North American cities, and then, in swift succession, she'd become a wife and mother. Now she was an actress who no longer acted, a wife without a husband, a mother without a child, a child without a father who never saw her mother. She had lost everything that had shaped and formed her identity.

Reluctant to go back inside, Emily sat on a bench on the veranda facing the sea. The wind whipped her hair into salt-coated strands. Sarah had noticed the change in her too. They'd been sitting on this same bench a couple of weeks before, drinking hot chocolate, their hands wrapped round their cups to warm themselves. It had been a chilly day but the sun was bright and it had felt as if spring had finally arrived.

'You appear different,' Sarah had said. 'I noticed as soon as you came back to us last year.' She'd taken a sip of her hot chocolate and huddled further into her coat.

'Different? In what sense?' Emily had asked, although she hardly cared to hear what Sarah's answer was.

A curlew called, a long and lonely sound.

'I couldn't quite place it,' said Sarah, still looking out to sea and not at her. 'You seem a paler version of yourself. More timid. But I think I know what it is now.' She turned to look at Emily. 'It's fear, isn't it? You're frightened.'

'All the time,' Emily whispered. 'I never knew how Charles would react. What he might do.'

'Oh, my dear.' Sarah put down her cup and squeezed her shoulders. 'I hoped that time with us would allow you to heal and become more like yourself. I told myself that you are young and strong and resilient. But it's not enough, is it?'

'I will recover,' said Emily more firmly, 'I will be myself again. One day. When all this is over. When I get Clementine back.'

As she remembered this conversation, she took out the packet of letters she'd written to Sarah and Ely that Charles had never posted. In the fine, fresh air of Cape Cod, her letters were heavy with heat, redolent with the exotic scent of jasmine at night, the chorus of frogs and cicadas, thick as a shroud. They were also dense with misery: the misery of the slaves' pitiful existence and her own deepening misery, writ large between each sentence in spite of how much she had tried to belittle it. They made her cry. She stood up and shook them into the breeze, which swept them from her fingers and scattered them across the sand. And then she took out the letter from Charles and tore it into pieces which she tossed into the air to fall, tiny white flakes as delicate as cherry blossom petals, shortly to be swallowed by the sea.

She went indoors. The Crawfords were having afternoon tea in the drawing room; they looked up at her as she walked in. Their faces were white. They spent too long pressed into their books without taking enough fresh air.

'I'd like to divorce Charles,' she said.

There was a long silence and then Theodore said, 'I'll speak to my lawyer.' His voice was expressionless.

'What's the matter?' she asked, looking from one to the other.

'We are on the brink of war,' said Sarah.

'Are you talking of Fort Sumter?' asked Emily carefully.

In her grief she had paid little attention to national events but Fort Sumter had obsessed the Crawfords. Earlier in the year a Major Robert Anderson had, without authorization, taken his troops and stationed them at the unfinished garrison, Fort Sumter in Charleston, Carolina. He was refusing to leave and the port was being blockaded by southern Confederate troops. The men had only a small amount of food left. Ely had explained that by early February a total of seven states had seceded from the

Union, forming a Confederate States of America. The outgoing President, James Buchanan, had declared, 'The south has no right to secede, but I have no power to prevent them.' Southern Carolina was one of the states that had seceded so the occupation of the fort by a handful of Unionists was tantamount to a foreign invasion.

The whole affair did not interest Emily much. It seemed a petty argument: Anderson had disobeyed orders in the first place. What she did understand more clearly was Ely's anxiety. The south had left the north precisely because Abraham Lincoln had been elected and he was against slavery. He had announced, 'I have often inquired of myself what great principle or idea it was that kept this Confederacy so long together. It was not the mere matter of the separation of the colonies from the mother land, but that something in the Declaration giving liberty, not alone to the people of this country, but hope to the world for all future time. It was that which gave promise that in due time the weights should be lifted from the shoulders of all men, and that all should have an equal chance.'

This strange-looking man had, like a tumbleweed from a wild frontier town, blown into Washington, and the south was afraid that their easy lives of whiskey and cotton, whoring and slaving, would be torn from them by this overly educated nobody from the north. But Lincoln, as soon as he accepted power, had not abolished slavery. He had said that he would not interfere with those southern states that already held slaves. Ely wanted her pamphlet to force their leader to remember his promises.

'Lincoln has sent the navy to resupply the fort,' said Sarah. 'The ships are carrying food. He's hoping that it will look as if the south is preventing hungry men from eating. But sending the navy is exactly what will trigger the firing of the first bullets. It's going to end in nothing less than civil war.' She put her head in her hands.

'It might not happen,' said Emily. 'No one may shoot. And if they do, it need not result in war.'

The three Crawfords were silent. She looked at their expressions and saw that they thought her naïve. What did she really know, after all, of America and Americans?

Theodore smiled stiffly. 'Come, sit down and have some tea and cake and let us talk of happier things,' he said, holding out a chair for her.

It was a cold, overcast day and they were eating a late breakfast of tea and toast and marmalade. The letter Sarah placed next to Emily was officious-looking but rather battered after its long journey. She felt nauseous. She put down her toast and opened the envelope with the butter knife. Charles's reply via his solicitor was prompt and curt. In the event of a divorce being granted, he would retain sole custody of Clementine. Emily would not even be allowed to visit her daughter until she came of age. The cruelty of it made tears start in her eyes. Speechless, Emily handed the letter to Theodore. He read it carefully and gave it to Sarah.

'We have been patient and conciliatory with him so far. Why not threaten him with publication of your pamphlet if

287

he refuses to allow you custody of your daughter? He's a coward at heart, Emily,' said Theodore.

'Do you truly believe that would work?' asked Emily, pushing away her toast and taking a sip of tea.

'We can but try,' said Theodore. 'We haven't gone to court yet so you won't lose anything by threatening him. My belief is that he will not want to be seen to be upstaged by a woman, to have what he considers his morals, his whole way of life called into question and dragged across the nation for discussion.'

'Even if the pamphlet is published anonymously?'

'He won't know that is your plan. Besides, you were famous enough for journalists to fathom it out and that is precisely what Charles will be afraid of.'

'It's happened,' said Ely, interrupting. He put down the paper, pale with anxiety. 'The Confederates fired the first shots at 4.30 a.m. on 12 April. And continued to fire until Major Anderson was finally forced to surrender. The siege is over.'

'And war has begun?' asked Sarah.

'I'm afraid so.' Ely glanced back at the paper. 'Apparently only one man was shot during the salute at the end. A Unionist. And a Confederate bled to death when one of the cannons misfired. Altogether remarkably bloodless, considering.'

'What will happen now?' asked Emily.

The Crawfords turned and looked at her blankly and in silence. And then all three started to talk at once. Emily stopped listening. If there was to be a war, travel between north and south would become difficult, dangerous and perhaps downright impossible. She must leave immediately.

Israel leaned on the paddle and pushed the boat off from the bank. It was hot and a cloud of black gnats danced around the bows. The swamp smelled fetid, of rotting seaweed and creek mud as Israel, accompanied by Frank and two more slaves, paddled up Buttermilk Sound through curtains of reeds.

Theodore had cautioned Emily that there was no telling how Charles Brook might react if she simply turned up at the house. She had suspected Charles would say no to any form of threat or negotiation but she was surprised. In response he had sent a telegram saying that she could visit and discuss arrangements for the child. Theodore had been triumphant but Emily was not convinced. It was not like Charles to give in to a rational proposition quite so easily. Preparations for her journey and negotiations between the lawyers had taken until late May and now, as she and Charles's slaves paddled towards the Brook Estate, it was the start of June.

Ely had insisted on accompanying her. The journey south had seemed interminable, especially since she was separated from him on the railroad. Ely had read the papers and talked to people constantly, trying to discover what was happening. As they journeyed south, Lincoln was assembling ten thousand troops in Washington and campaigning for every Unionist state to raise an army. They met many teenagers at the railway stations, waiting to travel north: lean, pimple-faced youths who had no concept of war but longed to hold a gun and wear a uniform. It made Emily despair; they seemed little more than children. The blockade of southern ports – the Anaconda Plan, as the newspapers called it – had started. The north would starve the south into submission by preventing them from selling their cotton. It was just as Charles had predicted.

Although Emily had now completed this journey twice, nothing could have made her grow accustomed to the lack of privacy, the dirt, the heat, the stench, the spitting and the appalling food. It had been a delight to reach Mrs Baker's establishment and be able to wash, eat well and sleep in a comfortable bed. But she had left Ely at the boarding house in spite of his protestations, for she suspected Charles would not react well if she turned up with her old abolitionist friend.

Now Israel starting to sing softly and the others joined in quietly. A sea eagle flew slowly overhead and the dark woods with their tangled creepers slid past. There was a faint trace of honeysuckle on the breeze. The beauty of the place was almost sinister: Emily began to feel a rising nausea. She had imagined, so many times, stepping off the boat and running towards her daughter, sweeping her up into her arms and spinning her around as the little girl laughed with delight. She pictured Clementine with long hair, almost to her shoulders, blonde and curly, wearing the white cotton dress Emily had sent her for her birthday. She could even smell her hot baby smell, feel the fine strands of hair against her cheek.

They passed St Annie's half hidden from view by the trees: acres of swamp with the white sentinels of egrets and, in the distance, the infirmary and the ruined hovels where the slaves lived.

'It be all right, missis,' said Frank suddenly.

She nodded at him. She had been afraid to ask him what had happened to him when he'd returned to St Simons.

They turned into Hamilton Creek and Emily looked across at the barren fields, the cotton bushes brittle and dark and broken. The slaves' houses were even more tumbledown than before, crumbling back to shells as if no one lived there any more. As they rowed between Sugar Island and St Simons, she saw Charles waiting for her at the end of the jetty, wearing a white shirt and cream riding breeches, his hat in his hand, shielding his eyes from the sun.

They moored and he strode forward and gave her his hand to help her out of the boat. He was leaner and more tanned than when she'd last seen him, the bones in his face more pronounced, his curly hair blonder, his eyes as pale as water.

'Where's Clementine?' she asked, looking round.

His face seemed to close in. 'She's not here.'

'Where is she?' asked Emily, running to the end of the jetty.

'She's safe,' he said.

'Where? I want to see her.'

'I thought it better that we had a talk first.' He strode past her towards the house.

'I want to know where she is.'

He clenched a muscle in his jaw. 'She's at Louisa's house. And that's where she'll stay until we're done talking.' He ran up the steps to the house and shouted for Bella.

Emily followed slowly. The house was a mess. Whiskey and claret bottles lay across the table, along with stained glasses, dirty plates and piles of papers and bills. Charles's boots, gun and various jackets and hats were scattered across the sofas and chairs. The place was filthy. There was the smell of decay, the faint odour of damp. She hesitated in the doorway, wiped away her tears and stepped over the threshold. At least she wouldn't have to confront Virginie and Sugar just yet.

'I had a dress made for you.' He nodded towards the stairs. Hanging from the banisters was a white gown. It had flounces over the bodice and frilled ruffles snaking down the skirt. There was something odd and yet familiar about it. Emily touched the soft fabric. It was a copy of the dress Louisa Hall had been wearing in the photograph of her and Charles when they were children. She snatched her hand away.

'Put it on,' he said, smiling.

'It's charming, Charles, but I have no maid with me.'

'Bella will help you.'

Bella was standing in the corner of the room. She looked frightened.

'I want to see you wearing it.'

'Please, Charles, can we talk first?'

He scowled. 'As you wish. Bring refreshments for Mrs

Brook,' he ordered Bella, sitting down and stretching his feet out across the table.

'How have you been?' she asked, with an effort.

He shrugged. 'The cotton is ruined. Not that there is any damn way to get it out of here with the blockade in place. The sugar harvest came to nothing. That damn bastard, Stewart, has run away to sign up and left me in the lurch. Not that you care. You picked a fine time to hightail it to the north, Emily, and leave me here to deal with all this on my own.'

'How's Clementine?'

He smiled, the tension in his face momentarily dissipating. 'She's enchanting. She's walking. She's got five teeth. She can say Pa.'

'But not Mamma.'

'No. She doesn't remember you, Emily.'

'Please, Charles, just let me see her.'

'Are you coming back?'

'Well, I thought we might discuss it.'

Bella came in and poured them their drinks.

'It's a simple question requiring a simple answer. Yes or no. Which is it to be, Emily?'

'No. But . . .'

He swung his legs round and kicked one of the chairs, sending it clattering across the room.

'I thought we might talk about Clementine. She needs her mother.'

'She's doing well. Virginie looks after her and Louisa helps when she can.'

'That woman has as much maternal instinct as a viper,' Emily said tersely.

Charles laughed. 'I can't say you've got much more yourself, my dear.'

'I want my daughter back. It's only right and natural she should be with her mother. We won't speak of divorce, Charles, if that's what you want, but at least let me have Clementine with me.'

'So you thought you'd let your little abolitionist friends try to frighten me into giving up my child by threatening to publish your damn pamphlet?'

'If I had Clementine, of course I wouldn't publish. I give you my word.'

'The problem is, Emily, I no longer believe you,' said Charles. 'You've betrayed me, more times than I care to count. So, no, I don't believe you wouldn't publish your pamphlet as soon as you got what you wished for.'

'We could have a contract,' said Emily desperately, 'you could arrange it with your lawyer.'

Charles snorted. 'No. But I will say this. If you don't publish for six months, then we can speak again.'

'Six months?'

'I knew you wanted to get that thing out to incite the northern masses.'

'What I was trying to say was, another six months until you'll even speak to me about Clementine?'

'Exactly.'

'And can I see her in the meantime?'

'No.'

'Charles . . .'

'This is the one time you won't get what you want, Emily. Let this be a lesson to you. There are always consequences for your actions and this time you've got to take responsibility for what you've done. Since you don't want to stay with me as my wife, I suggest you leave right now. If you're quick you'll catch the last steamer.'

'The last steamer?'

'Yes. She stops running tonight. Once you leave here you'll never be able to return to the island – unless I choose to send a boat for you.'

She stood up slowly as if she were old and followed him out of the house. A crowd of men and women were standing waiting for her: Bella and June, Dianna, Psyche, Edward and Molly, Charlotte, Jane, Sophy, Abraham and Joshua and numerous women whose faces she recognized and ailments she remembered. They stood silently and as she walked past, weeping, they touched her gently.

'Get back to work,' said Charles roughly.

The slaves slowly dispersed; only Israel and Frank remained.

'Charles, may I buy Frank from you?' Emily asked.

'You? Become a slave-owner? Now that would be a turn-up for your abolitionist friends.' He laughed shortly. 'The problem is, Emily, you can't buy him because you haven't got any money. If you had, it would be mine. When I married you I thought you were smart but you've never seemed to grasp that one simple little fact.'

She looked up at Charles, whose face was shadowed by his hat.

'You don't want a dress but you do want a damned nigger.' He suddenly pushed Frank towards her. 'Have him. He's my parting gift to you. But I can't spare Israel or a boat. If you want to catch that steamer, I suggest you walk fast.'

'Walk?' said Emily.

Charles turned on his heel and strode away.

Emily stood for a moment looking at his retreating back.

'It's miles to the other end of the island,' she said quietly, almost to herself.

Frank squinted at the sun. 'We best go, missis.'

She nodded slowly, without moving, and then started to walk along the dirt track that led through the Brook plantation, Frank following behind. It was mid morning but already hot. Emily loosened the lace collar of her dress and tipped the brim of her hat forward to shade her face. Ochre-red earth quickly powdered her boots and the skirt of her dress and she felt sweat trickle down her back between her shoulder blades.

Preoccupied with thoughts of Clementine, Emily barely took in her surroundings. It was only when they were on the road running down the centre of St Simons that she began to notice the island felt different. She looked around. It was the emptiness, the silence, that struck her first. On either side of her were fields full of rice but there were no slaves tending it. The young rice quivered and rippled in a faint breeze. The crop was riven with weeds, morning glory blooming in glorious profusion. In some fields the rice stood almost up to the tips of its leaves in fetid water, a cracked glaze of putrification on the surface; in others, the stems were already withering and turning yellow, their roots in fissured mud. Many of the great trees that lined the road had been felled, leaving raw stumps oozing rust-red resin, and on the horizon were columns of smoke and the red heat haze of fires. They hadn't passed a single person.

Emily began to feel uneasy. She was tired, hungry and thirsty. Her tongue felt as if it were swollen and her mouth was dry. She wished she'd eaten the cookies Bella had brought. It was early afternoon by the time they reached the middle of the island and that was when they first heard the drums. The sound was faint at first but grew in strength and was unlike anything Emily had heard before. The drums beat with a lethargic intensity, vibrating in her ribcage, savage and atavistic, a single refrain repeated.

'What is that, Frank?' she asked.

He shrugged but he looked frightened. His face was dark with sweat. Without looking at her he increased his pace slightly so that they were walking side by side.

As they neared the Taylor plantation, the acrid smell of smoke grew and glowing embers and flakes of soot wafted towards them. One of the many absentee landlords, the Taylors' large house stood near the road and although empty since Emily had been on St Simons, it had always looked immaculate with freshly painted clapperboard and a clipped lawn, a giant magnolia partly shading it. Now she saw with dismay that the house had been almost burned to the ground. The charred remains glowed dully and smoke and ash blew in their faces as they walked past. A partially destroyed rocking-horse, weeping singed hair-stuffing and a single shoe lay among the white embers. The magnolia had been hacked down and the lawn was covered with leaves and branches. The hibiscus hedge had withered to blackened twigs in the heat; only one blood-red flower remained at the far end with a corolla of green leaves, like a wreath, surrounding it.

The smoke made her cough and her eyes water. They walked past as fast as possible. A little further down the road a group of Negroes were sitting round a fire in an old oil drum. There were empty whiskey bottles lying in the road. One man lay sprawled in the dust, his hat partially over his head, the tattered remnants of his shirt open to reveal grizzled white hair matted over his chest. They gave the men a wide berth. One took a swig from the bottle he was holding and held out his arm to detain them.

'Where you gone to?'

'Just walking her to the Drummonds', catch the steamer,' said Frank.

'You bout the last white woman on this island,' said the man, gazing at Emily.

He looked as if he were in his twenties, hard and muscled. His eyes were bloodshot and he fixed her with a malevolent glare. She could smell the alcohol on his breath.

'Mrs Hall and Mrs Drummond are here too.' She felt frightened. This was the first time a Negro had been anything other than subservient towards her.

'Not for much longer,' he said. 'Soon gone be no white people on this island.'

'Where's your overseer?' she asked sharply.

He laughed, revealing tobacco-stained teeth. Slowly a couple of men sitting on the ground on either side of him rose to their feet. 'He gone fight in the war. Left us folks here.' He waved with his bottle in the general direction of the ruined plantation house. 'This island gone belong to we people.' Now he took a step towards her. 'Seem mighty keen to leave this place,' he said softly, leaning closer.

She held herself very still, forcing herself not to flinch.

'I am,' she said firmly. 'I never wanted to come here.'

'You all the same, you white folks,' he said, looking away and taking another swig from the bottle. 'Don't want to live here, don't want to work. But you do want what we get for you.' He rubbed his index finger and thumb together and his skin rustled dryly. He swayed slightly. 'You know what gone happen now?'

Emily stared at him, trying to slow her breathing.

'The army gone come here from the north. They gone free us. Soon we all gone be free men.'

'For your sake, I hope that is true,' said Emily, and turned and started to walk away from them. Slowly, almost reluctantly, the men stood aside and let her pass.

'You don't have to go with her. Stay with us. Have a drink,' called one of them after Frank.

The two of them kept walking as fast as they could. Emily was breathing rapidly and shallowly. In the distance the drumming continued, a monotonous and menacing beat. She could hear chanting and singing too, not the sad and gentle lullabies the slaves sang as they worked, but something altogether harsher and fiercer.

It was early evening by the time they reached the Drummond Estate and Emily was light-headed from lack of food and water. Her legs ached and her feet were tender. They crossed the lawns towards the avenue of live oaks. The grass was longer and more unkempt than normal. There was an aura of decay about the place. The panes in the glasshouse had been smashed and the roses in Ann Drummond's beautiful garden had collapsed under the weight of the blooms, scattering petals across the paths. Chickens stalked and scratched their way through the beds. It was so quiet Emily wondered if the Drummonds were even at home.

When she knocked on the front door a maid led her into the drawing room where the Drummonds received her.

'My dear,' said Mrs Drummond as the couple rose stiffly to their feet, 'how kind of you to call.'

Her voice faded as she took in Emily's dishevelled, dirty appearance. For the first time since Emily had met her Mrs Drummond looked her age. Lines were etched more deeply around her eyes and she had a haggard air. The brilliance of her bright eyes had dimmed. Mr Drummond also had an unhealthy pallor and his features were sharper than ever, his thin lips white. They tried to be their usual hospitable selves: the maid brought tea but Emily could smell that the milk had turned and the cornbread was stale.

'Has there been any alteration in your relationship with Mr Brook?' asked Mrs Drummond.

Emily burst into tears. In between sobs she explained what had happened. Mrs Drummond shook her head sadly and said how utterly shocked she was that Charles had made her walk from one end of the island to the other.

'He thinks the war will have blown over within six months and then your pamphlet will be irrelevant,' said Mr Drummond.

'Do you think that's true?'

'No, I certainly don't.'

'We fear for our lives,' said Mrs Drummond quietly. 'There are almost four thousand of them and so few of us. We are planning to travel north. Joel Hall is leaving to fight soon.' She hesitated. After a moment she continued with difficulty. 'We found a woman lying outside the hall a few days ago. One of Mrs Hall's involuntary servants. We took her in and cared for her but we'll have to leave her behind.'

'She was in a terrible state. Never seen anything like it,' said Mr Drummond grimly.

Emily looked from one to the other in confusion.

'She'd been beaten,' said Mrs Drummond gently, 'so badly we didn't think she would live. She survived but she lost her baby.'

'Which was the point of the beating,' said Mr Drummond.

'What do you mean?' asked Emily slowly.

'The girl said that Mr Hall had forced her. When Mrs Hall found out, the girl was eight months gone. She whipped the child herself. I doubt Mrs Hall will be able to remain on the plantation on her own.'

For a few moments no one said anything.

Eventually Mrs Drummond said tiredly, 'We need to finish packing. We're leaving on the last steamer too.'

As the night drew in, the three of them waited by the jetty for the steamer. Frank, the Drummonds' maid and two of their slaves stood a little further back with the luggage. Cicadas and frogs chorused and in the distance, carried on the breeze, came the sound of the endless drumming and chanting.

Eventually they heard the low, guttural note of the ship's horn.

'Thank goodness,' said Mrs Drummond, her hand nervously at her throat.

A few minutes later they saw the lights flickering through tree branches as the boat slowly approached. Once they'd boarded, the Drummonds immediately retired to the salon but Emily remained on deck as the steamer cumbrously turned around. She watched the flicker of lights and the red haze from myriad fires blotting the sky above St Simons as they headed back to Savannah.

The port was curiously silent, boats packed together alongside the quay. Seagulls perched on the rigging and a few fishing boats off-loaded creels of crab and lobster. A couple of men were painting their boat; an old man crouched over a net, mending the holes. It was the following morning and she and Ely were walking through town.

'What will you do?' asked Ely.

'I don't know. I thought I would stay here. Perhaps Charles will change his mind. Maybe he'll let me see Clementine. I feel if I go north I may never set eyes on her again. I'm sorry, Ely, I can't publish the pamphlet.'

'You can't stay here,' said Ely, running his hand through his hair distractedly. 'It's not safe.'

'Look at it.' Emily gestured around her. 'It doesn't appear so very different to me.'

There was no sign of fighting nor even of soldiers. Savannah was eerily quiet with a distinct absence of men. The larger boats that would have carried cargoes of cotton, rice and sugar were languishing idly in the dock. It was as if the rumour of war had been enough to frighten the plantation owners into leaving their plantations and at the same time the rumour had been enough to embolden the enslaved.

'It's a powder keg,' said Ely. 'It might be safe now but it won't remain so. What if we are trapped here? Unable to return to the north.'

'I wasn't expecting you to stay.'

'I'm not leaving you,' he said firmly.

'Then let us wait and decide. Charles may have changed his mind by then,' she said desperately. 'Anything could happen – there might not even be any fighting. It could all end peacefully.'

Ely was about to speak but thought better of it. 'I'll send a telegram to my sister,' he said, 'and perhaps I should see about hiring us some horses.' He looked grim.

*

For the next few weeks Ely worked on his abolitionist literature and Emily rewrote her diary, in case a more substantial
booklet than her pamphlet should ever be needed, and
continued her lessons with Frank. They started to read
Uncle Tom's Cabin, which made them both cry. Ely visited
Charles's lawyer to try to find out news – in this he was
unsuccessful, for Charles had not communicated with his
lawyer in some time – but he did procure the paperwork to
show that Frank was now legally owned by Emily. Ely read
the newspapers, his brow furrowed, and corresponded
almost daily with his father and by that fact alone she knew
it would not end well. And sometimes there were gangs of
slaves hanging round Savannah. They were not doing anything, simply sitting and watching, but they had not been
there before and as Emily walked past them she felt the first
stirrings of fear.

And then one day in July soldiers started to arrive. They
were a haphazard bunch of men, some in grey, some in
navy, others in homespun butternut-coloured coats, with
a ramshackle assortment of weaponry. They gathered on
street corners and in bars, drinking and smoking. She and
Ely were sitting on the veranda. Ely was, as usual, reading
the newspaper and she was watching the men parade
through the town, wondering how long it would be before
they started to kill the Negroes they were harassing. She felt
her throat tighten and her palms grow slick. Ely looked
from his father's letter to the newspaper and back again
and then set both aside.

'Emily,' he said, and cleared his throat.

She looked into his kind blue eyes and thought, This is where it all ends, this is where I have to decide to abandon my child.

'Emily,' he began again. 'The war has begun in earnest. There has been a battle, just outside Washington. The Confederates won. The Unionists had to retreat. And Lincoln, to stop any more states seceding and joining the Confederacy, has issued a resolution. He says the war is not about slavery. It is about upholding the Union and preventing its dissolution. Emily, I've forborne from asking you about your pamphlet because I know how much is at stake if you publish it and what you stand to lose, but, Emily, please, this is our last chance. If we do not strike a blow now then the war will be in vain. Lives will be lost, blood will be shed and yet no Negro will walk free at the end of it. You yourself have seen with your own eyes the misery and degradation of slavery. I don't have to tell you, you have seen worse things than I can imagine. We must publish. There will be more fighting and it will spread south. And even if it does not, the two of us, northerners in a southern town, will attract attention of the worst kind. Please come home with me before it is too late. My father has promised to hire a lawyer to fight for custody of Clementine and is prepared to do and pay whatever it takes.'

'As long as I publish the pamphlet,' she said.

Ely merely bowed his head. Emily had wondered how long it would take before he could no longer put the happiness of one little girl above the plight of a million men and women born into servitude.

305

'I should like a little time alone,' she said.

Ely stood and looked at her as if he had more to say, as if he wanted to reach out towards her, but he merely nodded and went indoors. Emily remained sitting at the table in front of the dregs of her cold coffee, pork fat congealed on her plate, a trail of crumbs across the tablecloth, and felt numb.

Two days later she was sitting on the veranda in the late afternoon with Caroline Baker and Ely, drinking a final farewell glass of Madeira, their luggage packed, waiting to board the night train, when she saw a strange-looking person running up the high street. He was wearing almost nothing, a tattered pair of trousers only, and no shoes. He was pale, the colour of dried mud, and his hair was wild and blond. Frank, who was on the street below them, perched on their trunks, jumped down and took a step forward and Emily rose.

'It's Caesar,' she said. 'Thank God.' Charles had sent a message at last. She felt as if her insides might dissolve into liquid. She ran round the side of the house and down the front steps and out into the street.

Caesar was breathing so hard he could barely speak.

'What does Charles say?'

Caesar shook his head.

Emily grabbed his scrawny arms and shook him. 'Charles sent you with a message. What did he say?'

Caesar shook his head again. 'It Virginie. She send me.' He rested his hands on his knees and bent double, dragging breath into his lungs. 'She make me row all the way here from the island. She say I must be quick.'

'What happened, brother?' said Frank quietly.

Caesar cut him a look out of the corner of his eyes and said to Emily, 'Virginie says you got to come now. Mr Brook, she expect him to die.'

'Die? What's happened?'

'He shot. He bleed to death. She say you must come now.'

Chapter 11

August 1861

Emily finally persuaded Ely to catch the train and take her pamphlet to be published as soon as possible. Once she had seen Charles, she would travel north and meet up with him, she promised.

'I'll have Frank with me. Please don't be anxious,' she'd said.

She could see that he had given in only reluctantly. Finally he'd said, 'Take this,' and handed her a Colt revolver.

'I don't need a gun,' she'd exclaimed, holding her hands away from it, as if it were tainted.

'Even if you're safe on St Simons, you have a long journey ahead of you,' he'd said.

And now as she sat in the boat, her palms resting on the gun in her purse, which lay across her lap, she wondered at Ely carrying such a weapon. She saw now that all the way from Cape Cod to St Simons, he had been protecting her.

It was a clear night and Caesar and the other slave,

Joseph, were able to navigate by the stars. The waves were as black as obsidian, stellar light sliding along their sharp edges. A purple bruise marked where the sun had set and then the whole sky deepened to the colour of a weighty burgundy. Emily could extract no further information from Caesar about Charles.

'Why did Virginie send you?' she asked him.

He shrugged. 'She say no one else she can trust.'

He curled up in the bottom of the boat, a thin tangle of arms and legs, and slept. Frank took over rowing. As the boat slipped through the water, Emily turned over the possible events in her mind. Why had Charles been shot? Would he live? She wondered whether he'd had a hunting accident.

It was late when they arrived at St Simons. Emily climbed stiffly out of the boat. She had still not grown accustomed to the truncated end of the island; one miserable orange tree left at the jagged edge of the bank. The house was black and silent, the only sound the wind whispering through the cabbage palms. Shells, the remnants of the driveway, grated against one another beneath her feet as she walked up to Brook House. She went inside. The sitting room smelled of whiskey and the sour tang of sweat. She slowly climbed the stairs. When she reached the room that had been hers and Charles's she hesitated. Then the door swung open to reveal Virginie, holding an oil lamp, Emily's white shawl wrapped around her. She was tall and thin and beautiful, her large eyes glowing, the soft light gliding over the fluid planes of her cheekbones and highlighting the gold gleam of her skin. She said nothing, only stood aside to allow Emily into the room.

Virginie had made up a cot for herself on the floor next to the large, dark rosewood bed. There was no sign of the baby. Emily bent over Charles. His face was deathly white and there was a rattle as he breathed.

'What happened?' she asked Virginie.

Virginie put the lamp on the bedside table. 'Mr Hall ask him to fight a duel. It very early in the morning. Mr Hall shoot him in the stomach.'

'What was the argument over?'

'Mrs Hall,' said Virginie with contempt.

'Has the doctor been?'

'Yes. He say he come back in the morning.'

'How bad is it?'

'Bad. I leave you with him now,' said Virginie.

'Wait,' said Emily. 'Thank you for sending Caesar to find me.'

Virginie nodded and silently stepped back into the shadows on the landing.

Emily carefully pulled back the sheet and Charles moaned. Virginie had packed the wound with Spanish moss and wrapped torn flannel strips around him but the bandages were sodden with fresh blood, dried blood cracked and flaking at the edges. How had it come to this, she wondered, Charles and Joel Hall with their pistols drawn at dawn? She imagined them standing shivering in the early morning mist, their guns rattling, cold and greasy in their palms, turning on their heel in the mud to line each other up in their sights. She thought of the picture in Mr Stewart's house, in that incongruous room with the crumpled silk sheet and the scent of perfume lingering in the air. Was this the penalty for a lifetime of betrayal, for a lingering love affair with a childhood sweetheart? Or merely boiling rage over a recent adultery, fuelled by gambling debts and brandy? How ignoble, to shoot a man in the stomach; how much worse to die a death calibrated in drops of blood.

Charles suddenly gripped her hand hard and half turned his head. His lips were dark, as if stained with wine. He tried to speak.

'I've something to tell you,' he said hoarsely.

She bent forward, struggling to hear him, her heart sinking. He was going to say that this was her fault. That she had driven him to seek solace with Louisa. That she must accept responsibility.

He coughed and groaned in pain and swallowed with difficulty. He said, 'I see you.'

'Yes, Charles, I'm here, with you.'

'I see you all the time,' he whispered. 'Sometimes I catch a glimpse of you through the reeds, fishing in your canoe, smiling when you catch a fish. I come across you on horseback in the woods, I see you standing on the beach looking out to sea. Since you left I still see you everywhere, on the stairs, on the veranda. I'm plagued by you. I loved you so much, Emily. I first fell in love with you when I saw you ride. I loved your passion. And I wanted to see you here. In my home, on my land, where I grew up.'

She knelt by his side and felt sharp splinters of wood dig into her knees. Her eyes filled with tears.

'I have always loved you,' he murmured. 'I'm sorry I never told you or showed you how much I cared. I thought if I kept Clementine, you would come back to me. She was all I had, all I had to try to make you change your mind.'

'And yet you and Louisa . . .'

'Louisa is nothing to me. I was so angry with you. You were so stubborn. I couldn't understand why you wouldn't behave like a wife, my wife, should.'

He coughed and moaned again in agony.

'Hush, you shouldn't be talking,' she said.

She wiped her eyes and poured him a glass of water. She sat on the edge of the bed and he winced. She supported his head and helped him sip a little.

'I thought,' he said, 'that it would teach you a lesson. You would realize that I was your husband. You would be proud of me. You would obey me. But, Emily, I've been so lonely since you left. I miss you. I miss you every day, more than I can say.'

He closed his eyes.

'Charles,' she said in alarm.

He squeezed her hand weakly. She continued to hold his hand although it lay slack in hers. He didn't speak again.

As the pale light of morning filtered through the shutters, Emily saw that he had gone. She let go of his hand and wiped her face. Quietly she pushed open the door of Clementine's room and looked down at her baby girl. She was still asleep, breathing fast and deep like a small animal might. She rested her cheek against her daughter's cheek, breathing in her smell, feeling her soft exquisite skin. She waited and watched until, as the sun rose and a cock started to crow outside the house, Clementine opened her pale grey eyes.

Emily picked her daughter up, still half asleep, and wrapped her in her blanket, savouring her warmth and unfamiliar weight. Emily felt like a shell, hollowed of all emotion, but in spite of this a curious sense of peace stole over her as she held her daughter in her arms. This was what life was truly about, she realized. All else – fighting for an end to slavery, fighting for equality within a marriage, fighting for her own independence – all that was as nothing compared to the life of this little girl. She threw open one of the shutters. A huge crowd of slaves had gathered around the house. They stood silently, their feet wet with dew, their heads bowed. Those who had hats held them in their hands.

Emily thought about what she had to do: send a message to Dr Walker and also to Christ Church so that they could prepare the grave – although now that she thought about it, the preacher was likely to have left. Edward should start making the coffin. She thought she might cry again but she felt entirely drained of tears. She wished that Ely was with her to give her some moral support. Clementine was walking about the room on sturdy little legs, chewing on a piece of toast. Her hair was longer, fine and wispy with little curls, and she had started talking.

Virginie was upstairs washing Charles's body. She had

taken Sugar with her, almost as if she didn't want to leave the child in Emily's presence. Emily had only glimpsed the baby. Virginie, she noticed, had moved into what had been Emily's room with her child. It made sense, she supposed, but it still made her feel angry. The slaves had melted away, where she did not know, for why work when their master was dead and the overseer had joined the army? They had left a row of candles burning on the veranda though, which emitted the delicate scent of eucalyptus and cloves.

She suddenly understood that she could leave. With her daughter. It was so long since she'd seen Clementine, the child couldn't possibly remember her, and yet she was happy to be held by her mother and stay with her while her nurse was out of the room. Perhaps she had an infant's memory of her mother's touch, her smell, the sound of her voice. And the slaves, she thought, she could free them all.

She was about to call Virginie and tell her to pack some clothes for Clementine when the maid appeared. She was carrying Sugar, and seeing her in Virginie's arms made Emily draw breath. The child was so like him, the shape of her sharp jaw mirroring his. She had dark, almost black hair and those same astonishing grey eyes.

'Someone come here,' said Virginie.

Emily picked up Clementine and the two of them walked out on to the veranda. The faint heat from the candles warped the air above them. Plumes of dust rose from the horse's hooves as it cantered towards them, stumbling to a halt before the house. She recognized the horse first – it was

Oak – with his wild, blue, brown and yellow eyes and his black and white patchwork coat, matted with sweat and dirt. The rider jumped down. He was lean save for a thick paunch. He removed his hat and walked over to them. It was Emmanuel.

'Where's my brother?' he said without any formalities, his face set in a grim frown.

Emily said nothing, only stared at him.

'He upstairs,' said Virginie. 'He gone.'

'Mr Brook,' said Emily finally and cleared her throat. Clementine started to wriggle and fuss but she gripped the little girl hard.

'Mrs Brook,' he replied with cold formality.

He walked past them and upstairs. They waited on the veranda for him to return. Emily put Clementine down and gave her a wooden toy horse to play with. Out of the corner of her eye, Emily saw Frank and Caesar, crouched at the corner of the house, waiting. She hadn't spoken to either of them, or the boy, Joseph, since they'd arrived.

She heard the creak of Emmanuel's footsteps in the bedroom and then his heavy tread as he came downstairs. He sat on one of the chairs and put his hat back on.

Emmanuel coughed and said, 'My condolences, Mrs Brook.'

'And mine to you,' she said quietly.

'Mrs Hall sent me a telegram to say there would be a duel. I came as quick as I could. Not fast enough, I see.' He looked out towards Sugar Island and a muscle clenched in his jaw.

Emily felt as if she were sitting with Charles. A cold chill swept through her.

'I hold you responsible,' he said bitterly, turning back to her.

Emily looked up, startled. Something instinctively made her reach behind her and touch Clementine's solid little body, to check she was still there.

'You were no good to him when you were here, then you left him. No wonder he turned to another man's wife. And that is the consequence.' He jerked his thumb upwards in the direction of the bedroom.

'How ridiculous,' she managed to say eventually.

He held up his hand. 'I've got more to say so it would pay to listen. My brother and I own this plantation jointly. Now that he's left us, I own it in its entirety. Everything.' He waved his hand around expansively. 'This house, those fields yonder, Sugar Island, the cotton gin, the sugar mill, every goddamn buck, woman and child on this estate.' He glanced at Virginie and then back to Emily. 'You're welcome to cast a look at the will if you wish to.'

She thought of her vision. Of seven hundred slaves walking free.

'Not very hospitable, are you?' he said. 'I've ridden all this way and you ain't even offered me a drink. Since it's all mine now I shall do as I please. You' – he nodded at Virginie – 'go fetch me some water and a glass of whiskey.'

Virginie got up and brushed past him.

'There's one more thing,' said Emmanuel, leaning a little closer to her. 'When I said everything that Charles owned I own, I do mean everything. That includes the child.' He nodded towards Clementine.

'No,' burst out Emily.

'The last time I checked with our lawyer, he said that Charles has custody of the little girl. I have the documents with me to prove it.'

'He changed his mind,' said Emily quickly. 'He apologized for keeping me from her.'

'I ain't going to contradict you but he was dying. He didn't make a new will, did he?' said Emmanuel.

There was a sudden movement and Oak snorted and wheeled round. They both looked up. Virginie was on Oak's back, clasping Sugar to her chest. She dug her heels into his side and the horse leapt into a canter. Where did she learn to ride? wondered Emily. And then it dawned on her, with some amazement: she's running away. And she's leaving me here with this monster.

'God damn it,' shouted Emmanuel and jumped to his feet. He pulled out a gun and aimed it at the girl's back.

Emily screamed and knocked him off balance but she wasn't fast enough. He fired and Virginie fell heavily from the horse and lay on her side. Oak, trailing stirrups and reins, continued to gallop down the road. For what felt like a long moment no one did or said anything. Then Clementine started to cry and Emily snatched her into her arms. Frank and Caesar burst from the side of the house and ran towards the fallen girl. Virginie tried to sit up. One arm was drenched in blood and dangled lifelessly at her side. Emmanuel ran to the end of the veranda and jumped down all the steps at once and followed the two boys. Emily walked towards them all slowly, as if in a dream, clutching her child and her purse, the gun cold and solid through the fabric.

When Emmanuel reached Virginie, he grabbed her by the hair and swung her head round to face him. 'First thing I'm going to do as the new owner is flog you within an inch of your life for taking my horse and trying to run away, you nigger bitch. Now get up.'

He started to drag her by the hair back towards the house. Virginie kept tight hold of her screaming baby with one hand. Her face had taken on the texture of chalk but she didn't utter a sound. Emily saw the fear in Frank's face, his fists clenched at his sides. She thought Caesar had gone to help Virginie too but now she saw that had not been his intention.

Emmanuel turned to the boy. 'Get me a whip,' he shouted.

Caesar, though he was thin, had grown tall in the past year. He was the same height as Emmanuel and when he looked into his grey eyes, with eyes that were exactly the same shade, he stood level with his father. His skin colour, his belief that he should be treated differently, his general air of superiority, instantly made sense. What he wanted, she realized, was recognition.

'No,' he said.

There was silence. Emmanuel dropped Virginie. He looked dumbfounded. No slave had ever spoken back to him. No slave had ever refused an order. No slave had ever looked into his eyes as if he were an equal. Caesar seemed equally stunned. His mouth started to form a new word. Perhaps it would have been 'Father'. Emmanuel pulled out a large hunting knife. Caesar stood looking at him, his expression bewildered. Emmanuel pressed the knife against the boy's neck and, drawing back his arm, he slit the boy's throat. For one moment, comprehension flickered in the boy's eyes. The wound suddenly opened and Caesar's expression died. He folded, almost in two, and his knees crumpled. Slowly, almost delicately, he collapsed on the ground, and his blood pulsed over the white shells.

In the turmoil, Emily had dropped her purse and the revolver fell out. Before she could react, Frank ran over to her and grabbed the gun.

Emily shouted, 'No,' but it was too late.

Emmanuel turned, still holding the knife, the blade dripping blood. He moved to draw his own gun but he was too slow. The bullets shook him as if he were a man of air, a man of feathers, and when their force was spent he buckled and fell and lay alongside his son.

No one spoke. A mockingbird gave an alarm call. There was the faint smell of sulphur from the gunpowder. Emily put Clementine down and gently took the gun from Frank and replaced it in her torn purse. She asked Frank to hold Clementine and then she called for Bella and June. Virginie was half unconscious with pain but she would not let go of Sugar. The bullet had shattered her arm and she was bleeding profusely. Emily wiped the blood from Sugar and her mother with the end of her skirt. Bella and June ran to fetch moss from the nearest oak and pressed it into the wound and tied a bandage tightly around her arm.

'What we do now, missis?' asked Bella miserably.

The three of them looked at Virginie. Frank stood next to them, unconsciously rocking Clem. It was hard to think with Sugar crying so loudly. There wasn't anywhere, she thought, she could take a slave who had been shot trying to run away and another who had murdered a white man. Slowly slaves emerged from the trees surrounding the house and gathered around Caesar's body. They began to sing softly and quietly, their voices mingling with the waves lapping at the ruined shore.

'Let's take her inside,' said Emily at last, 'and wait for Dr Walker.'

Four men carried Virginie into the house and laid her on the sofa. She groaned when they picked her up and set her down but otherwise made no sound. June carefully prised the child from her mother and held her while Bella bathed Virginie's face with cold water. She was shivering feverishly.

The sound of hundreds of men, women and children singing was mesmerizing. Clementine and Sugar both stopped crying.

'Missis, what gone to happen to we?' asked Bella.

'I don't know,' said Emily, 'I don't know who owns you now.'

'You say we ought to be free,' said June quietly. 'Once, I hear you say them words.'

'Yes,' said Emily, 'that's right. That's what I believe.'

'I'm free,' said Frank suddenly. 'Mrs Brook made me free.'

'Why you still here?' said Bella sullenly.

'I chose to come here,' he said with quiet dignity.

When Dr Walker finally arrived, it was early afternoon and Virginie was dead.

'What happened?' he asked.

'She stole my gun and my horse and tried to run away. Mr Emmanuel Brook shot her in the arm but she fired back and killed him.'

'I am deeply sorry,' said Dr Walker. 'To lose your husband and your brother-in-law on the same day . . .' He passed his hand over his brow. His face was drawn, his complexion pallid. 'It was difficult to get here any earlier . . . I'm sure you can imagine.' He paused awkwardly and then said, 'I found your horse though. He was by the Drummonds' plantation at the other end of the island. I brought him back with me.'

'Thank you, Dr Walker. Thank you for coming.'

He nodded and poured them both a large glass of brandy.

'It's not safe to stay here any longer, Mrs Brook,' he said. 'You are the only white woman on the island. The steamer, as you know, has stopped operating.'

She smiled. 'Thank you for your concern, but I am safer here than almost anywhere else I could be.'

The doctor was rowed away by his slaves in the late afternoon. Emily, with Frank, who was still carrying

Clementine, stood on the end of the jetty and watched him leave. She waited until she could not see him any more and then she turned to Edward who was standing on the shore.

'You once asked me if I would like to buy your canoe.'

He nodded.

'You can have my horse, Oak, in exchange.'

Edward bowed his head. 'Thank you, Mrs Brook,' he said quietly. 'I get something for you too,' he added. He put his hand in his pocket and drew out a tiny, wooden canoe. It was smooth and slim and perfectly carved. It was made of pine and the wood had darkened with time to the colour of coffee. 'Frank make it for me when he just a small child. I carry it with me every day,' he said and he placed the miniature canoe in the palm of Emily's hand.

Later that afternoon Emily curled up on the sofa with Clementine sleeping on her lap and watched June wash Virginie's body. She was sobbing and occasionally stopped to wipe away her tears on the back of one hand. Virginie's skin was already stiff and waxen. As Virginie's beauty slipped away like some rare and scented oil, Emily was all at once conscious that in front of her lay the body of a vulnerable young woman, practically a girl, who had worked tirelessly in a white household. She knew nothing about Virginie, how long she had lived here, where she had come from, who her family were, how she had learned to ride, what Charles had forced her to do. Emily felt utterly ashamed.

Sugar started to wail and Emily automatically eased Clementine from her lap and went to pick up the child and soothe her. She held the baby's warm, soft body in her arms, her chubby limbs meltingly soft; she smelled of wood smoke and milk and cornbread. Virginie had never left her alone in Emily's presence. Yet now, as she rocked Sugar, she knew she could not leave the baby here.

Some of the slaves dug four graves side by side in their cemetery. Emily stood and watched and saw how first the water seeped and then flowed freely into the clay-sodden pits. In the end, Emily saw no reason why Charles should be buried any differently than his slaves. As it grew dusk, they carried the bodies, wrapped in white sheets, over to the graveyard and laid them on the rough, rush-infested grass. Edward led the service, reading openly from his Bible.

'We brought nothing into the world, and we take nothing out. The Lord gave, and the Lord has taken away; blessed be the name of the Lord,' he said.

They slid Caesar, Virginie, Emmanuel and Charles into their watery graves and the men heaped clay and sand over them. It was only when the last spadeful obscured the white shroud covering Charles's face that the enormity of what had happened hit her.

'We commit the bodies of Caesar, Virginie, Emmanuel and Charles Brook to the ground; earth to earth, ashes to ashes, dust to dust; in the sure and certain hope of the Resurrection to eternal life,' said Edward in his soft, sonorous voice.

They planted a small wooden cross at the head of each

grave and Emily lit four candles and scattered wild rose petals across the raw earth.

Edward prayed:

> *Our days are like the grass;*
> *we flourish like a flower of the field;*
> *when the wind goes over it, it is gone*
> *and its place will know it no more.*
> *But the merciful goodness of the Lord endures*
> *for ever and ever toward those that fear him*
> *and his righteousness upon their children's children.*

And then they sang:

> *Free at last, free at last,*
> *I thank God I'm free at last,*
> *Free at last, free at last,*
> *I thank God I'm free at last.*

Epilogue

November 1861

*H*er mouth was dry and she had a familiar sick feeling in the pit of her stomach. She'd been unable to eat a bite of the lobster or drink the champagne. She could smell the boards, pine sap popping from the wood, dust in the heavy drapes and molten candle wax. Her dress felt cool; as she moved, the satin flowed over her skin. It was white and cut to expose her shoulders, with a train of red roses cascading from the bodice to the floor and she wore roses in her hair. What was different though, was that this time there were no other actors and the odour from the audience was not of oranges and oil lamps but the distracting and delicious aroma of roast goose.

It was Thanksgiving and the Quaker Society was hosting a dinner for the elite of Boston to raise money for wounded soldiers and their families. Emily was the star attraction in between the lobster first course and the main. She'd had several speaking engagements based on the success of her pamphlet but this was the most prestigious. She was planning to reveal extracts from her new diary, which was about to be serialized in the *New York Times*. The organizers had advised her to keep it short.

Ely was fiddling with his cravat. She rearranged it for him.

'I used to do this for my father,' she said, 'and fasten his cufflinks – but you appear to be more dextrous,' she added, inspecting his wrists.

She watched Ely from the wings. She had come to recognize that he was quite remarkable. Studious, quiet and academic, he was luminous with passion when he spoke of the rights of all men to equality. Ely reminded the audience of Emily's illustrious career as an actress and then described her pamphlet, based on her unique, first-hand experiences living on a cotton and sugar plantation in the deep south. The pamphlet, he said, had shown the American people that this was not merely a war about the union of American states, it was a war to safeguard freedom, the freedom of all peoples no matter what their colour or culture in this great continent. It was a war to prevent wealthy southern landowners from continuing to enslave men, women and children stolen from Africa and forced to work in utter degradation against their will. He said that today the pamphlet was about to be published in England and he hoped that the working men and women of that land would rise up in revolt against slavery and would not join in the war on the side of the southern slave-owning states. Today though, he said, the reading would not be from the pamphlet but from an intimate diary that Miss Harris had kept while she was living on the plantation and was shortly to be published. The diary described scenes that would be of a distressing nature but were a record of daily life among slaves such as had not been witnessed or detailed before.

'Miss Emily Harris,' he said.

Emily walked on to the stage to tumultuous applause and bowed to her audience. Ely smiled and stepped down to join the rest of the Crawfords at a table in front of her. Emily opened her book and read.

'As I skirted one of these thickets, I stood still to admire the beauty of the shrubbery. Every shade of green, every variety of form, every degree of varnish, and all in full leaf and beauty in the very depth of winter. The stunted, dark-coloured oak, the magnolia bay, which grows to a very great size, the wild myrtle, a beautiful and profuse shrub, and, most beautiful of all, that prize of the south, the magnolia whose lustrous dark green foliage would alone render it an object of admiration without the queenly blossom whose colour, size and perfume are unrivalled in the whole vegetable kingdom. Under all these the spiked palmetto forms an impenetrable covert, and from glittering graceful branch to branch hang garlands of evergreen creepers, on which the mockingbirds are singing and swaying even now.'

She looked up to see Theodore, Aunt Mathilda, Ely and Sarah smiling at her. Clementine and Sugar sat on the younger Crawfords' laps. They were striking little girls:

Clem with her porcelain-pale skin and curly blonde hair, Sugar with her dark kinked hair, aristocratic nose and skin the colour of polished pine; both of them with their daddy's eyes. It was only just over a couple of months since Emily had left the island with the two children and every day she struggled with her anger over losing precious months of her daughter's life. She found it hard to love Charles's other daughter.

Emily disliked seeing Virginie in the child and she loathed the girl's slave name. She worried for Sugar's future. How would she ever be seen as Clementine's sister by a people who treated an African less humanely than a dog? She hated the responsibility and she hated Charles for having creating this impossible situation. Yesterday Ely had lit a fire on the beach at Cape Cod and they had sat on logs in a circle around it. In spite of the heat from the flames, Emily had started to feel a chill spread across her back. Behind them the ocean was grey-green and in front of them the forest blazed with colour – in between the deep sea-green pines were larches vivid as sulphurous fungi, maples burning vermilion, beeches turning crisp old gold. If it hadn't been for Sugar she would have felt supremely blessed.

'I was thinking of changing her name to Sarah,' she'd announced. 'It seems so much more fitting for a free child.'

She'd expected Sarah to be touched but instead her friend had frowned.

Ely had said almost forcefully, 'She can't help who she is or what she was called. She's the result of generations of injustice. Look at her mother. And her mother before her, sold to the highest bidder before being chained in the hold of a ship in a space the size of a coffin for weeks and then auctioned like an animal at a slave market. Nothing we can do will erase the past. All we can do is love this one little girl.'

Now Emily smiled at her two children and, looking over at the rest of the audience, she said, 'But, ladies and gentlemen, beautiful as the south is, and in particular my little island, the magnificence of the shrubbery is not what you have come to hear me speak about. Rather, though, instead of reading from my diary myself, I have decided to engage someone else to carry out this onerous job for me.'

There was a murmur, almost of disapproval.

'This gentleman was there with me and he had first-hand experience of what I witnessed. More than this, he experienced slavery in a way that I never could and, thankfully, never will. For this young man was born into slavery and until recently never left those few acres that comprised the plantation where he was raised and toiled his entire life. Ladies and gentlemen, it is illegal to teach a slave to read. He risked his life to learn what every white child takes for granted. No longer a slave but a free man, Mr Frank Wilson.'

Frank stepped forward with a dignified smile. Tall and slim, he looked handsome in a fitted black suit, his hair shorn almost to his scalp, his eyes burning. He took the book from her and commenced reading. An extraordinary hush spread across the audience who, wine glasses and champagne flutes in hand, ceased even to sip their drinks. Frank had a perfect reading voice, soft, yet resonant and able to carry to the furthest reaches of the theatre. Emily had coached him well and he knew the passage almost by heart and paused for dramatic effect in all the right places. It was even more poignant as it was Emily's description of Frank and his life on the plantation, how he longed to learn to read yet was denied even the simple pleasure of reading from the Bible; how he slaved in the cotton gin every day on a diet of cornmeal. He only stuttered once but quickly recovered and composed himself; this slight mistake was even more moving since it occurred when he came to the part where his mother was raped by the owner of the plantation; an owner whose parting gift to his own son was to slit his throat.

When Frank finished reading there was deathly silence and then as one the audience rose to their feet and clapped as if they would not stop. Some of the ladies were weeping into their handkerchiefs. As soon as the applause died down people started to ask questions, mainly directed at Frank.

'How did you learn to read?' asked a gentleman.

'Miss Harris taught me,' said Frank.

'What would have happened if you'd been found out?'

'I expect I'd have been flogged,' said Frank simply.

'Have you been flogged before?' asked another.

'Yes, sir.'

'Is it so very painful? Surely owners would not risk damaging what in effect are their commodities?' said the same man.

Frank slowly unbuttoned his jacket, loosened his cravat and took off his shirt. He turned to show the audience his back. It was a tangle of welts, the flesh raised either side, the scar tissue livid pink. There was a gasp. He put his clothes back on, all without a word.

'How much did Miss Harris pay for you?' said a man in a tux and pince-nez five tables back.

Emily stepped forward. She said, 'I did not pay for Mr Wilson. His owner gave him to me as a gift and I freed him. As you know, all free slaves have to carry papers at all times signed by a white man to prove that they have been liberated. I have no idea how much Mr Wilson was worth to his owner. But I believe there is no price that one can put on a man's life.'

She turned to Frank and took his hand. The two of them bowed. Ely joined them on stage, his eyes moist. As they stepped from the blazing stage servants entered the room carrying platters of roast goose and tureens piled high with squash, creamed corn, mashed potato and jugs of cranberry sauce and gravy. Several women surged forward but they paid no attention to Emily. Instead, they surrounded Frank.

'I think,' said Emily, as she regarded the rest of the diners who, almost as if released from a spell, were pouring wine and staring in delight at the arrival of their lavish supper, 'I would prefer to go somewhere quiet, just the two of us, and our little girls.'

'It would be a pleasure,' said Ely. And he smiled and held out his arm to her.

Notes on Sugar Island

I have worked every day through dew and damp, and sand and heat, and done good work; but oh, missis, me old and broken now, no tongue can tell how much I suffer.

Female slave speaking to Fanny Kemble, 1839

I first became fascinated with Fanny Kemble when I was writing a book on sugar (*Sugar: The Grass that Changed the World*). Sugar, when it was cultivated on a vast scale during the eighteenth and nineteenth centuries in the Caribbean and America, was grown by slaves originally captured in Africa. Fanny's story was an extraordinary one and although she never made it into the finished book, her tale stayed with me and eventually became the inspiration for *Sugar Island*. Fanny was a young intellectual Englishwoman who in 1834 (a quarter of a century after Britain had abolished slavery) married a dashing American gent. Shortly into their marriage Fanny discovered to her horror that she had wed a slave-owner. The shocking irony of Fanny's predicament captivated me.

Fanny was born into one of the most celebrated acting families in Britain. She grew up in Bath and London and was partially educated in France. Her eccentric mother, Marie-Thérèse De Camp, had been tiny and used to enact the part of a trapped fairy beneath a glass bell jar at dinner parties. She was bitter about the loss of her looks and her parts and jealous of her daughter's beauty and success. Fanny's father, Charles Kemble, grew increasingly successful as an actor at the same time as his Covent Garden theatre accrued a mounting debt. In desperation he asked Fanny to read for the part of Juliet in *Romeo and Juliet*. Three weeks later, at the age of eighteen and without any desire to act and with utterly no training, she was put on the stage. She was an overnight success. Men vied to paint her portrait, her picture was printed on fine china and neckties, and money poured into the genteelly bohemian Kemble family. Fanny, because she adored her father, continued to act, although she hated it.

I went a couple of nights since to a little party . . . I met everyone, including the terrific Kemble herself, whose splendid handsomeness of eye, nostril and mouth were the best things in the room.

Henry James, 1872

However, in spite of her fame, her father still could not shake off his debts and determined that he and his daughter, accompanied by her aunt, would seek their fortunes in America. In the States she was, again, a sensation.

Unfortunately, a year later their carriage overturned and her aunt suffered severe internal injuries and died. Not long before this Fanny had met a young man, Pierce Mease Butler, who was enamoured of her. He followed her around from city to city, even playing in the orchestra during some of her performances. Without the support of her aunt, whom she had dearly loved and utterly relied upon, she succumbed to Pierce's southern charm and they married.

This turned out to be a terrible mistake. For a start, Fanny was used to working and having independence, fame and fortune. She was young, headstrong and opinionated. She was in love with culture, literature, ideas and art. She was also a published author and had had a play written, performed and published when she was still a teenager. Although Pierce had fallen in love with her, what he demanded from a wife was abject subordination. She was not allowed to work but merely to play the role of a good wife. He insisted that they move to the country outside Baltimore where Fanny, who gave birth to a daughter (Sarah, nicknamed Sally), felt she would die of boredom. Their marriage was already starting to disintegrate: Fanny, in a fit of pique, packed and left, only to find that she was in the middle of nowhere, had nowhere to go and no money.

Then came the bombshell. Pierce's grandfather, Major Pierce Butler, originally from Britain, had married an American slave-owner and thus came into possession of a large slave plantation. After his death, he left the plantation in trust to his unmarried daughter. It was to be bequeathed to his two grandsons, Pierce and John, if they changed their name from Mease to Butler. Pierce Mease Butler had obliged. When Fanny discovered that her husband was a slave-owner, this led to conflict not only with Pierce, but with his brother's family, particularly as Fanny started to work on an anti-slavery pamphlet until Pierce and his brother put a stop to it. Pierce had refused to show Fanny the plantation or even talk to her about it. When his aunt died, he had little choice but to take Fanny, their daughter, Sally, their new baby girl, Frances, called Fan, and a white Irish nursemaid with him.

> *I used to pity the slaves and I do pity them with all my soul; but oh dear! oh dear! their case is a bed of roses to that of their owners, and I would go to the slave block in Charleston tomorrow cheerfully to be purchased if my only option was to go thither as a purchaser.*

Fanny Kemble, 1839

The Butler plantation was located on St Simons Island in Georgia. Pierce also owned a tiny island called Butler Island and what is now known as Little St Simons Island, which housed a penal colony called Five Pound. The slaves were sent to this pestilential swamp if they attempted to run away or talked back to their owners. Pierce owned seven hundred slaves and grew rice.

Fanny was appalled and horrified by the conditions of the slaves. She kept a diary of her four-month stay, two months of which were spent in rudimentary conditions on Butler Island and two on St Simons Island. Fanny became distraught, and her relationship with Pierce deteriorated dramatically. She tried to leave him as she found life on St

Simons unbearable, but their marriage limped along for several more years.

Over the course of the next thirty years a devastating and traumatic game of cat and mouse ensued. Fanny tried to leave Pierce and also tried to publish her diary. He threatened to prevent her from ever seeing her children again. She would back down, he would relent, she would arrive in America to see her daughters, he would refuse to let her into the house. She would apologize, he would book the family into a boarding house but only allow Fanny to see the girls in the public bar. So it went on until Pierce eventually divorced Fanny in 1849 and, as part of the contract, stipulated that the girls should not see their mother until they reached twenty-one if she published her diary. Although Fanny refrained from publishing the diary, Pierce still made it difficult for her to see her daughters. Emotionally bereft and unable to have a meaningful relationship with her children, Fanny returned to England for good. Once her elder daughter reached twenty-one and came to visit her, Fanny finally felt able to publish.

The diary, *Journal of a Residence on a Georgian Plantation*, was published in 1863, during the civil war. It is debatable what impact it had. Certainly the British were shocked to read about slavery first-hand. It is one of the most intimate contemporary portrayals of slavery since it was written by someone who was neither a journalist, a tourist nor a slave-owner and, as a woman, Fanny had witnessed events and had conversations with female slaves that a man would not have done. Some argue that her book helped to sway

British opinion away from Britain's support of the south and that Americans rallied around the northern cause as a result. Others say that her book was published too late to change the course of the war and that Britain did not support the south for reasons that had little or nothing to do with Fanny's writing.

Regardless of this, Fanny's diary is a remarkable account that is unparalleled in historical terms. It is also beautifully written and affords us a glimpse of Fanny's character.

In *Sugar Island* I have changed a number of events. The biggest change is that I have telescoped the time-frame. Fanny married in 1834, visited the plantation in 1838 but did not publish her diary until 1863. In *Sugar Island* she meets, marries and publishes her diary over the course of two years. She thus only has time (in fiction) to have one child. The reason I did this was to make the narrative more dramatic. In real life the endless to-ing and fro-ing, getting her hopes up and having them dashed as she tried to retain and obtain custody of, and then simply to see, her children must have been heart-breaking. But it could seem monotonous, stretching over twenty years, to a modern reader of a novel.

I owe a great debt to Fanny's story and relied heavily on her diary. Still, this is a novel not a biography (of which there are already a great number) and so I have felt at liberty to deviate from Fanny's story and tell my own. To show this most clearly, I have changed the names of the characters – Fanny Kemble becomes Emily Harris and

Pierce Mease Butler is Charles Earl Brook. To begin with, as I thought about my story, plotted it and began writing, I kept calling my characters Fanny and Pierce in my head. But, quickly, the characters of Emily and Charles asserted themselves, owing something to their antecedents, but in my mind living and breathing their own thoughts and desires.

I've kept the island's name the same, St Simons, but ignored the fact that the Butlers owned Butler Island. Instead, Sugar Island becomes what is now called Little St Simons. Little St Simons, unlike Sugar Island, is not linked to the main St Simons Island. I did this because having a connection to an island and then seeing it severed is a physical way of heightening Emily's feeling of isolation and her sensation of being trapped. It is also a tangible way of showing that nature will out: no matter what, the wilderness will prevail, as it has at the abandoned settlement of Fort Frederica. It is, too, a way of signalling that human nature also triumphs. By this I mean both that good will eventually conquer evil, and in real life capitalism always seems to win – slavery had to die out because it was monstrously unjust but also because the system increasingly became uneconomic.

The Butler family grew rice. Originally Georgian plantation owners cultivated sugar and cotton but switched to rice in the early to mid 1800s when these crops became less profitable. I kept the Brook plantation growing sugar and cotton as a way of indicating Charles's stubborn and unyielding nature and to show how he believed his ideals would surely be victorious, for he thought that he could trade cotton for arms and help win the war for the south. Nature, of course, will out and his crops succumb to diseases, which were common in genetically weak monocultures such as sugar cane and cotton at the time. This is a way of hastening Charles's impending demise, itself symbolic of the forthcoming end of slavery.

I have occasionally borrowed Fanny Kemble's beautiful prose, for instance, when Emily writes in her pamphlet against slavery:

> *The principle of the whole is unmitigated abominable evil; moreover the principle being invariably bad beyond the power of the best man acting under it to alter its execrable injustice, the goodness of the detail is a matter absolutely dependent upon the will of each individual slaveholder, so that though the best cannot make the system in the smallest particular better, the bad can make every practical detail of it as atrocious as the principle itself. It is in short a monstrous iniquity.*

And she says in her lecture in Boston:

> *As I skirted one of these thickets, I stood still to admire the beauty of the shrubbery. Every shade of green, every variety of form, every degree of varnish, and all in full leaf and beauty in the very depth of winter. The stunted dark coloured oak, the magnolia bay, which grows to a very great size, the wild myrtle, a beautiful and profuse shrub, and most beautiful of all, that prize of the south, the magnolia whose lustrous dark green foliage would alone render it an object of admiration without the queenly blossom whose colour, size and perfume are unrivalled in the whole vegetable kingdom.*

The rest of the time the words are my own. I visited St Simons Island, now a holiday resort with some of the wealthiest zip codes in America. I was stunned and shocked by some of what I saw. One day I cycled through the rain to the far end of the plantation where Fanny had lived for those brief months all those years ago. Now this area, in spite of its Butler Road and Fanny Kemble Street, was a suburb of enormous houses set back from the road in between live oaks. And then I saw something curious. A ruin on the lawn in front of holiday condos. It was surrounded by railings and I peered through them in the drizzle. There in front of me, crumbling to dust, trees and creepers growing through their midst, in someone's front garden, without so much as a plaque, were the remains of Pierce Butler's slave cabins.

I visited Little St Simons Island too, which is now a nature reserve and even more exclusive resort, famed for its wildlife and, in particular, spectacular bird-watching. Luckily my naturalist guide was sympathetic and, in between ornithological lectures, led the whole group off piste. He showed me the exact spot where Fanny had canoed to Little St Simons and alighted on the island. Right there were the remains of a slave cabin where one of the head slaves had lived and offered Fanny such help and refreshment as he could afford. We followed Fanny's path through the dense woodland, a Rousseau-esque mass of live oaks and red bay, swamp privet and saw palmetto, to the wild white beach in front of the Atlantic Ocean. It was here that Fanny had stood and thought how poignant it was that her slaves were unaware how close to the Caribbean they were, where their brothers and sisters now lived in freedom.

Fanny's story moved me unbearably; I hope that *Sugar Island* has the same effect on you too, and that perhaps it will encourage you to investigate the inspiration for Emily Harris, a free-thinking, courageous and fiercely intelligent woman who fought hard against all that she believed to be wrong.

Reference

Journal of a Residence on a Georgian Plantation in 1838–1839 by Frances Anne Kemble, edited and with an introduction by John A. Scott, Brown Thrasher Books, University of Georgia Press, Athens, Georgia, 1984

Acknowledgements

My thanks as ever go to my friend and agent, Patrick Walsh. I'm also grateful to the team at John Murray and, in particular, Morag Lyall for her meticulous copy-editing which, here as in her edit of my previous novel, *The Naked Name of Love*, saved me from several embarrassing factual errors. Dee O'Connell and Bethan Evans read and made useful comments on an earlier version.

For help with research I'd like to thank the library staff at the Fashion Museum and the American Museum in Britain, both based in Bath. Taylor Schoettle, author of *The Naturalist's Guide to St Simons*, and Scott Coleman, ecological manager of Little St Simons Island (which I have renamed Sugar Island), both lent me their time and expertise to discuss the natural history of St Simons. My trip to St Simons Island was facilitated by Patrick Saylor who went above and beyond the call of duty in his endeavour to answer all my questions and make my trip profitable and memorable.

Last but not least, I owe a debt of gratitude to Kate Parkin, my editor at John Murray, for her guidance throughout the creation of *Sugar Island*.